An Ordinary Drowning

LeAnn Neal Reilly

ZEPHON
BOOKS

Boston

Zephon Books USA
3 Billings Way
Framingham, MA 01701

First published in the United States by Zephon Books in 2012.
First Kindle edition: December 2012

AN ORDINARY DROWNING was originally published as Volume One in The Mermaid's Pendant. The characters and events portrayed in this book are fictitious. Any similarity to real persons, living or dead, is coincidental and not intended by the author.

Book design by LeAnn Neal Reilly
Front cover image by Olena Pantiukh /Shutterstock

Text set in Cambria.

Printed in the United States of America.

To Laurie, Amy, Raffaella, and Nancy

For never doubting me

The whole world has now been so ransacked that there is little room in these times for the imagination to play; but in mediaeval days travelers brought back such wonderful stories, some of them true, and others, perhaps, a little wanting in that respect, of the things that they had seen, that almost anything seemed a possibility.

F. Edward Hulme, Natural History: Lore and Legend

One
୧୫

IT TOOK TWO HOURS AND TEN MINUTES for John Wilkerson's fantasy about escaping to paradise to evaporate in the dry Caribbean air. Two hours on a ferry and a short walk around Culebra, a small island off the east coast of Puerto Rico, and John had to face up to the truth. But then, it was his own fault. He should have known that any island that resembled Disney's Neverland from an aerial photo must, at ground level, have more than a few flaws. He should have known not to invent something too fantastic to believe.

Unfortunately, he'd spent months conjuring up images of Culebra, known as the Last Spanish Virgin. Months invested in visions of dark-haired, buxom wenches with castanets on their slender hands and tiers of flounces swirling around their ankles. For weeks before he left Pittsburgh, he heard Spanish guitars thrumming and waves rushing when he drifted off to sleep at night, his girlfriend Zoë coiled around his body. Once or twice he even saw the sheen on the forehead of an *hacienda* owner in his mind's eye. When he and Zoë went to the Squirrel Cage after their day's research at Carnegie Mellon, he now drank rum instead of Yuengling's. And every now and then he caught the delicate scent of frangipani entwined with the mineral intensity of saltwater. He always darted a glance at Zoë whenever he remembered the scent of frangipani. His first love in high school, a bubbly artist named Tilda, had worn frangipani.

These visions stayed with him until he got to Puerto Rico. Instead of chartering a flight to Culebra from San Juan, John spent two bucks on the sleek double-decker ferry from Fajardo. When he arrived at the ferry dock, he found dozens of beachgoers lounging on hard-plastic coolers, holding beach towels and floats, and chatting with more energy than he had at eight a.m. Many drank Medalla or Bud Light, already getting a start on their beach weekend. He heard a toddler's cries and witnessed a mother in tube top and shorts, her thighs pockmarked with cellulite and a bandana around the curlers in her hair, shush the child. John's images of an island paradise wavered a bit but still held.

For the first hour on the ferry, he saw nothing but a steely smudge along the eastern horizon where Culebra should be. There wasn't much to do except listen to a CD of Van Morrison and watch the Caribbean, but then his batteries ran dry and he discovered that he hadn't packed replacements. Dropping the CD player in disgust, he ignored the smells of fried food and the rapid flow of Spanish around him. As he leaned over the ferry's railing on the upper deck, John studied the pixelated surface of the ocean, surprised at how much it resembled a poorly compressed movie. Choppy shades of blue, gray, and white jerked and resolved into water and foam and then fractured again into blocks of color. He blinked, rubbed his eyes and lifted his gaze to the horizon.

The steely smudge lingered and without landmarks to confirm the ferry's passage, John's mind played tricks on him. The constant sounds of wind and rushing water convinced him that the ferry labored on a watery treadmill—one which he feared would break down any moment like the taxi he took to the dock—but gradually he discerned the smudge growing and clarifying into a mountainous outcropping of sere green and dusty brown. Except for a smattering of white structures along the northern shoreline, Culebra appeared unsettled. A frontier outpost.

As they approached Dewey, Culebra's one and only town, the last rosy tinge faded from John's vision and reality settled in. No winsome *señoritas*, no Spanish guitars, no *haciendas*. Old men in tank tops sat on two benches in front of a short block of shops painted in dusty pastels. The small plaza with its tree benches, picnic tables, and old-fashioned streetlights across from the squat terminal with its wall of glass-block windows only made John long for the more stately colonial plazas in Old San Juan. Just beyond the main block, red-and-white columns for a drawbridge reared up behind the tired shops.

As he waited behind a father laden with sand pails, a mountain of beach towels, and an open Medalla, John shifted from foot to foot. At last the father lurched away and John shouldered his backpack, grabbed his bag, and disembarked into paradise, two hours and ten minutes after getting on the ferry.

After a quick tour of downtown Dewey, he returned to the *público* stop near the dock. Four people waited in the sparse shade across the street, talking and drinking beer. Half a block away, a liquor store did a brisk business from foot traffic, including some graying *gringos* who looked more than a bit pickled from sun and drink. When the *público* finally came, John walked all the way to the back, slid into a seat, and stared out the window. His dreams of colonial villas teeming with bougainvillea and surrounded by lush green landscaping had died, and they'd died hard. He glared at the arid and hilly terrain during the whole ten-minute ride to Playa Flamenco, supposedly one of the world's ten best beaches. The architecture relied on the ubiquitous cinderblock and no amount of bright-red blooms softened their angles. At least Wean Hall, in whose bowels his networking lab resided, daunted. These homes just depressed.

When he saw the rusty chain-link fence around the camping area and the sandy field that stood for a parking lot, John almost went back to Dewey. The backpack and bag weighed his arms down and he propped himself against the fence with his eyes closed until he could bring himself to rouse the dozing Culebrense in the shack identified as the camp office. The man shrugged when John asked about renting a locker. John rolled his eyes and turned on his heel, dragging the bags with him. He halfway hid them among some guinea grass near a tree trunk.

Through the palms and over a small rise, laughter and loud music from the mob of weekend beachgoers repelled John from Playa Flamenco and back to the *público*. He'd eaten *huevos rancheros* hours before and his stomach demanded more *cocina criolla*, more Puerto Rican food, before he headed off for snorkeling. The Pepto pink of Señorita's, a two-story guesthouse, drew him in the glare of early afternoon. He enjoyed lunch there so much that his disappointment in not finding paradise began fading and when he rented snorkeling gear, the primitive machine for swiping credit cards only added to Culebra's growing rustic charm. It was time to find out if the snorkeling and diving around Culebra redeemed it altogether.

Half an hour later, he strode toward the trail to Carlos Rosario, a reef that the dive-shop owner had raved about. At the trailhead, he stopped long enough to read the sign posted on the chain-link fence that warned against straying off the trail and into an area littered with U.S. Navy ordnance. John's chest tightened, threatening a familiar panic attack, and he took a step back. Three carefully controlled exhalations seemed to relax his breathing, but he took three more for good measure and stepped onto the lonely, risky path.

A strip of white sand and ocean met him at trail's end. Nothing but the delicious sound of waves sighing against the shore and an occasional wild cry overhead from a seabird. The crystalline color of the water seduced his screen-weary eyes and something let go of him, some grip of asphalt and glass-walled office buildings, and he breathed in deeply. Even if he saw nothing but rocks and hermit crabs, the surreal blue saltwater against a clear Caribbean sky redeemed his trip, made Culebra a paradise, cellulite thighs and cinderblock eyesores be damned.

A hundred feet out he saw the shadow of coral reef. To the south, a narrow canal separated Culebra from a large cay. The dive-shop owner had recommended the canal for a first snorkel dive. Of course, the guy had warned against snorkeling alone, but alone with nature was *exactly* what he wanted to be. He'd return to the Carlos Rosario reef after he'd gotten his feet wet in the canal. Grinning at his weak joke, he whistled a short tune. Even weak jokes were funny when Zoë wasn't around.

To get a better idea of what he was getting himself into, John dropped his gear on some bare ground among the clusters of cactus and guinea grass near the trail and climbed a twisted mangrove to look out over the canal. From this height, he saw clumps of turtle grass in the shallow waters where fish of all sizes darted in and out of the swaying blades. Besides the fish and dozens of birds surfing along air currents, not another soul intruded upon his peace. Satisfied with his reconnaissance, he climbed down, stripped off his t-shirt and snatched up the snorkel, goggles, and flippers.

John hadn't snorkeled since senior year at Berkeley, but once he plunged his face underwater he wondered why he'd waited so long to do it again. He'd descended into another world, vast and silent except for the regular gurgle of his breathing in the tube. All around him, organic shapes defied right angles and straight lines, flat planes and intersecting sides. Colors ranging from subdued to garish—but never dull as concrete or bland as limestone—enticed his city-weary eyes. There was a mystery here, a truth so sublime that it defied easy expression into variable and quantity.

He swayed on the current, gazing at parrotfish with their hooked beaks darting among the blue tangs. A squadron of sergeant majors soared over the reef south of him, their black stripes flashing as they banked and turned. Copper-colored squirrelfish with their big brown eyes, ocean surgeonfish, and slender needlefish swarmed ahead of him. Here was primeval life, unaware and unconcerned about the self-important ambition of computer scientists in their office cubicles overgrown with cable and whirring disk drives.

An image of Zoë, tall and sinewy, wavered to life in front of him. His chest tightened and memory overlay his view of trumpet fish hovering among tan sea whips as thick as fingers. Darkness overwhelmed him. He tugged at remembered covers that clung to his torso and legs, but they only entangled him more tightly. Yanking at edges, clumps under his back—anything he could grab onto—he kicked out and then his vision cleared until he saw that a flipper had snagged on some turtle grass.

He panted into the snorkel and waited, his heart racing. Behind him, Zoë's weight shifted and she coiled her arms around his torso, binding him. John blinked and the underwater tableau reappeared. Large yellowtail snapper, a bright yellow stripe racing down their sides to their yellow tails, drifted past. As John turned to follow, an octopus lunged from nowhere at a yellowtail. Writhing arms pinned the hapless fish to the ocean floor. In seconds, it was all over. The octopus injected the yellowtail with poison and stuffed it into its beak.

John flinched. His heart stuttered and thudded. He kicked away from the violent death, but a flipper again caught on turtle grass. His arms thrashed. Spears of sunlight, bubbles, sea grass upended his vision. Then a terrible thing happened. His lips lost their seal on the breathing tube. Saltwater choked him. He flung his face above the surface and spit out the tube. Gasped a breath. Choked and sputtered. Flailed under again, losing the goggles. Struggled out into sunlight, coughing and sucking at the air. He slipped under; pushed up again. Missed a breath, slid down. Inhaled more water. Ears ringing, he popped up a final time. Then he swatted once at the water before slipping under the surface. The heaviness of saltwater filled his lungs just as two arms grabbed him from behind and pulled him free of the water. The pressure in his lungs eased and the pounding in his brain faded to black.

Dizzy awareness returned to him. He couldn't focus his eyes. Everything was a blur. His shoulder and side hurt. His chest spasmed. He coughed weakly, but something soft and firm wrapped his mouth. He wanted to lift a hand to brush it away, but his arm refused to move and he coughed again. The pressure on his mouth lifted and then he retched warm saltwater until nothing came up. He continued to heave and shake. Someone laid a hand on his back; a gentle vibration spread through his torso, soothing his retching.

The hand remained while he breathed. The dizziness subsided gradually. He had no idea how much time had passed and cared only for the implacable ground beneath him, the concerned fingers on his back. When he felt that he could move without causing the world to spin, he rolled to see his rescuer. The hand dropped away and he felt bereft. His eyes, still clouded by saltwater, refused to focus on her face. He had an impression of luminous skin, and two bare breasts peeking through a curtain of dark hair.

"Thank you." The words croaked from his ravaged throat. Then he passed out again.

ఇళ్ళ

John's savior sat some minutes, watching him. Then she leaned forward and pressed several fingertips to his neck, feeling for his pulse. It was there, strong and steady. She let her hand slide along the skin of his jaw, brushing the hair away from his cheek. She put a light fingertip on his mouth, now a warm red. Her lips tingled and she leaned her face closer—perhaps she could press her lips there again? He moaned and rolled his head against the stones. The mermaid snatched her hand back and waited, her breath held, but he didn't move again. She didn't touch him a second time; instead, she caressed the hard muscles of his calves with her gaze. She looked away from his feet though. One still wore one of those pseudo-flippers that always made her shiver.

She had, of course, seen countless humans before—snorkeling and diving, on shore and on deck. But she'd never *touched* one before, never felt the dry skin that prickled with fine hairs. This man overwhelmed her. Already the sun had evaporated most of the water on his chest, which was covered with dark hair. Not like a merman, smooth and sleek and slender. His chest, shoulders, and hips were wider and his frame bulkier. His flesh was a different color, too. He was pale but not shark-belly pale like the *mer* people. His skin held warmth, the warmth of sun-bleached wood. Only his long dark hair resembled a merman's. Her nostrils flared at his scent. She had no words to describe it other than hot and dry, but she used those words for the shore and he didn't smell like the shore. He smelled like the wind from distant lands.

A voice, sandy and familiar, abraded her thoughts. "What have you done, young one?"

The mermaid looked up to see an ancient woman as gnarled and twisted as the roots of the trees that grew at the shore's edge. The woman picked her way across the stones toward the place where the mermaid sat. She stopped a few feet away. Freeing her bag, which the mermaid had always seen at her waist, the old woman rummaged around for a few moments before withdrawing something. Then she came forward and nudged John with her foot. He didn't stir.

"Pulled him out of the water, did you? Cough up all the water he breathed in?" The mermaid nodded. "And his heart's beat is still strong?" The mermaid nodded again. "He'll live then."

She bent and tugged the flipper from the man's foot. When it came off, the mermaid let a sharp sound escape her.

The ancient one laughed, a sound like dry stones shifting. "You think he's strange? No wonder you find him so interesting, girl." She smiled. It spread like seal oil on water. "I can help him, if you'd like." She paused and waited. The mermaid stole a glance at the man and nodded. "This herb tincture will rouse him. I'll see to it that he's recovered his senses and can walk. You'd best get going. I'll tell him I found him here."

The mermaid nodded again. After one more look at the unconscious man, she propelled herself backward with her hands, her tail lifted slightly above the stones. Once she was in the water, she paused, her gaze taking in the wide stance of the ancient woman, who stood over the stranger as though he were *her* bounty from the waters. Was this all there was to saving a man's life?

Before she could lower herself underwater and speed away, the old woman called to her.

"Oh, yes, young one, I need some turtle grass, and a sea cucumber. And one of those pink sea urchins, you know the ones."

There was nothing of the usual promise of a human artifact or any stories about the human world on this island. The mermaid nodded. It was the old woman's price for keeping her secret.

෴෴෴

When John regained consciousness, he found a wizened old woman hunched over him holding what looked like a mini-bar liquor bottle. But its rank liquid was no whiskey that he'd ever smelled. Upon seeing her wild, white hair and a burning right eye in a face like a walnut, he sat up quickly. She chortled and hunkered down, her ragged skirt splayed across her bony knees.

"So, you don't like the smell? Strong it is. Just be glad you aren't dead, then, and can smell it." Her voice crackled. Her accent was odd, not like the locals.

John shook his head, trying to clear the confusion that still hung over his thoughts. "Who ...?"

The old woman just sat there and looked at him. He cleared his throat and began again.

"Who pulled me from the water?"

"You were pulled from the water?"

"Yes." A cough interrupted him. "Almost drowned."

"What'd he look like?"

He shifted his position on the rocky shore, bracing himself and pushing his hair out of his eyes. "Not he, she."

"She? Then you did see her?" The woman's voice was sharp.

"No." He shook his head. "Not really."

The old woman at first said nothing; instead, she wrapped the top of the bottle with a bit of cloth and then tied that with a bit of string. She dropped this bottle into a bag that lay on the rocks behind her before turning to face him again.

Finally, she spoke. "You were lying on the beach. You were breathing; you weren't dead. That's when I put my tincture under your nose."

John recalled the foul odor of the tincture, grateful that she hadn't poured it down his throat. "Thanks."

"It's little enough I did." She shrugged. "If you want a doctor, there's one in the *pueblo*, across the plaza from the dock. But you're all right."

Without waiting for him to agree, she picked up her bag and slung it over her shoulder. She headed toward the east and the low-growing shrubs there. Not sure what he should do or say next, John sat watching her go. As she reached the edge of the rocks, the old woman turned for a parting shot.

"You should thank God for your life." She raised her chin toward the water of the canal and continued, "The ocean is as lethal as it's lovely. You'd do well to remember."

She disappeared into the shrubs and darkening shadows, going who knew where. John, feeling chastised, sat for a long moment before studying the rocks near where he'd been lying. There was nothing to show how he'd gotten ashore, no footprints, no drag marks. No way of knowing where his rescuer had come from or gone to. Why hadn't she stayed around?

Two

❧

John leveraged himself to his feet before shaking gripped him. He sat down again, hard, on the stony shore. His heart seized up and he flushed hot and cold before it resumed beating. Turning to look at the canal, he thought that he saw his snorkel floating north but the fractured sunlight dazzled him and he couldn't be sure. His second flipper and mask had disappeared into the deceptive water. The shaking intensified. He'd almost lost his life in an out-of-the-way corner of the Caribbean. The silence of the empty shore confirmed how fantastic his rescue had been.

Maybe his rescuer was still close. The thought impelled him to his feet and a mad, yet fruitless, search of the scrub around the shore. Whatever girl? woman? superwoman? had pulled him to safety must have hightailed it along the path back to Carlos Rosario. Or maybe there was access from the nearby Tamarindo Estates. Zoë would have stood over him, hands on hips and smirk on lips, until he'd stumbled upright with his head hanging. Frustration filled him, drowning his

19

shock. He couldn't remember what she looked like. A bleary memory of long, wet hair that could have been any color swam across his mind's eye, panning out into a clearer image of breasts, small and strangely vulnerable. If ever he saw those breasts again, he'd recognize his rescuer—and cover her up. Given that he wasn't likely to see any other breasts than Zoë's for the foreseeable future, his frustration magnified ten-fold.

A nagging bladder drew him from his predicament and the mundane act of pissing behind a tree brought him back to himself. He felt as empty as the stony shoreline, as blank as the impervious waves, drained and hollow from his struggle. He couldn't stand here all day, longing for an ephemeral sprite to reappear and finish saving him. Maybe he wanted some magical creature to enter his life so badly that he half-believed that she had, but nothing had changed from the time he'd gone under to the time he'd awakened on shore: the sun would still set tonight on dreamless sleep and tomorrow it would rise on unfulfilled fantasies.

He looked around, trying to get his bearings. Directly opposite him rose the jagged outlines of a cay. He'd have to take the path back north toward Carlos Rosario where he'd left his gear. There was no way he was getting back into the water. He'd gone only a couple of feet along the path when a prickling sensation along his spine caused him to stop. Yet when he looked behind him, he saw nothing but the regular lapping of water on stone. No one watched him.

By the time he returned to the Playa Flamenco campground, his frustration and emptiness had bottomed out into resignation. He was accustomed to the hilly terrain of Pittsburgh but had no stamina for Culebra's dry heat or the uneven trail. His head hurt and his throat had constricted around a layer of dust. He'd earned a sunburn from going so long without a t-shirt. All he wanted now was air conditioning, low lights, and a cold drink. A shower was out of the question. He wouldn't get one of those until Zoë arrived in two weeks and they stayed at Tamarindo Estates.

Against all expectation, there weren't any places to retreat to near here, not even a stand to buy a bottle of water or a soda. He'd known that Culebra was undeveloped, a "hidden jewel in the Caribbean," but why hadn't someone set up at least one thatched-roof shack with an ice tub filled with drinks and a hot-dog steamer? No wonder all those people on the ferry had lugged those huge coolers with them. One of the world's ten best beaches and you were on your own. He'd hiked into wildernesses with more civilization.

He consulted the island map that he'd gotten at the dive shop. The closest restaurant outside Dewey was at Tamarindo Estates, but it only opened on the weekend for lunch and dinner. He suspected that it was what passed for nice on Culebra. He didn't want to wait two hours while covered in trail dust to order a beer there. Tamarindo Estates *was* the only place near where he'd almost drowned, but he couldn't be sure that his rescuer had any connection to it. And really, what would he say? Any of your guests like to swim topless in the canal?

There weren't many other options. On the way back into town, there was only The Happy Landing Café near the airport. Beyond that, there appeared to be only two or three standalone eateries in Dewey. Either way, he was on foot. The prospect didn't appeal to him, but he decided that he could kill a few birds with one weary trip: he'd rent a bike, report the lost gear, and get a beer and dinner. So he settled on Isla Encantada, which was back near the dive shop. It sounded more appealing anyway, even if Culebra had turned out to be far from enchanted.

He regretted his decision to walk into Dewey after taking an hour to get there. If he hadn't stopped at The Happy Landing Café for a bottle of water, he might have passed out along the way. A lone black stallion standing along the highway oddly tempted him, but when he took a step in its direction, it bolted.

The bike shop owner had just stuck his key into the shop's lock when John came limping up. He smiled and opened up anyway, chatting the whole time it took John to fill out a form and for him to swipe John's credit card. John didn't have the same luck with the dive shop, however. It was already closed even though it was only four-thirty in the afternoon. He didn't mind. If he didn't get a cold Medalla in the next ten minutes, he might combust and his ashes float away on the wind over the harbor, Ensenada Honda. He was that dry.

Isla Encantada had none of Señorita's refinements. That is to say, it wasn't pastel. It didn't have strings of white Christmas lights and tropical flowers. There was no Hemingway doppelganger at the bar. The tables were wooden, their surfaces pockmarked and oiled by countless palms and fingers. It didn't serve Nuevo Caribbean cuisine with thin-sliced plantain chips and entrees drizzled with garlic-scented sauce. No, Isla Encantada served traditional *tostones*, monstrous *pastelillos de carne*, *paella* teeming with shrimp and spiny lobster, and heavy *arroz con dulce*. This was a place Culebrense sons came to eat when they couldn't eat their mother's cooking. John, who wasn't a Culebrense son but the boyfriend of a virulent vegetarian, restricted himself to *estofado de garbanzos*, a thick chickpea stew with pumpkin and cabbage. He washed it down with Medalla and ice water. He tried to pace himself, but he drank more beer and water than he'd ever consumed at one sitting.

He sank against his chair back and looked around the dim restaurant. A barrel-chested Culebrense with a hairy caterpillar of a mustache stood talking to a younger Culebrense behind the bar. Four young men sat at one of the ten tables in the dining area. A small dance floor with worn, sooty parquet took up the rest of the space. John grimaced at his reflection in the floor-to-ceiling mirror on the far wall. He wondered what kind of musicians used the stands waiting in the corner.

Too bad no lovely *señoritas* sat sipping *sangria* at the bar. Not that it mattered, anyway. He wasn't as smooth as his friend Stefan. Or maybe not as carefree and immoral. He could never seek out a one-night stand, Zoë or no Zoë. At the thought of his girlfriend, John looked around the bar even though she wasn't there. That's when he saw the old woman at a table by the door. She nodded at him and raised her beer bottle. John nodded back and shifted his gaze away. Something about her gave him the willies.

The barrel-chested man approached with a Medalla.

"*Hola, mi amigo.* Medalla?" He didn't wait for John's answer, just set the bottle next to John's empty. "May I?" He gestured to the chair across from John.

John shrugged and nodded.

"So, you like our island, *señor*?" The man had brought an extra Medalla for himself. He sipped it and waited.

John shifted in his seat. His backside ached and he found himself thinking about the hard campground where he planned to sleep tonight. "I dunno. Haven't seen much of it yet."

The big man nodded. "Not much to see, unless you like seabirds and turtles."

"Playa Flamenco as amazing as they say?"

23

"*Sí, señor.* Not so much when the beachgoers from the mainland infest it like sand fleas. They will be gone tomorrow. Then you will see for yourself."

"Weekend only?"

The man nodded. "My name is Tomás. I own Isla Encantada. You like my wife's cooking, no?"

"*Sí.*" John smiled, his first since he'd gotten to Culebra. "My name's John." They shook hands. "So, what's there to do around here at night? Any good music?" He indicated the music stands with a sideways tilt of his head.

"We have a four-piece group. A guitar and kettle drum. A trumpet. And *maracas*, of course. It's the best on *la isla*. You stay and listen, no?"

"Is there a lot of music on Culebra?"

"Sometimes at Señorita's. No one is there now." Tomás sipped his beer. "We are *muy rústico* here, *señor*. There are more roosters and wild horses than *turistas*. I am the only one open past eleven on the weekend. An hour."

"Wow. Zoë's gonna love that."

"*Cómo?*"

"Oh, nothing." He shrugged. "It's not what I expected is all."

"You came to snorkel perhaps? The reefs, they bring many *norteamericanos*."

"Actually, I came to scuba dive. I'm going out over the Trench in a couple of weeks."

"Treasure hunting? The Trench is graveyard to many Spanish galleons."

"No, no. Too deep, *amigo*. It's a research trip. Underwater geology." John laughed. "Of course, I almost drowned in the canal today so maybe I shouldn't go."

Tomás appeared shocked. "The canal? Luís Peña?"

24

John nodded, sheepish. "Long story, Tomás. Never would have made it back to shore without somebody pulling me in."

Tomás frowned. "You snorkeled alone then? You are *suerte*, lucky, *señor*, that someone came along at the right time. As I have already said, not many *turistas* come here and the *puertorriqueños* stay on Playa Flamenco. The Culebrenses, they don't often snorkel."

"Well, whoever she was, she saved my life."

Tomás started. "She? A woman pulled you from the canal?"

"Yeah," John laughed. "Must be some kind of superhero to pluck me out of the water and drag me to shore so fast."

Tomás looked thoughtful. "What did she look like, this woman?"

"Don't really know. My eyes were full of saltwater. I was throwing it up, too." John paused. "Actually, now that you ask, I'm getting this distinct image of her." He frowned heavily, concentrating on the startling and clear vision that popped into his mind.

"She's got outrageously curly hair"—here he demonstrated with two hands hovering around his head—"the color of an old penny and eyes the color of the shallows around Culebra. And ..." here John hesitated, "and she didn't have anything on. No shirt. No swimsuit. *Nada*."

"You saw her?" Tomás sounded excited. "You really saw this woman, *señor*?"

John's confusion mushroomed. "No. No." Anger sharpened the edge of his voice and he shook his head. "*Lo siento*, Tomás. I'm not angry with you. It's just that I know I didn't see her clearly, but I have this distinct image of her. Like I already know her."

Tomás pursed his lips and nodded. He sipped his beer and then, his gaze directed at his beer label as though seeing for the first time, he asked, "What happened to her, *Señor* Juan? Did she tell you her name?"

"That's the odd thing. I passed out. When I woke up, she was gone. But that old woman—" John inclined his head toward the old woman, who sat smoking and reading a book—"was there. Stuck a foul-smelling liquid under my nose. Claims she found me on the shore, no one else there."

Tomás's gaze slid toward Ana and back. "Ana?"

"You know her?"

"Yes, everyone knows Ana, *señor*. Some more than most. Some wish they knew her less."

"What's that mean?"

Tomás kept his gaze on his hands, which were wrapped around his empty Medalla bottle. "Some say she is a *bruja*, a witch, *señor*."

John looked at the other man for a moment, trying to gauge his meaning. "You're kidding? A witch?"

Tomás shrugged. "One man's superstition is another man's explanation."

"She's just some sort of herbalist. Crossed with a bag lady. Scary looking, but a witch?" John heard incredulity twist his voice.

"Some say she is also *del mar*."

"'*Del mar*'? 'Of the sea'?"

"This woman, the one who pulled you from the sea. Perhaps she was not altogether a woman."

"What's that mean?" John studied the other man's face but saw only seriousness in his eyes. "What else is there? A mermaid?" He laughed and looked away.

Tomás looked at Ana. He picked at the label on his bottle and shook his head. "Sí, *loco, loco*. Just a crazy explanation for your mystery, *Señor* Juan. A story to tell your friends when you go home."

John frowned. "I'd rather know who she is, Tomás. I just don't have any idea how to track her down."

"You could post a flyer here. Nearly everyone comes here at one time or another."

"A flyer?" John pursed his lips. "Sure. Why not?" He tilted the last of the beer into his mouth. "Time for me to head back to the campground. I'll catch the music another time. Nearly drowning has worn me out. What I owe you?"

After he settled the bill—trying without success to pay the friendly Tomás for the last Medalla—John biked back to Playa Flamenco. The heat had fled with the sunset and a languor slowed his peddling. He passed a few Culebrenses enjoying the evening from their porches. They waved and called hello and he answered in kind. There were only a handful of cars on the road to the north, and none past the airport. The acrid smell of dry thorn acacia and asphalt subsided beneath the cool mineral scent of ocean water. The sky was the color of honeydew, oozing thousands of white seed-stars. Bougainvillea, its rich red muted, added mystery to the dusk. John thought the world looked unutterably lovely, tranquil and complete. He was alive and he had no one to thank. His gratitude wouldn't stay inside though.

"I'm alive!" he yelled into the gloaming. Startled horses whinnied and broke across the highway in front of him. He bellowed, a pure animal sound of pleasure, and coasted down an incline, his hands fluttering above his head.

Later, as he lay listening to laughter from the weekenders still partying on the beach, he wondered again how he was going to find her, the vulnerable woman with the crazy hair and haunting eyes who'd saved him from drowning. He tossed on the sandy ground for more than an hour, replaying the rescue. Where was she, this woman *del mar*? Something tickled his thoughts and ran down his spine.

He popped up in his sleeping bag. Again, he had the feeling that someone was watching him, but he could see nothing, just dark shapes of trees and snoring bodies. He strained his hearing, but only voices and waves reached him. He might have sat up half the night, waiting, but a breeze caressed his face. Its touch urged him to slide back down, to close his eyes, to dream.

⊷⊷⊷

Ana climbed the hidden path beyond her house toward Playa Tamarindo. Overhead, sooty terns fluttered like kites without string. Before she reached the summit, her rooster crowed, but her sleepy hens would ignore him. They wouldn't leave their straw-lined beds until she jostled them looking for eggs. She paused at a small stand of tamarind trees and studied the full-length pods hanging from the branches. Their pliant shells needed another six weeks to fill out with a sweet-sour pulp and become brittle enough to pluck. Given the number of pods, she'd have pulp for a dozen vials of diarrhea medicine, a jar of burn salve, and a vial of abortifacient—and still have enough to make three or four kegs of tamarind ale. If she didn't harvest them quickly, the birds might feast on them first. Her cadre of laughing gulls forgot their training as messengers and spies every spring to gorge on ripe tamarind pods.

While she stood there, one fluttered to a branch at her head. Seaweed affixed a lace murex shell to its leg.

"What's this, Ai?"

Ana slipped a small pair of scissors from the bag at her waist and snipped the seaweed. The lace murex dropped into her palm. She fingered it, turning it over and studying its lacy spines and ridges. Then she rubbed it around her palm several times, humming and chanting under her breath. When she'd released the message, she put the shell into the bag. The gull cocked its head and opened its beak, laughing at her.

"Of course you did well. The midwife in Guadaloupe still watches. She'll signal when the winds turn ferocious. All right, all right." She reached into a pocket of her skirt, pulled out a rectangle of dried tamarind pulp, and broke off a corner. "Don't be so greedy or you'll shit yourself silly, Ai."

She tossed the bit into the air where the gull snatched it. As she walked on, a sea of thorny acacia and guinea grass, unremarkable yet as familiar to her as the thicket of lines on the back of her hands, rolled away. She didn't have to look over her shoulder to know the acacia and guinea grass swallowed up her steps. No one could follow her unless she wanted him to.

At the shore, she sensed the mermaid, maybe close, maybe far—but not too far. So she squatted at the water's edge and rummaged through the wet stones. She'd gathered five when a shift in the air tingled her ears. The mermaid had released her glamour, the magic spell of disguise used by the *mer*.

"It's good you returned." Ana spoke without looking up from her work. "You must be warned." She swiveled to face the mermaid. "That *idiota americano* is looking for you."

He'll see what I mean him to.

"Then careful what you mean, young one."

But ....

"No buts. Stay away until he's gone."

The mermaid tossed her head, reminding Ana of the proud stallion who nipped the wild mares and shied away from everyone, even her. She launched herself from the water, arcing over backward in defiant grace, her sinewy tail slapping the water's surface. The air wavered around her and she swelled into a portly manatee as saltwater and foam

29

showered Ana. A sheet of droplets glittered in the early sunlight, but Ana saw the mermaid torpedoing through the canal anyway.

Ana sat back on her heels and studied the mermaid's wake with narrowed eyes. She must continue to follow the stranger, but more importantly she must find some way to distract him. She'd heard him at Isla Encantada, she'd heard his desire to find his rescuer. He would never find the mermaid on his own, of course, but his thoughts would be open to her. The besotted fool would linger around the edges of Culebra, hoping to catch his thoughts. He would draw her, like a homing pigeon, to him.

A smile lifted her face. Perhaps she, Ana, could call him to *her*. She'd caught him thinking of dark-haired, dark-eyed Spanish beauties and long limbs entwined, glistening as they moved against each other. He would soon forget the mystery woman who'd saved his life when he'd become intoxicated with a flesh-and-blood siren. It would be done.

She plucked up her skirt and waded into the shallows to gather more stones, shells, and seaweed. Muttering, she placed these around the edge of the small beach. She returned to the water and searched until she found a small sea star. At her touch, it flexed its arms but could not move fast enough to escape. She carried the dripping animal to the largest stone on the beach and laid it there. From the bag at her waist, she pinched a bit of dried cactus powder and, muttering again, outlined the sea star.

It poured its life into her hands and into her plans.

Three

ଔଷ

WHEN JOHN WOKE AT SIX A.M. the next morning, cool sand and crisp light buoyed him. Sometime in the night, he'd freed himself from his sleeping bag, which lay in a heap at his feet. He stretched and grunted, reaching overhead and breathing deeply. He sighed and released the stretch. Overhead, terns and gulls fluttered, their sharp cries counterpointing the rhythmic *shoosh-shoosh* of the waves. Palm and acacia leaves tangoed with a flirty breeze tangy with salt. John closed his eyes and sighed again. All his senses had heightened. Sounds were clearer, smells sharper. Even his sunburn had cooled.

Sitting up, he scooped some sand and let its powder slip through his fingers. It was as fine as confectioner's sugar and almost as white. An urge overcame him and he scooped up more and rubbed it into his stubble. The sand felt less gritty than he did. He grinned. He was alive and he'd never felt better.

His stomach rumbled. He was hungry. He rummaged in his backpack and found a Snickers bar. Breakfast of champions it was not, but it would do for now.

It wasn't until he bent over his sleeping bag, smoothing it before rolling, that he remembered the dream. It was less a vision than a memory of movement, a flowing along dark, swift currents studded with lights and teeming with music. Infinity swirled at his feet and forever arched over his head. He'd been without form, yet he'd been everything. He'd traveled alone, silent—yet not alone. A multitude of others swam beside him. Together, they swam always, yet they needed no destination. Once recalled, the dream disappeared like smoke on the breeze. Even though he'd lost its details, it left a sense of fulfillment in its wake.

He hummed and stepped over snoring campers toward the Portajohns. That's when Zoë's absence hit him. He hadn't slept away from her in nine months. A shadow crossed the sun and he glanced up reflexively. The morning brightened even before his eyes adjusted, but his peace faded. He shook himself. He needed to find the mystery woman.

Not knowing what else to do, John decided to return to the scene of his rescue. Perhaps, in the clear light of early morning, he'd be able to spot some clue that he'd missed from the day before. The hike over the Carlos Rosario trail only added to his perplexity. There was no good reason to think that a stranger happened to be hiking along this trail, heard his floundering in the canal, dove in and pulled him out, and then returned to her hike post-haste. It just didn't make any sense at all. The Luís Peña Canal was a destination, not someplace anyone would just pass by. And what had brought Ana, the local witch woman, to the shore with her pungent herbal medicine?

The trail ended near the quiet little beach where his rescuer had brought him. John searched the perimeter of the shore again, but the only thing that he found out of the ordinary was a shriveled sea star lying exposed on a large rock. He was the last one to know anything about sea animals, but it seemed a strange place to find a sea star. There was something forlorn about it. He touched it with the tip of his finger. Out here, it was nothing but some tern's morning meal. He cradled it on his palm and turned to face the canal.

The last thing that he wanted to do was go back into the ocean. He stood for a minute or two, studying the impervious water—water that had nearly swallowed him. He looked again at the sea star, desiccated when it should have been moist, living. He was too late to save it, but he couldn't leave the sea star lying on the stones. Returning the helpless creature to the ocean was the best he could do to set things right. He owed it to the woman who'd risked her life to save his. Holding his breath, he took a step into the canal. The water was blood warm and silky. It caressed his thighs and urged him deeper. He sighed and sank to his knees. Beneath him, the sand shifted to accommodate him. He lowered the sea star below the surface and watched as the water lifted its husk off his palm and carried it away. The current swirled around him, alive and tender. Like being naked and draped in satin sheets. He knew that he was alone. He saw nothing through the crystalline water, not even a darting fish, yet fingers stroked his calves and thighs, toyed with his hair, caressed his shoulders. A hallucinatory torso pressed against him, arms encircled his neck and he bent forward....

The water turned playful, rolling and ducking him. John, water sheeting over his face, laughed and began splashing. Somewhere in the back of his mind, he realized that he'd look totally bonkers to anyone who stumbled upon him, but he didn't care. Nothing held him back, entangled him, under this infinite sky.

"Where's my lady *del mar* when I need her?" He didn't realize that he'd spoken aloud until he heard an answer.

"Will I do?" Ana stood at the mouth of the trail; her wild white hair spun wisps around her face. "Or are you looking for something else? You seem recovered."

John hung suspended in the water, which had lost its charm. He felt vulnerable to the old woman's sharp gaze. "I am."

As dainty and graceful as a mountain goat, the old woman picked her way across the stony shore. She squatted down and toyed with some broken bits of shells. "Saw your flyer at Isla Encantada. Think to catch your mermaid, eh?" Her rough voice stayed even, but John heard the scorn in it.

"I never said that."

"Tomás thinks you did."

John sighed. "No."

"Don't believe in mermaids, do you? Why not? Maybe one is swimming right beside you." The old woman's right eye glittered. "Close to us vile humans, eh?" She chortled.

John squirmed. "Look, you see who pulled me out of the canal or not?"

"I saw no woman. Either there's a lady *del mar* or you made the whole thing up."

"Why would I do that?"

"Hm." She picked at some seaweed on the sand, swirling its limp strands on the stones. "Ask yourself."

He had to get out of the water, fast. He lurched upright and strode to the shore, water spraying from his quick arms. He stopped next to her, but she didn't look at him. "I'm not making this up. I didn't imagine nearly drowning. I didn't

34

imagine the woman who saved me." He paused and then braved a question. "Do you know more than you're telling?"

She swiveled and looked up at him. A sly smile oiled her wrinkled cheeks. "Maybe I pulled you out."

John ignored her. "How'd you happen to find me?"

Ana shrugged, stood up, and brushed her hands on her threadbare skirt. "Came here to gather this and that for my remedies."

"Maybe you're not the only one who gathers 'this and that' for her remedies."

"Perhaps." She shrugged again. "Whatever makes you happy."

John watched her bend over the stones, dismissing him. He didn't need to stay and watch her pick over rocks, to have her pick over his story. What did it matter what she thought? He'd already passed her and reached the trail before something in her manner made him turn around. She seemed to scour the rock where he'd found the sea star. After a minute, she turned to stare at him.

"Maybe Tomás has found her for you."

"I'll ask. Good hunting." He nodded and turned back to the trail.

If he'd felt perplexed before, now he felt angry. He stopped walking after ten minutes and closed his eyes. The memory of saltwater filling his lungs choked him. Fresh panic shocked his heart into erratic beating. His eyes flew open. Brilliant light haloed his vision in the rising heat. He *had* almost drowned. But. He tried to recall the feel of her arms around him or the sound of her voice. All he summoned was a feeling of warm security, of relief from suffocation. Had his oxygen-starved brain hallucinated her? The inexplicable image of curly hair and brilliant blue eyes returned as if to confirm this.

John returned to his campsite. He couldn't go to Isla Encantada for hours. He didn't want to read. He couldn't snorkel. He wanted to know who had pulled him out of the water. He wanted to know why she'd left him. He stuck the island map into the waistband of his shorts and hopped onto the bike. He would distract himself with a tour of the island. He pedaled so furiously that he lost himself under the hard blue sky until a headache pounded its way into his blank mind and made him acknowledge his need for water.

When he got back to Dewey, John headed for Isla Encantada where water and a cold Medalla waited. Tomás nodded and smiled when John caught his eye and brought a bottle over before John could order.

"*Gracias.*"

"*De nada, Señor Juan.*"

"Some water too, please."

"*Sí.*"

John noticed a woman at the bar. He couldn't see her face, but her dark hair cascaded over her shoulders; her flamingo-pink skirt and white blouse popped against the brown of her skin. He stole looks at her through lunch. No one came to meet her. She flirted with the bartender and made Tomás blush. Her husky, Bette Davis voice drifted across the dining area and insinuated itself into John's ears. He began to wonder why he'd never picked women up in bars. He'd just worked up the courage to motion Tomás over when a man slid onto the stool next to her.

John watched as the newcomer leaned into the woman's shoulder and said something. The woman answered, shaking her head and shifting away. She lit a cigarette and propped her elbow on the bar between them. From John's vantage point, it was a clear rejection. He waited for the other man to take the hint, but he didn't. Instead, he snapped his fingers at the bartender and ordered something without taking his eyes off of the woman. The bartender set two beers down, his eyes sliding from the woman—who'd grown into John's Caribbean fantasy—to the man, who ignored the bartender to lean again toward the woman. The bartender hustled away but not before John saw the nervous flash on his face.

When the newcomer put his hand on the small of the woman's back, she shrugged it away. The man put it back. That's when John acted. His chair scraped against the floor and he stood before he knew what he was doing. The newcomer turned and stared at him.

"*Una problema, señor*?" The man's flat dark eyes telegraphed a challenge.

It wicked all the moisture from John's throat. He stood there, suspended between his seat and a certain confrontation.

The woman swiveled and looked at him, smoke painting a ghostly filigree around her. She smiled. White teeth brightened her face. "*No problema*, Jesus. This is *mi amigo*, the one I was to meet. Right?" Her dusky voice never rose yet John heard her across the room.

His own voice returned. "Yes."

The lithe Caribbean beauty slid from her stool and slinked toward him. John saw bare feet with peeping pink toenails. She met him, slipped her arm through his, and winked. "Buy me a beer, my friend?" She smelled of cloves and something hot and fecund. John nearly swooned.

"Of course." He started to guide her to a chair when Jesus blocked the way.

"*Gringo*." Jesus' breath stank of hops and something sour. "I never forget. Never. " His flat eyes regarded John. He looked at the woman. "You and I will meet later, *mi alma dulce*."

She laughed, a throaty, wild sound. "I will be all the sweeter, *mi guapetón*."

Jesus stroked a fingertip along her forearm. "*Igual que la fruta.* Until then." He shot a final glance at John and left Isla Encantada.

John let a shaky breath out and helped the woman into a seat. She reached for the dregs of his Medalla and tilted the bottle to her mouth. John watched as she swallowed. She kept her eyes on his.

"So." She passed a hand across her lips. John noticed that they were the color of pomegranate seeds, slightly swollen and glistening. "You are visiting Culebra?"

He nodded.

She smiled at Tomás who brought over two frosted bottles of Medalla. "*Gracias.*" He stuttered a nearly inaudible reply and left. "The beer is in my hand, my friend. Now, perhaps, we share names?"

John grinned. "I'm John."

"*Hola*, John. I am Raimunda." She tucked a strand of dark hair behind her ear, which was oddly shriveled against her smooth cheek. "You have come for the beach and the fish, my friend?"

"That's the plan. What gave me away?"

She shrugged and tipped up her bottle to drink. "That is why most *norteamericanos* come. Others? They run away from their demons and hide here on the Island of the Snake."

"'Island of the Snake?'"

"*Culebra.*" It sounded slightly dangerous when Raimunda said it. "Did you not know that you are on the Island of the Snake?" She watched him closely. Her right eye drooped a little. John found it enticing.

"And? *Are* there snakes here?"

Raimunda looked at him from between lowered eyelashes. "Not enough, some would say."

John's eyes widened. "And what do *you* say?"

"I say, my friend, there are always snakes if you know how to find them."

"I bet you're a regular snake charmer."

She tipped a modest face and the hair behind her ear slipped free. John wanted to reach over and push it back but he couldn't bring himself to touch her.

"You see my flyer?" He tilted his head toward the wall next to the door. She followed his motion with her gaze.

"That was you?" It was her turn to widen her eyes.

"'Fraid so. Do you like to swim?"

"Sometimes. *Por qué*?"

John looked at his hands, which were wrapped around the half-empty Medalla. She didn't match his mental image of his rescuer, but he wanted her to. "Someone pulled me out yesterday. I would've drowned."

"Oh, no! That is terrible, my friend. No, no I could never save you." She shifted so that she leaned closer. Her husky voice lowered. It caressed his jaw on its way into his ears. "I am *muy débil*. How you say? Weak. I am only *una mujer*. How pull I such a big man from the water?" Here she touched his arm.

John lifted his Medalla and drained it. At the moment, finding his mystery woman seemed less compelling.

She slid the bottles to the side of their table and took one of his hands in her own. "It matters not, my friend. I can make you even more glad to be alive."

≪≪≪

The mermaid circled the canal over and over and over, long after a glaring Ana left the shore. She worried the water over the hapless sea star. A hot, foul stench rose off of it, poisoning the water for a tail's length around it. Its death stank of cruel purpose, not natural release. She hovered over it for long seconds and then darted away toward the spot where the man last treaded water. Here, a different kind of echo altogether colored the water's essence. It was soft, luminous, and warm still. When she'd had more than she could stand from the sea star's final resting spot, she returned to the man's echo and renewed herself.

She'd hardly touched him last night. She'd found him after hours of searching along the coasts until she'd detected him on the northern shore. She'd drawn upon the dark energy of the earth and walked on temporary legs to his sleeping place. His sleep was hollow and yet heavy, devoid of nurturing dreams. He'd come from a far place where something had bound his soul, delicate as a sooty tern chick, in a filament as light and unbreakable as whale sinew. She tested this binding, finding that it had loosened a bit. There was hope then. She could send him dreams and free him entirely.

She lay next to him and sent visions into him as he slept. His dark hair covered her cheek and tickled her nose. She nuzzled the musky hollow beneath his arm. He smelled rich, his salty body excretions becoming his own human cologne, the breath of plants, and cool night air. He smelled like the promise of life. Next to his sharp odor, the *mer* males she knew smelled faint and diffuse, pale and unreal.

In the time between night and day, before the sky lightens with the sun's approach, the mermaid drew away from his warm, dry body. He sighed and she watched his sleeping face as long as she dared. When the shifting light sharpened his features, she stole away to the ocean. A gossamer thread connected them now. It was enough. She could trace him, could follow where he went.

She'd followed him to the place where she'd left him the day before. That's when she realized that he was looking for her. The gossamer thread binding them grew a little sturdier, a little more permanent. His thoughts were open to her and she urged him into the water. He came, bringing the lifeless sea star. She felt his pity and sorrow for the small animal and it moved her. When he lowered its husk, she sent it away on the current. She couldn't restrain herself any longer and she swam around him, running hidden hands along his thighs and up his flank. He radiated heat. She wanted it to weld them.

As soon as he sensed this, she backed away and they began to splash and roll. His deep laugh surprised her. She'd never heard laughter quite like it before and that too captured her. If she could elicit that again and again it would never be enough.

When he said, "Where's my lady *del mar* when I need her?" she knew that it was time to reveal herself.

At that moment, the old woman spoke. The mermaid's glamour wavered, but it held steady under the old woman's jagged gaze. The gossamer thread linking her and the man attenuated and flattened but didn't break. Heart skipping, she swam between him and the old woman, who came closer to the water, squatted, fingered bits of shell. The old woman radiated menace. Then she asked the man the unthinkable.

"Don't believe in mermaids, do you? Why not? Maybe one is swimming right beside you. Close to us vile humans, eh?" The old woman laughed, a sound of broken shells tossed on stone. The mermaid knew that she laughed at both of them. When the man wriggled behind her, she looked back at him. She recognized embarrassment. And denial.

Disconcerted, the mermaid swam to a safe distance where she observed as the man spoke to the old woman, saw him stop and scrutinize her search. She felt his perplexity when the old woman reached the rock where the sea star had lain. Unlike the stranger to whom she'd given her heart, this search troubled the mermaid. It troubled her a great deal.

Four

☙

ON MONDAY MORNING John awakened with an implacable urge to go to the cay across Luís Peña Canal, an urge that went far beyond any desire to be alone on his own private rock, beyond the fear of the ocean crouching in his brain stem. It had all the force of ravenous hunger, of raging thirst, of insatiable lust. After nearly drowning, he would have put off coming back to the dive shop to schedule diving lessons—his stated reason for coming to Culebra—except that he needed to rent a kayak *today* to quell this urge.

So he returned to Chris's Sunken Reef Dive Shop, a dusty storefront carpeted in beige and lined on one side with racks of snorkels, masks, and flippers, as soon as the shop opened, which happened to be ten a.m. Chris, a slouching tanned man with a phone cradled between jaw and shoulder, waved him in before disappearing into the back room. While he waited, John studied the shop more carefully than he had on Saturday. An assortment of artifacts—links of rusty chain, several spikes embedded in worm-eaten planking, and disintegrating portholes—studded the opposite wall along with other less certain items. What appeared to be a palm-size, dark-orange cannonball served as star to a solar system that included ancient handles and a dozen verdigris lengths of metal that may have been fasteners (of what, John had no clue) before the sea laid claim to them. The real treasure, presumably from Chris's underwater adventures, resided in a glass case that divided the shop. Inside, three dark gray plates—pewter, John guessed—lay in state along with flat oval gold rings and several heavy coins stamped with a cross surrounded by lions and what looked like castle towers. An emerald, the size of a teardrop, and flakes of gold held the place of honor in the center of the case.

John tapped his fingers against the smudged glass, his lips compressed and his chest tight. Chris had been friendly and chatty on Saturday, saying it was good to see someone from the States in the off-season, and told John that his diving schedule was wide open for the next two weeks. John knew that getting certified to dive was more important than satisfying an insane need to spend the day on a deserted cay, but he just couldn't think beyond renting a kayak. Would this genial guy deny him one after he confessed that he'd lost the snorkeling gear in Luís Peña Canal?

He found out two minutes later when Chris, his mutt Murphy at his heels, strolled through the doorway from the back office. He carried a flat wooden box that looked like it had been rescued from the wreck of a Spanish galleon. John would love to see what was inside.

"Hey," Chris said. He set the box on the counter between them. "I thought I'd see you today."

That made John nervous. "Why?"

Chris pursed his lips, opened the box. It contained receipts for the shop. John's disappointment couldn't

44

overshadow his anxiety at Chris's next words, however. "I saw the flyer at Isla Encantada. I figured you lost the gear."

John closed his eyes, took a breath, squared his shoulders, and looked at Chris. "Yes, I did."

Chris shook his head slightly. Sighed. Then he pulled out the top receipt and noted something on it. "Shoulda made you wear a vest. I'm gonna have to charge you for the gear."

For the first time since the near-drowning, John felt like an idiot. "I still have these." He held out the mesh bag that stored the gear and the lone flipper.

Chris accepted them, his face thoughtful. "Well, I can use the mesh bag, but no one's lost a leg to shark bite in years." He grinned at John's dumbfounded look and laid the items aside. "A new set will cost me seventy dollars."

"No problem." John handed Chris a credit card, simultaneously relieved that his stupidity was out in the open and angry with himself for the cost. And then he remembered that the cost had nearly been his life and he let the anger go. Instead, while Chris swiped the card, he screwed up his courage. Time to ask. "I don't suppose I can talk you into renting me a kayak?"

Chris dropped the card machine into the box and shut it with a satisfying snick. He studied John while scratching his stubbly chin. "Kayaking alone? Depends. Where you plan to go?"

That was the best John could hope for. At least Chris hadn't said no outright.

"To the cay across the canal." He paused, took a breath. "Listen, I've been white-water kayaking with friends since high school. The trip to the cay will be a piece of cake after all the rapids I've gone over."

Chris nodded. "I believe you, but I'm gonna need to know what happened the other day, before I take you out in open water. That is, if you still wanna dive."

John looked out the window. He'd gotten the kayak, but he still needed the lessons. All the coursework and confined diving in Pittsburgh meant nothing without the open-water dives. What else could he say about his accident? He returned his gaze to the lanky instructor and then looked down at the glass case. The emerald winked at him.

"I have these attacks sometimes. They've always been at night before so I didn't expect this one."

Chris's large eyes grew larger. "Attacks? Like your heart? Man, that's not something I think we should mess with."

John's mouth went dry. How would he make what happened sound mundane? "No, nothing like that. I just wake up sometimes feeling like the room is going to swallow me." He sounded weak. He spread his fingers on the counter, forced an easy grin and some apology into his voice. "What can I say? Thought of my girlfriend and suddenly I couldn't breathe. Got some water down my gullet and suddenly I was drowning."

Chris frowned. "Tell the truth, that makes me a little nervous." He turned, pulled a thick navy binder down from a shelf behind him, and plopped it onto the counter between them. "But it's probably covered under the standard release form."

John nodded. He waited while Chris considered the situation out loud.

"You won't be diving alone, of course."

"Right." John nodded again.

"And you gotta do well on my quiz before we go out."

"No problem." John knew he could ace any written test—he always did well on paper.

Chris scratched his chin again. It sounded like sandpaper. After what seemed like forever but was probably only ten seconds, he made up his mind.

"If you start to feel that way again, give me a sign—hands at your throat works for me—and I'll drag you up. Also, you gotta wear a full-face mask." He waited for John's nod before grinning. The lantern of his large white teeth lit up his long face. "Now that's settled, I gotta ask: is it true that some woman pulled you out?"

"Afraid so." John shifted his feet, shrugged, and smiled. "Any idea who she was?"

"Maybe. What'd she look like?" Chris's eyes had taken on a funny light, especially given how serious he'd been only seconds before. Later, John would wonder uneasily if he'd misread Chris the whole time or if he'd turned into a whack job only after hearing John's story.

"Not sure. I was a little out of it."

"Did you see breasts?" Chris sounded eager; breasts might do that, but the fact that he'd even asked the question stunned John.

"Y-yes," he said. "Is that relevant?"

Chris's grin had grown excited. "Maybe. I've seen one or two of them but never so close to the island."

"Of who?" The change that had come over Chris surprised John. Worse yet, he couldn't follow Chris's narrative. "How many women swim alone and naked around here?"

Chris blinked as though the question caught him by surprise. "Women? No women swim alone and naked around here."

John began to feel exasperated, but he pushed it down. It would do no good to let it out; who knows how Chris's mood would shift. "I'm sorry. What are we talking about then?"

Chris's expression lightened. "The *gente del mar*. I've seen them several times."

"'*Gente del mar*'? People of the sea?" Even when he translated it into English, John didn't understand as quickly as he should. When he did, incredulity flickered through his thoughts, and then died down. He smiled. "I see you talked to Tomás. He teased me too."

Chris, who'd been staring out the window and muttering to himself, a little smile curling his mouth, stopped and focused on John. "No one's teasing you. I *have* seen mermaids. And so have other Culebrenses. Pablo and Jorge, the guys who work on my boat, talk about seeing mermaids. ..."

"The oceans are such a huge mystery," John said, choosing his words carefully.

Chris's smile faded. "You think I'm one of those people who believe in UFOs and the Bermuda Triangle, don't you?"

John couldn't meet Chris's eyes. "I didn't say that."

Awkward silence padded the space between them. John looked down at the consent form that Chris had left on the counter. One man's fish might be another's mermaid. Who was he to decide? He looked at Chris, who watched him, shrugged again, and smiled.

"A mermaid's certainly better than a giant squid."

Chris smiled back. "I bet you see her again. I'd take you out, panic attacks and all, just for the chance to be with you when you do."

❧❧❧

After leaving the dive shop, John spent the rest of the morning in Dewey. Chris, although he'd agreed to rent a kayak, had stipulated that he needed to check on John for his own peace of mind. What that meant was that John had to wait until tomorrow. So he shopped for supplies at the *mercado*, picking up a Caribbean soda made with tamarind syrup, peanut butter, a loaf of bread, and a half a dozen oranges. He'd brought a camp stove and enamelware for some of his meals but only halfheartedly tossed four cans of beans into his basket. He'd suspected that camping would test his devotion to Zoë's diet, but he hadn't expected the dearth of good vegetarian convenience foods. He'd have to make do with fruit, imported chips and candy bars, and purified water from the main island. One good thing about Zoë's visit in twelve days: breakfast came with their room at Tamarindo Estates.

When he came out of the *mercado*, he stopped on the sidewalk, clutching his bag of supplies and blinking in the brilliance of the late morning. For perhaps the first time in recent memory, he had no agenda, no goal to accomplish or activity to pursue. Even the intense desire to go to Luís Peña had lost its edge. As he stood there, an unexpected tide of nostalgia surged in him. At 26, he couldn't be justified in missing his youth, in missing the free hours frittered away during summer. Or weekends. Or holidays. The lazy, hazy time spent daydreaming on soft spring mornings instead of tapping away at his keyboard or reading a textbook. But he did miss his youth. More often than not, he turned away from the beckoning green world outside his graduate office. More often than not, he spent hours below ground in a bunker euphemistically called a research lab.

He'd brought a book, of course, Lewis Thomas's *Late Night Thoughts on Listening to Mahler's Ninth Symphony*, but at the moment it seemed like pulling it out qualified as an assignment. A must-do, focused and probing. He wanted— no, he hungered for—diffuse, unplanned, open-ended wandering. After some time, a man pushed past him, lifting his reverie for an instant. Rubbing his forehead in a vain

49

attempt to control his thoughts, he saw his bike and understood that he needed to get on and ride. Unlike his almost-frantic tour of the island yesterday, he pedaled only strongly enough to keep the bike going and gradually his thoughts unspooled into emptiness.

His surroundings melted and merged into a living Impressionist artwork, a stained-glass filter that blocked out details of baked asphalt and dusty scrub. He'd lost two hours this way when a nagging ache in the pit of his stomach brought him back to the needs of his body. In his moving meditation, he'd managed to bike back to town—a very good thing because the back of his neck and his forearms had started to burn even though he'd slathered them with sun block.

He walked slowly into a deli, blinking his dazzled eyes in the sudden dimness. A plump, middle-aged American woman in an apron stood muttering with a clipboard before a cooler. She glanced up and smiled; her large eyes and upswept wrinkles promised old-fashioned hospitality and good cheer. She piled shredded carrots on top of a mound of hummus and feta, jabbed an olive-adorned toothpick into the sprouted-grain bun, and grabbed a large handful of plantain chips to wedge into the basket next to his sandwich. Seeing him settled at a table, she returned to her inventory and left him to his book.

John read through the heat of the afternoon, sucking in Thomas's essays with all the fervor of a man dying of thirst. Here was a kindred mind, a scientist and music lover driven beyond the myopic world of hypothesis, controlled setting, calibrated instruments, and precise measurements. To life beyond lab specimens. Even though Thomas's palpable fear of a nuclear holocaust no longer held the urgency it must have once excited, his genuine sense of wonder at the beautiful complexity of the natural world more than made up for its appearance in the lead essay. His willingness to tackle the dark side of modern technology, to pull back and consider the intricate connections among humans, life, and science both gratified and disturbed John.

He left the deli, stuffed in body and in thought. This time when he pedaled toward Punta Soldado at the tip of the southern peninsula, coasting on the downhill stretches, he returned again to Thomas's observations about the Earth. At the end of the paved road, he left his bike at the top of a steep hill and picked his way down a rutted dirt path to the rocky beach. He snapped a few photos and then sat down on a boulder near the water. The sun hung low in the sky, its reflection a golden fractal.

After a minute or two, he dug the essays from his backpack and flipped again to a sentiment that had grabbed him:

> Of all celestial bodies within reach or view, as far as we can see, out to the edge, the most wonderful and marvelous and mysterious is turning out to be our own planet earth. There is nothing to match it anywhere, not yet anyway.

Lewis Thomas was right, of course: the Earth was one of the seven wonders of the modern world, one hidden beneath the feet of all those urban souls who tramped unconsciously upon its skin, forever busy with their self-important tasks. His own vision had long been clouded, his own soul long troubled. On impulse, he rose and climbed back up the hill where he could look out at the blue horizon and marvel at its vastness. No one noticed it, this vastness, sitting inside a cubicle or walking along a sidewalk surrounded by houses or office buildings. But here, where there was nothing to obscure his vision, to bring the world down to his size, it was clear just how wide the sky was and just how small *he* was.

He glanced at his watch for the first time in hours. There was still time before the sun set to write a few postcards. He thumbed through glossy photos of old San Juan with its Spanish colonial fort and images of Caribbean parrots, orange and green and yellow like sweet-and-sour lollipops with beaks and claws. What should he send to Zoë? Historic buildings or living creatures? What would he write in the two-inch by two-inch square that would strike the right balance between "having a good time" and "it's no big deal that I'm here without you"?

After shuffling through the postcards, he sighed and decided to put off writing. Instead, he pulled out one of Punta Soldado that he'd bought this morning and scrawled a note to Stefan, who'd joked about John never returning to Pittsburgh:

> *They named this point of land after a soldier*
> *who went AWOL when he came to Culebra. I*
> *feel like going AWOL, too. The beauty of the*
> *ocean calls to me, like a siren.*

What would Zoë think if he admitted that Culebra answered some primeval need in him? She'd take it personally, of course. An image of her large black eyes radiating angry hurt flickered to life in front of his eyes. Perhaps he'd better keep his note chatty and impersonal. After staring toward the setting sun for ten minutes, he finally wrote this on the back of a postcard of Ensenada Honda, Dewey's harbor:

*Jackpot! I've found the last unspoiled spot in
the Caribbean. No casinos, no swanky resorts.
I'm up with the rooster, literally. Lots to see,
do. The food's great and the locals are
friendly. I'll call this weekend to talk about
our plans.*

He'd filled the four square inches; his writer's block had unfrozen once he'd discovered the appropriately casual tone supplied by the exclamation "jackpot." There was hardly room to sign his note, but he hesitated anyway. He never wrote a closing in an email to her, but a handwritten note demanded one. If he signed just his name, would that be intimate enough? Did she expect a "love" or would "cheers," just squeezed in, do? He waited for the answer and when it came, he knew that he couldn't write "love" no matter what she expected. If he was going to fall in love with her, it hadn't happened yet. He was still falling. So he signed only "John."

He stayed at Punta Soldado until the sun sank into the water, its brilliance extinguished in the rhythmic blue. Afterwards, he biked in the deepening dusk through town until he reached Isla Encantada. Standing just inside the entrance, he searched the dim interior, but only a handful of customers sat at the bar drinking. Tomás looked out from behind them and when he caught John's eye, nodded and returned to drying a rack of glasses.

The scent of hot corn oil and fried dough made John's stomach grumble. He ordered *arepas* stuffed with *queso* and a Medalla. The dumplings' flaky crust tasted so wonderful that he found himself ordering more. Tomás grinned at him when the waitress brought over a second plate heaped with extra *arepas*. John ate these so quickly that the bubbling cheese burned his palate, but still his stomach felt hollow.

Perhaps he'd better order something more sustaining, something more basic like rice and beans. When the waitress set the bowl of *arroz con habichuelas* in front of him, he started to sigh until he caught sight of the chunk of ham, a dark pink iceberg floating in a sea of rich brown. Even then, he almost tasted it. His mouth watered while he struggled against the complex scent of cilantro, garlic, and smoked meat. The waitress, who'd come to check on his food, saved him from himself. He sent the bowl back untouched.

Tomás came over looking concerned. "The *arroz con habichuelas*, they are bad, *señor*? They are *una especialidad de mi esposa*."

John squirmed and made an embarrassed face. "I'm sure they're *deliciosa*, Tomás. But I don't eat ham."

Tomás's face cleared. "Oh, I see, *señor*. *No problema*. I will tell her to make you some without."

"You don't have to do that."

"Oh, it's *no problema*. Many people, they don't like ham. We often eat it without ourselves."

Thankfully Tomás hurried away before John could protest again. He longed for the ham, but everything tasted so good here that he shouldn't give in to his baser cravings, even though the hollowness in the pit of his stomach had spread down his thighs. To distract himself while he waited for the vegetarian beans and rice, he pulled Zoë's postcard out and laid it on the table to consider.

Fifteen minutes later, the waitress deposited another bowl in front of him with a *thunk*. John looked at her, but she'd already turned, disapproval in her meaty shoulders. John shrugged and scooped up a mouthful of the savory beans and rice. Before he could stop himself, he'd shoveled the contents of the bowl into his maw. Afterwards, he still felt empty. He'd hardly begun to study the menu when

Raimunda, pink and brown and luscious, sauntered into his line of vision. She stopped at his table, a hand-rolled cigarette dangling from her fingers. She smiled, her dark eyes bold.

"Find your mystery woman yet?" He couldn't believe how attractive he found her husky voice. The hollow feeling spread to his chest.

"Nope." John hoped that he sounded casual. He nodded toward a seat. "You'll have to do."

Raimunda sat down and pulled her chair closer to his. "Buy me a beer?"

John waved the waitress over and ordered two Medallas. Raimunda put soft fingers on his wrist. He felt rather than heard his stomach growl.

"A plate of *alcapurrias*, too. You do not mind?" She smiled. "I am ravenous."

When the basket of deep-fried yucca fritters arrived, John's stomach did rumble aloud. He smiled and shrugged and focused on his order of *sorullos*, a cornmeal "log" stuffed with cheese.

Raimunda picked up one of the *alcapurrias*, broke it in half, and offered it to him. John shook his head, but his gaze stayed on the tantalizing deep-orange pocket filled with what looked like ground beef. Raimunda took a dainty bite from her half, and John could almost taste the savory meat-and-yucca.

"Have some, my friend," Raimunda said and brought the *alcapurria* nearer to his nose.

They sat that way for an eternity while John's heartbeat filled his head and hunger filled his whole body. He leaned over and took a deliberate, large bite from the fritter. It was his first taste of beef in almost a year and it tasted out of this world. He took another bite, his lips brushing Raimunda's fingers as she popped the last of the *alcapurria* into his mouth. She said nothing, just pushed the basket closer to him.

He ate three more orders of *alcapurrias* before the hollowness inside him had been satiated. He'd had no idea how hungry he'd been until the relief at not being hungry left him drowsy and unfocused. He slouched in his chair and played with the label that he'd stripped from his Medalla bottle. Through its brown glass, he saw Zoë's postcard lying under an empty basket. Grease spots speckled his handwriting. He found that he didn't care.

They sat drinking and talking for another half an hour. A few more customers wandered in and the conversation at the bar grew lively, but no one looked their way. John let words slip from his mouth, too overwhelmed by Raimunda's scent, her throaty laugh, the hollow at the base of her neck, to have more than a passing interest in the sound of his own voice. He floated just outside his head, detached from himself and yet aware of how hot he was, how slick his palms were on his thighs. When Raimunda edged her seat closer, he knew only the reality of the pulse fluttering in her throat.

"Let's leave." She spoke low, sending a thrill through him.

"You got someplace in mind?" He heard the tremor in his voice.

She stood up. Held out her hand. "Come, *gringo*."

They left his bike outside Isla Encantada. She held his hand in her warm, dry one and led him through Dewey, past the disapproving Catholic Church and the darkly officious post office. A few Culebrenses congregated on lit porches drinking beer and listening to tinny radios, their warm laughter muffling John's steps. Raimunda padded along on cat's feet. On the far side of the plaza a couple of sailors sauntered into the liquor store, but the *pueblo* was otherwise deserted at this hour. No one called out to them or even looked their way—they were wraiths. Near the clinic, Raimunda turned west and headed away from town. John tried to picture where they were going, but a fuzzy Culebra map only flickered and died in his memory.

They walked close to each other, Raimunda's arm grazing his every so often. As she moved, she exuded the spicy scent of cloves and musk that he already associated with her. It made him lightheaded. Perhaps Raimunda clicked no castanets nor seductively twirled any long skirts, but in her company he had no desire to meet a *señorita*. He'd just begun to wonder where she was leading him when he saw the sign for Playa Melones, a small stony beach near the southern tip of the canal. Except for a red navigation light glowing at the tip of a thin tower on the point, only the sound of lapping waves and the pungent odor of seaweed and salt greeted them.

Before John could speak, Raimunda sank down onto her knees and tugged at a sandal strap. She braced her shoulder against his thigh and lifted his foot to remove the loosened shoe, running her warm fingers lightly up his calf afterwards. John let his hand drift to her shoulder where it rested among soft dark hair. He leaned into her as she stripped the other sandal off. Again she caressed his calf. Gooseflesh sprung up in the wake of her fingers, which traveled as far as his shorts. Just as they tickled the skin under the hem, she jumped up and pulled John toward the water. As soon as their feet touched the wet stones, she ran ahead of him on the thin strip of beach.

John stood, gasping faintly.

"Catch me, *gringo*," Raimunda called over her shoulder.

His legs carried him forward before his mind had chosen to act. As John ran after her, she swerved into the ocean. Water swirled around his ankles before he realized what he'd done and stopped. She appeared not to notice and continued until the water reached her thighs. She turned around to face him.

"You must follow me to catch me, my friend," she said. The warm huskiness of her voice made the night intimate. "Rescue *me*."

The soft sibilance of her *rescue* twined around him, tugged him toward her even though the rush of the water urged him to stay safe on shore. Heart pounding, he waded deeper, his eyes locked onto Raimunda, her head dark against the night sky and her face hidden in shadow. And then she turned and headed toward the path of flickering moonlight caressing the waves. Without warning, she slid under the surface and disappeared. John's heart lanced his throat and he lunged toward the spot that she'd last been standing. Water cascaded over his head as he plunged into the suffocating ocean and grabbed for her. His hand closed on her hair. He snatched her head up and stumbled back until his feet touched the bottom.

They stood there, panting, faces dark and streaming.

"What did you say last night about making me glad to be alive?" The words tumbled out of him. Beyond recall.

For an answer, Raimunda pressed her chest against his and leaned in to kiss him. Her hot, salty mouth clung to his. The water tugged at their shoulders, pulled at their legs. But it could not separate them.

৵ ৵ ৵

John woke up late the next morning, headachy and stiff—and bemused. He'd only had three or four beers last night, but the fuzzy feeling between his ears and along his tongue testified to former intoxication, as though the forbidden beef, or Raimunda, had made him drunk. He sat up and rubbed his temples, squinting against the light. He'd slept heavily, dreamlessly. A sense of regret filled him as he realized this. He'd missed something. Or someone. Regret and peevishness sharpened the ache between his eyes, but he managed to shoulder them aside as he ate a cold breakfast of bread and cheese. He had the campground to himself now that the weekend beachgoers had returned to the mainland so he left his sleeping bag unrolled when he left to go kayaking. He biked into town, passing parents kissing children good-bye at the school. It was a familiar, if unexpected sight. That sealed it. No paradise contained a school.

He arrived at Luís Peña around nine-thirty and paddled around to the north side of the cay to the small beach there. Like much of the larger Culebra, the uninhabited Luís Peña Cay was covered with low-growing vegetation, stunted trees and dense shrubs; at its highest point, south of the beach, it reached nearly five hundred feet. Even though it was a nature preserve, day trips for hikes, snorkeling and swimming were allowed. Still, he was almost guaranteed to have the entire cay to himself on a Tuesday morning in March. He'd maneuvered his kayak without any difficulty, gliding smoothly and silently over the innocuous seawater, its clear depths hiding no dangers. After securing the kayak, he set out to explore the cay, taking forty-five minutes to walk its perimeter. By the time he returned to the beach, the fuzzy fatigue had burned off in the morning sun, taking his black feelings with it.

While he drank some water, he imagined that he was Robinson Crusoe. Castaway and forced to survive by his wits. No hard drives. No fluorescent lights. No windowless lab space. Just him, his hands, and what God and nature provided. An image of himself, woolly bearded and tanned sinew, filled his mind. He laughed. He wouldn't last three days let alone twenty-eight years. Still chuckling, he stripped off his sweaty t-shirt and shorts, leaving them to dry on a rock. After a few minutes, he added his sweaty underwear, too.

He considered the ocean before him. Unlike the fear that had gripped him last night when Raimunda beckoned him into the water, this gently lapping expanse promised peace. As long as he went no deeper than waist high, he should be fine. He wandered fifteen feet into the water, which was too warm to cool off in, and swam across the length of the small bay twice. The desire to separate from his body as it moved, to recapture the sweet blankness that had freed him as he'd cycled yesterday afternoon flitted in his thoughts, but a shadow on his spirit stoppered them inside his head. He flipped over onto his back and floated, his hearing muffled by seawater and his eyes dazzled by the sun. Seabirds streamed overhead like bits of windblown confetti. He tried to distinguish different species, but outside of the laughing gulls he was familiar with and a variety of pelican, the rest remained unknown—just as his rescuer remained unknown. She was one more element of nature, inextricably linked to Culebra's beauty and serenity.

As if conjured up by this thought, an upside-down face blocked his view of the sky.

"Ahhh!" He pulled his feet to the sandy bottom to right himself. His heart zigzagged and his breathing sped up.

Saltwater streamed into his eyes and blinded him. He swiped at the water running down his forehead. When he could see again, he realized that a young woman swam nearby.

"You scared the shit out of me." Even as he said this, his heart righted itself and his breathing calmed.

She flinched and backed away from him.

He regretted his words, the sharpness of his voice. He extended a hand toward her. "No, don't go. I didn't mean to yell at you. You just surprised me, that's all." Could this be his mystery woman? Only her face, her hair plastered to her head, appeared above the water's surface. Hard to know if she had the hair or the breasts to be the one.

She stopped backing away and came closer. She certainly had the eyes, though. Her eyes mirrored the color of the sea. "I'm sorry," she said. "I wanted to make sure you're all right." Innocent concern turned her musical voice grave.

"All right? Why wouldn't I be all right?" Confusion and discomfort tangled his voice. His thoughts were as opaque as the water around him, full of the sand that he'd stirred up, shielding his nakedness only temporarily. He refused to look down, to call her attention to it.

"The last time I saw someone floating alone, she—well, she didn't need any help." Something in her voice, some slight hitch, alerted him. He saw unhappiness cloud her wonderful eyes.

"I take it she'd drowned?" He asked this gently, as if the word might startle her into darting away. She couldn't go until he knew for certain if she were the one that he'd been looking for, if she were the one who'd saved *him* from drowning.

The unhappiness surged into tears; she nodded but said nothing. He wanted to wipe them away, but he didn't dare touch her. He tried to console her with words instead. "It wasn't your fault, you know."

Again she nodded and the tears shone on her cheeks. He looked beyond her and then over his shoulder to the beach. He saw no other kayak and he was sure that he would have heard a water taxi or other boat.

Seeing him searching, she looked away and said in slow words as though uncertain that she should admit to such a fabulous tale, "I swam from the other side of the cay." She'd stopped crying. Her brief tears struck him as natural as a summer shower.

"Really? I was told no one swam alone around here."

"I don't do it often. My father doesn't like me to go far from my family." Her remarkable blue eyes, like stained glass, held his. An electric shock leapt between them.

"Ah." It was his turn to look away. He knew that the water around him had cleared and he was entirely at her mercy. He knew what she would see if he didn't get a handle on himself. He had to keep her talking, had to work up the courage to ask her if she'd pulled him from the canal. "So you live around here?"

"Yes." Her eyes slid away again, fortunately not down. "My father's a fisherman."

So far so good. Time for introductions.

"I'm John." When she said nothing, he continued, "Do you have a name?"

She bit her lower lip, reminding him of his sister Cassie when she was in high school. He wasn't any good at guessing a woman's age, except for some vague sense that she was too young or too old, some rough guideline for the tenor of their interactions. The lip biting signaled extreme youth. Surely too young to have the breasts he'd seen. Too young to pull a grown man, thrashing and gasping, to shore.

"Never mind. I'm sure your parents wouldn't want you to tell me your name."

Her next words confirmed his suspicions about her youth. "I don't care what my father wants and my mother's dead." Still she didn't tell him her name. Instead, she asked, "Where're your pants?"

Heat rose in John's cheeks. He looked down, not to verify her statement but to hide his embarrassment. Nothing like exposing himself to a pubescent girl. At least he'd controlled himself in time—he didn't have *that* on his conscience. "I thought I was alone. I was sweaty after walking around."

"Oh, so it's not your custom to swim naked?"

"Now that you mention it, I'd like to get dressed."

With as much dignity as he could muster, he swam to the beach and stood up, walking toward the rock where his clothes lay without turning to see if she'd followed. He pulled his briefs and shorts on before looking over his shoulder. She remained behind.

"Aren't you coming out?" Perhaps she feared him. They were alone, after all.

After a moment, she swam closer and stood up. When she did, John understood why she'd hesitated. Except for a pair of tan cargo shorts that looked a lot like his, she wore nothing else. Heat flooded John's face again.

"Here." He tossed her his t-shirt. She caught it and looked at it before looking back at him. She didn't seem nearly as disconcerted as he felt. "Please put it on."

Shrugging, she pulled the t-shirt over her head. Her hair left large dark patches on the shoulders and the shirt clung to her wet breasts, negating the concealment of the cloth and testing his theory about her age. *She's too young*, he repeated to himself. *Dangerously young*. Every aspect of her behavior pointed to innocence and vulnerability. She walked over to the rock and sat down and began to comb out the tangles in her hair with her fingers.

"And you asked why I was naked? No wonder your father doesn't want you to go too far from your family." John stopped, thinking. "Maybe you should get back to him. I'd hate for him to show up and see you're wearing my shirt."

She looked down. "He wouldn't be happy, no." She made no move to leave, however.

John frowned at her. She seemed too slight to pull a flailing man out of the canal, but he couldn't help himself. Too young or too slight, everything else fit. He had to ask.

"Did you save me from drowning a couple of days ago?"

He watched her toy with a strand of damp hair; her eyes followed the pelicans walking stiff legged through the shallows not far from them.

"Yes, I did," she said at last without looking at him.

At her words, a thrill sparked the tender of his curiosity and ignited some strong emotion in him. He damped it down, as much to calm himself as to keep from scaring her. *Go slowly*, he told himself.

"Please, I'd really like to know your name."

She looked at him and he fell into the immense blue of her eyes. In that instant, he recognized the face that he'd described to Tomás. Why had he ever doubted it? "Tamarind. I'm Tamarind."

"Like the trees?" When she nodded, he thought, *How fitting. A water sprite with a wood nymph's name*. She really was the embodiment of a natural element. He went on, "I'm sorry if I sounded rude a moment ago, Tamarind."

She cocked her head, looking for the world like an inquisitive bird. "Are you going now, John?"

"No." He couldn't say *I can't go now that I know who saved my life. I need to know more about you*. Instead, he said, "I brought lunch. Would you like some?"

"Lunch?" She sounded perplexed.

"It's not much. Just some oranges and peanut butter sandwiches." He retrieved his backpack from the kayak and pulled out the food. She hadn't moved from her perch. He held up an orange in one hand and two peanut butter sandwiches in the other.

When Tamarind said nothing, he came over and sat on the sand at her feet. She watched him slide a sandwich out of its clear baggie and bite into it.

"Would you like to try some?" he offered, holding out the other sandwich.

"Yes!" A smile transformed her small face, which was tucked into a bed of drying hair that already showed signs of wildness. John thought he saw bits of seaweed in it as befitting a water sprite. Just like a sprite, she was small, perhaps only as tall as his shoulder, and delicately built. She was definitely too young. Maybe not even in high school.

Ignoring the proffered sandwich, she leaned over and bit into John's. After a few chews, she started coughing and gagging.

"What?" Fear clutched John's chest. He leaned in and put his hand on her shoulder. "Are you choking?"

In response Tamarind began digging into her mouth. John watched her with mixed astonishment and fascination. Bits of peanut butter and bread clung to its corners and flecked her cheeks. She spit without turning her head away, her tongue pushing the tenacious paste that had been her sandwich out of her mouth. At last, she wiped the mush away with the back of her hand. She appeared totally unaware that her actions could be perceived as curious at best, disgusting at worst. John surprised himself by finding her lack of social awareness appealing. Clearly she hadn't been molded yet in the rough world of adolescence.

"Mmmnuhh!" She screwed her face up. "What *is* that?"

John's own sandwich lay forgotten in his lap. "All that because you've never tasted a peanut butter sandwich before?"

Tamarind tossed her head a little and the tangles of her hair fluttered around her face. He wanted to brush it away, like a big brother taking care of his kid sister. He'd fixed Cassie's hair when she was little. "It clung to the inside of my mouth, like a tongue crab."

"Tongue crab? What's that?"

Tamarind's brow creased as she thought. "A tiny crab that crawls into a fish's mouth. It latches onto the fish's tongue and drinks its blood. The tongue shrivels up and falls off." She caught his expression and laughed. It was a delightful gurgle. "Don't worry. The crab becomes the fish's tongue."

"I can see you're going to be a bundle of fascinating facts." John smiled and put his sandwich away.

Tamarind didn't seem to hear him. She dropped off the rock and waded out into the water.

"Hey, I'm sorry. I don't mind your stories," he said, standing up.

She waved a hand toward him. "I'll be right back."

He sat and watched as she entered the water and began swimming what looked like the butterfly but so fluidly and gracefully that she appeared to glide through the water. She swam out about fifty yards and disappeared. He waited, his chest tightening and his throat closing, but she popped to the surface before his head began to pound. This time, when she swam back, she didn't use her arms, which she held in front of her as though she were a human torpedo. She managed to get her feet beneath her and rose in one smooth movement, her hands cupped together. For no reason, John thought of primordial life emerging from the oceans. He kept his eyes on her face and avoided looking at her transparent t-shirt.

Tamarind approached him, her liquid blue eyes bringing some of the sea with them. She held out her hands. John peered at them. At first, he thought that she'd brought back a jellyfish, but then he realized that it was a mess of translucent, worm-like creatures with little round white eyes with black centers—like those wiggly eyes children used in crafts.

"Your turn," she said and held up one of the creatures pinched between forefinger and thumb.

"Uh, what is it?" John asked, stalling. The creatures were squirming.

"Baby reef fish," she said and popped a whole handful, like peanuts or popcorn, into her mouth.

Could he tell her that he didn't eat fish? But he'd eaten beef last night. In for a penny, in for a pound. Besides, she'd clearly never had peanut butter before and *she* hadn't hesitated. Maybe he could just spit his out, too? John swallowed and reached for one of the larvae, grasping its slippery body. It squirted from his grip and dropped in the sand.

Tamarind laughed, leaned over, and dropped several into his mouth, as though he were a seal. Or baby bird. He didn't chew. He swallowed. It was like swallowing salty noodles. Not so bad after all, but he'd pass on doing it again.

"Thanks." His voice came out as a croak.

She finished eating the tiny fish from her palm, sucking the last three between her lips. John shrugged; he'd watched enough cable television to know that people of different cultures ate all kinds of things. Fish seemed rather benign in comparison to insects. Or snakes.

She lifted her face to the sky and smiled, an unself-consciously happy upturn that rendered her eyes half moons of pleasure. Particles of food still outlined the corners of her mouth and there was a smear of peanut butter in her hair, but she was oblivious to them. Instead, she started humming a tune. John had never heard anything like it before. The vibrations thrummed through her torso as if her ribcage were a tuning fork. He heard variations in pitch emanating from her throat, serving as a nice counterpoint to the bass of her body. She clicked her tongue against her teeth at the same time. John sank his feet into the warm sand of the beach and closed his eyes to listen. His spirit soared into the cerulean above them. When she stopped, he dropped back into himself.

"Why'd you stop?" He looked at her. Whatever she'd done, she'd gifted him with the sweet blankness that he'd experienced on his bike ride.

"Do you ever fly up with the birds?" she asked. In the space of a heartbeat, she went on, "Do you ever go underwater, I mean, way underwater or do you only use one of those tubes and stay near the surface?"

"I'm trying to learn to dive, but—"

"Where'd you come from? Is it far from here?"

"I'm from Pittsburgh, which takes two short flights to get here. I—"

She didn't wait for more but leaped up. "It was very pleasant meeting you, John. Thank you for the shirt. I hope to see you again."

She laid a cool, moist hand onto his cheek and looked at him unsmilingly. After a moment, the spectacular smile split her face again and lit her eyes, and then she backed away from him without looking at the ocean.

"Wait!"

But she only waved and turned to run into the shallow water. When the water reached her thighs, she flung herself into the next wave. John saw a tangle of arms and hair as she surged away from him.

"Wait," he repeated to himself. He didn't know what else to say.

When she looked back at him, her laughter danced like sunlight on waves. And then she disappeared around the point toward the canal.

ॐॐॐ

That evening, John ventured south over the drawbridge to the Dockside, as much to avoid running into Raimunda as for a change of culinary pace. Isla Encantada was small and intimate, and he'd be a sitting duck if she showed up. He'd had all day to consider what he'd done last night and he still didn't know how it had happened. He wasn't a saint by any means, but he knew where his boundaries were. At least, he thought that he'd known. Raimunda had waltzed right over them as if they didn't exist. As if she had a secret code that bypassed his system programming. The question was: would Zoë believe him? Would she forgive him? They lived together; it mattered a great deal what he did with another woman, to himself as much as to Zoë. Stefan, if he knew, would grin and offer to buy him a beer.

John asked the waitress to seat him as far from the entrance as possible and she led him to a small table next to the canal. While he waited for his order, he drank iced tea and composed a speech to Zoë, but no matter how many times he tried, nothing he said sounded plausible or defensible. He stayed there all evening trying to find the words, sitting in an ever-increasing cloud of mosquitoes who dined on his penitent flesh until the waitress gently shooed him out.

Five
☙

WHEN IT FINALLY CAME TIME for John to strap on an oxygen tank and drop sixty feet to the ocean floor, he found that nearly drowning no longer dominated his thoughts. He couldn't look at the Caribbean without seeing Tamarind's luminous eyes—everything else about the sea receded into meaninglessness. He hadn't entirely lost his fear. It had just moved inside a plexi-glass box inside his mind: he could see his irrational self pounding and mouthing words, but it had been reduced to wild gestures that he ignored.

He met Chris at his shop. Chris had lost the feral gleam in his eyes and never mentioned the *gente del mar* while they loaded gear with Pablo and Jorge onto his boat. His no-nonsense demeanor and thorough checklist turned the lights out in John's anxiety box. As they worked, he told John what to expect at Amberjack—the reef southwest of Culebra named for the silver fish that clustered in schools there. The currents were variable, for good and for bad, but nothing that a neophyte couldn't handle. John started to look forward to it, to see himself surrounded by water and breathing fine.

They'd boarded the boat and were casting away when he caught sight of Raimunda slouching against a corrugated building on shore, one knee bent under her tiered skirt. Even from a distance, warm, spicy smoke from her cigarette drifted over the cool smell of saltwater, mesmerizing and insistent. A familiar hollowness filled John. He nearly cried out to Chris to reverse course and tie up again, but he clinched his jaw instead and wrenched his gaze forward to the brilliant horizon. The scent of clove lingered like regret until Culebra had shrunk into a dark speck.

While they sailed, an ominous patch of clouds obscured the sun. Pablo and Jorge shielded their eyes and muttered to each other, but as quickly as it had appeared, the patch blew away. Chris pulled out photo albums with hundreds of pictures of fish, crustaceans, coral, and seaweed from dives he'd taken throughout the Caribbean. John nodded and murmured over as many pictures as he deemed polite. Perhaps it was the protective sheet overlaying the images, but the sea life looked plastic and posed.

Chris closed the creaky cover on the last album. "I've been everywhere. Always come back to Culebra though. It isn't the best diving in the world, but there's something about the waters around this little rock in the ocean. It's not just that they're so clear. There's something, I don't know, something *eternal*. Something bigger than us here."

John, who'd let the sound of the engine lull him into a trance, stirred and stretched. He'd been thinking of Tamarind's crazy hair and infectious laugh. The outrageous way she'd spit out her food, the graceful speed of her swimming. He'd tried to recall her humming, but he could

71

only identify its absence. He tugged himself back to the present and Chris, who sat rubbing the album cover.

"I guess Culebra really is the 'Enchanted Isle,'" he said. It was the first thing that came to mind.

Chris looked at John out of the corner of his eye. His introspective mood visibly changed. "Think you'll see your mermaid?"

The question didn't surprise John. It didn't bother him as much as it would have two days ago. "Maybe."

"Ah-ha! You've already seen her again." Chris studied him. "She's pulling you under her spell."

A dolphin broke the surface of the water. John watched as it leapt beside the boat, racing them. An image of himself riding on its back filled his mind, echoing his dream from the morning after his rescue. "I met the girl who pulled me out, yes."

Chris beamed. "What'd I tell you?"

John smiled at him. "She's a scrawny young thing." He almost said, *Too young for me*. He didn't. Instead, he pointed out the obvious. "With legs."

Chris grinned. "Oh, yeah. They can put on legs, walk on shore. I'll bet you cold cash you won't find it easy to go back to Pittsburgh next week."

It was clear that Chris couldn't be talked from his irrational belief. But how irrational was it? How had Tamarind pulled him, a 165-pound male, from eight feet of ocean? She'd grabbed him as he slipped under that last time. Perhaps that explained it....

John shoved the doubt aside and ended their debate with a joke. "Don't tell my girlfriend that. She'll come down here and kick my ass all the way back if I don't."

Chris shook his head and stowed the albums away in watertight bags. As he headed below decks to put them into a locker, he called over his shoulder, "I came to Culebra to escape my girlfriend. Best thing I ever did."

৵৵৵

At Amberjack, they descended through warm, clear water to a bottom where tan-colored soft corals sprouted, sheltering tiny black-and-yellow-striped wrasses. A sharp, brief twinge of fear erupted through John's mental restraint, but it was too late. He succumbed to the press of water overhead, gave into it—and found himself free to mingle with a teeming world of alien life. Even as John watched, the wrasses set up cleaning stations there to rid barracudas and orange hogfish of parasites. Not far from the coral lay a long line of rocks where delicate sponges and red and black deep-water gorgonians blossomed in a rich brocade, large French angels gliding among them. At the end of the row of rocks a cabin-sized boulder jutted off the flat sand. A school of amberjack swirled around John, many of them larger than his torso. Here Chris urged him to shoot some photos.

As John floated over the boulder with his waterproof disposable at his eye, he heard—or rather felt—humming like the song Tamarind had hummed the day before. The weight of the water around him disappeared and colors brightened. Yet when he looked around he saw nobody but Chris, who hovered nearby. Chris turned his palm up, questioning. He grabbed at his own throat with two hands before repeating the upturned palm. John shook his head vigorously and brought the camera again to his eye. No panic assailed him now. He'd shed his fear as easily as a sea snake shed its skin.

৵৵৵

In the warm air afterwards, his body weighed more and the nerves in his skin tingled, exposed. The fiberglass deck burned his bare soles, but John scarcely noticed. As he moved around the deck, he swayed to the rhythm of his afternoon dive even though the boat rocked little. When they returned to Chris's dock in the harbor, they tied the boat up and began stowing gear in the lockers. Voices further down the dock, the thin cries of seabirds, and the sawing of outboard motors out in the harbor all washed over him after the deep silence of Amberjack.

"John." Tamarind's odd voice startled him.

Looking up, he saw her standing on the dock in his t-shirt and the same pair of cargo shorts that she'd worn the day before and still barefoot. Copper-colored hair corkscrewed around her face, obscuring her eyes in the breeze. A smile radiated through the mess.

"Hey, Tamarind! And here I was afraid I'd never see that t-shirt again."

Chris paused behind him at that moment and said in a low voice, "I'd be afraid I'd never see what's in that t-shirt again." Raising his voice, he said, "Go on. I can take care of the rest of this. See you tomorrow then."

John nodded, grabbed his backpack and slipped on his sandals before stepping up onto the dock.

"Your father anchor somewhere close by?"

"Yes." She matched his pace as he walked. "What were you doing? Fishing?"

"Nope. That guy—Chris," here he gestured behind him, "is keeping an eye on me while I dive. We went out to Amberjack today."

"Keeping an eye on you? What does that mean?"

John looked at her, but it was a serious question. "Watch. Dive with me in case I try to drown myself again."

"Oh. Well, then, that makes sense. You obviously have a lot to learn."

"Gee, thanks."

She stopped. "Did I say something wrong?"

John sighed and turned toward her. "No, no. I guess I'm not used to hearing such brutal honesty, except from my— my friend Zoë. But she enjoys it."

"Enjoys it?" She appeared to think for a moment. "It's not that I enjoy or don't enjoy it. I just tell the truth. We were all babies once."

John looked at her for a long moment. "I believe you." He heard the surprise in his voice and hurried on. "Do you dive?"

She looked away and started walking again. "Yes."

"Do you want to dive with me tomorrow then? Chris won't mind." He didn't say that Chris would salivate at the chance to dive with a mermaid. He didn't think that he could say that with a straight face.

"I haven't ... with the things you use."

"Really?" They walked along in silence while he pondered what she meant. He imagined Chris grinning. He went on slowly, thinking aloud, "You dive like pearl divers? That's amazing! How long can you stay down?"

She looked at him, her eyes wide, but said nothing.

"Well, I don't know much about them, but I think there are some people who can dive pretty deep and stay there for a minute or two to look for oysters. Where'd you learn to dive without equipment?"

"I don't know." She looked away from him.

"You don't know?"

"We've always dived without things, all of us."

"All of you?"

"All of my family."

"Why? Why does your family dive? Is it for your livelihood?"

"'Livelihood'? What's that?" Again, the eyes that haunted his dreams jolted him as she turned to look at him.

"To bring up stuff to sell. Like the pearl divers."

She shrugged. "We just do. We dive because we can."

"Oh, well, that's a good enough reason." He looked at her, but her crazy hair hid her features. He rushed on. "I think it'd be pretty cool to see you in action. That's if you'd show me."

She didn't say anything, her head bent to look at the street onto which they'd just stepped. John changed the subject.

"Can you do that humming thing again? It was unbelievable! I felt like I'd just had a full night's sleep *and* a massage. I can't remember being so relaxed and alert."

Without answering, Tamarind began humming. This time, the throat-level hum skipped along in a decidedly upbeat melody. They walked for several minutes with the heat of the afternoon rising from the pavement around them. John, looking at Tamarind's feet, wondered if they'd developed protective calluses or if her humming blocked out all burning sensation in them. He was about to ask her if she wanted to join him for lunch when she abruptly stopped humming. He glanced aside. Her gaze had frozen forward.

"I've got to go. Perhaps I'll see you tomorrow." A note of panic sounded in her voice.

"Wait! Tell me where I can find you."

She didn't answer; instead she turned down a side street and hurried away. John started to call after her when a small movement caused him to look ahead. Ana sat cross-legged under a palm tree forty feet away, a large mat in front of her. Sunlight glinted on numerous small objects around her. When John's gaze met hers, she folded her hands into her scrawny lap and nodded. The lightness following Tamarind's humming drained away into the scorching pavement. A gull laughed overhead. John looked up reflexively and bird crap dropped onto his bare shoulder.

That night, Raimunda found him at his camping spot at Flamenco Beach. When she finally slept, John lay on his back staring at the stars for a long time. He found that, if he focused on the distant wash of wave on shore, he could remember Tamarind's song. He imagined that it sounded like the music of the ancient seas, of the primordial ooze that birthed every living thing.

ৡ ৡ ৡ

When John went out on his second dive with Chris, he looked for Tamarind at the dock, but she never appeared. This time, no humming reached him underwater, but he played the memory of her last tune over and over in his head like that refrain by Sheryl Crow—*All I wanna do is have some fun*. Whether it actually kept his panic at bay or only acted as a placebo, he had no way of knowing. On his third and final dive on Friday, he hummed to himself behind his mask. Chris flashed him a thumbs-up at the end of the dive and John knew that he'd earned his certification. He looked for Tamarind again after they docked, but she didn't show up. Much to his relief neither did Raimunda that night.

Now that he'd completed his training, John had several days to explore other areas of Culebra, especially its National Wildlife Refuge—and to lose himself in its dusty isolation. He planned to check out Playa Brava and Playa Resaca on the north coast where leatherback turtles swam ashore every spring to lay their eggs in sandy nests. But his trek wouldn't soothe him: his inexplicable unfaithfulness simmered in his unquiet spirit. He prayed instead that hard hiking might exorcise Raimunda. A part of him, the altar boy part, the part that cared that he hadn't been to Mass since his grandmother died, sought absolution on the hilly terrain east of Flamenco.

But first, he had to call Zoë. To hear her voice for the first time in a week, to tell her. He woke too early, anxiety curdling his stomach. Forgoing breakfast, he tried to read to pass the time. He'd already finished *Late Night Listening to Mahler's Ninth Symphony* so he read through the proposal for his research mission again, trying to focus on the marine geology, which wasn't his area. When it was late enough, he biked into Dewey to use Chris's phone. Chris, his large eyes drooping, yawned and led him to the room in the back where an old black phone sat on a metal desk. He waved at John, yawned again, and left.

Zoë sounded groggy when she answered. "God, John! Do you have to call so early?"

"Sorry. I forgot you're in the middle of your paper." Had she been too busy to notice that he hadn't written to her?

"You don't know the half of it." Already she sounded alert. True to her nature, she warmed to her subject in zero to thirty. "Dan's decided we need to run some new simulations before we submit the final paper and I've been working eighteen-hour days all week."

Sympathy, played well, could distract her. "He's out of his freakin' mind. Who does that any way?"

"A man who knows everyone in the security world and can get all the extensions he wants. I'm sleeping in today as an act of rebellion." She paused. Her voice turned silky. "When I get down there next Saturday, there's no way I'm sleeping at the beach. This island of yours might be paradise, but I don't need to do penance to be let in, do I?"

"No, of course not. I've already booked a cottage." Let her think that Culebra was a 'paradise,' something from a travel brochure. *He'd* be doing penance when she arrived. "It overlooks the ocean."

"Beautiful." She paused. "Had any luck diving?"

"Yeah, it went much better than I'd hoped. I won't have any trouble." The truth hadn't found its way to his tongue so

78

he chattered on. "I saw some amazing sea life last week. It was like I'd descended into a Disney theme park, the colors were that bright."

"I told you there's nothing like snorkeling along a reef." Zoë's familiar smugness nettled him; he seized onto it to keep from drowning. "I'm looking forward to getting in some snorkeling. How's Playa Flamenco? Every bit as beautiful as you read?"

He counted to three, let out a steady breath. When he spoke, he sounded casual. "Oh, absolutely. A mile of pristine white sand, which unfortunately is crowded with drunk campers on the weekend. I took the ferry over with a few hundred last Saturday. They start drinking at eight a.m. and sleep at the beach."

So much for letting her think Culebra was a paradise. At least he'd told the truth. Maybe it would be easier to admit that he'd slept with another woman now.

"Okay, I'll cross Playa Flamenco off the list, then. Too bad, I was looking forward to sunbathing topless." The silkiness returned, inviting him to banter, but he couldn't respond in kind. He changed the topic to get his legs under him, to give him control.

"I've been going over the proposal again. The geology, what I understand of it, is incredibly fascinating. These guys don't really know what they're going to see down there, and it's rife with speculation. I'm beginning to appreciate just how important this is. It's like we're going to the moon for the first time."

"Not thinking about changing careers, are you?" It was a throwaway question.

More truth leaked out, surprising John as he said it. "I wonder sometimes."

If she'd understood him, she would have mined this vein for all of its worth, but Zoë didn't follow up. She appeared to have another, more serious issue to confront.

"So, have you met anybody on Culebra? Any sassy *señoritas*?" Her voice was light, playful, but John knew better.

Now was the time to tell her. He squirmed, grateful that she couldn't see his face. He couldn't see hers, either, and in that moment he knew that he couldn't tell her over the phone. He'd have to take his punches in person.

"Except for the weekends, this place is pretty quiet. There's a guy here who is Hemingway's double. He was talking to a couple of American college students the other day. I guess I could've sat at the bar with them, but I just satisfied myself with speculating about what brought them here. Other than that, I've spent most of my time with a guy from the dive shop."

Zoë must not have heard the tremor in his voice, only the escapism.

"You've got a week ahead of you with nothing to do except visit some sea-turtle nesting grounds and drink beer? I really wish I could've gotten away sooner to be with you. But *I'm* not blessed with an advisor who thinks it's okay to start spring break a couple of weeks early."

"What?" John feigned exaggerated ignorance. He could hide in humor now that the crisis had passed. "I'm here preparing for my mission."

"Yeah, yeah. Save it for the envious geeks you call friends. What are you *really* going to do with yourself? Daydream about what you're going to do to me when I finally get there?"

John ignored the question. "When *are* you getting here?"

"I'm flying into Dewey at 10 Friday morning where I'm sure you'll be waiting impatiently to see me."

"Impatient isn't the word," he said—honesty hidden in humor. Another relief to his sore conscience, even if it was indirect. "I'll see you on Friday then."

"Okay, I'll see you on Friday. And John—I love you." She'd slipped it in, just when he'd thought that he was home free.

John mumbled good-bye and hung up. He took the ponytail holder out of his hair and raked his fingers through the thick strands a couple of times, looking out toward the horizon. He shrugged and twisted the holder around his hair again. He'd delayed the catharsis of confession; now all he could do was to throw himself into his hike.

He picked up his backpack and set out for Playa Resaca, the nearest of the two nesting beaches. As he hiked the tortuous mile and a half, his mind emptied and he soaked in the mid-morning sun like a solar cell. He wasn't serene and detached as he'd been on the bike ride; on the contrary, he experienced an exquisite awareness of his body in its surroundings. The sun burned the back of his neck and forearms and that knowledge consumed him until he focused on his straining hamstrings and calves. He felt the heaviness of his footfalls on the steep boulder-lined trail that led him 650 feet upwards through a forest of cupey and jaguey, whose stilt-like roots shaded orchids, succulent bromeliads, and agave with their stiff, sword-shaped leaves. The still air clung to him like a wetsuit and he stopped frequently to drink water and shoot photographs. Once he arrived at the eastern side of the mountain, the trail plunged to the shore; and by the end of his hike, he panted and his skin was slick with sweat.

Playa Resaca—"bottom of the sack" in Spanish—was nearly as beautiful as Playa Flamenco; Mount Resaca and the rugged terrain that he'd hiked sheltered the beach and it remained deserted, even this late in the morning. John surveyed Playa Resaca for several minutes, resting from his trek and sipping water. He could well understand why the leatherbacks would avoid the noisier Playa Flamenco for this beach; he himself preferred its solitude. When his breathing had evened out, he continued through the thorny scrub toward the other main nesting beach, Playa Brava, where he would take a quick dip.

Playa Brava was much like Playa Resaca: sheltered and deserted. Here, however, the surf was much stronger; hence its name: "the rough one." John walked along the length of beach, imagining awkward turtles swimming onto the shore. Once they had cleared the water, their powerful flippers would be nearly useless in the clinging sand; they would manage to propel themselves across the beach with the drive to bury their eggs on land.

John paused in mid-stride.

Why do female sea turtles split their lives between sea and land? Why do they leave their eggs alone and vulnerable? Surely beaches are no safer than the sandy ocean bottom?

He looked up at the bright, flat sky.

There must be hawks or something who like turtle eggs. Come to think of it so do people and other animals. Why do leatherback turtles risk the survival of their species by leaving the ocean?

No answer came to him. As he stood, caught by these sudden questions, a lone seagull glided overhead, arcing over his spot. John watched, turning to follow it. The gull laughed and sped away toward the west.

Hot, hungry and unable to sustain a coherent mental struggle, he strode back to his backpack, which he'd left under a tree. He sat with his back against the trunk and pulled a sandwich and chips out. As he ate, he glanced idly up at the tree, which had numerous small green fruits resembling crabapples growing on it. He'd seen fruit trees all over the island: orange, lime, banana, guava, and mango. Perhaps the fruit of this tree was also edible, even if he wasn't familiar with it. He'd take some back with him to Dewey and ask a local what it was and if he could eat it.

He'd finished his lunch, including an orange and a banana, and stood up to pluck one of the fruits when a woman's voice behind him said, "No, don't touch it."

His fingers slipped from the fruit, which fell to the ground at his feet. He turned to face Tamarind, who stood fifteen feet away.

"Tamarind! You surprised me." He heard the happiness in his voice but didn't have time to wonder at it.

She stepped toward him. "The fruit of the *manchineel* tree is very poisonous."

John shook his head, smiling. "I wasn't going to eat it, if that's what you thought. I'm not *that* stupid."

She frowned, her eyes a vivid blue-green. "It's dangerous even to touch. It bleeds white. It burns."

John stood and gazed at her. She held his gaze for a moment but then tilted her head and stared off into the tree line. Strands of damp hair lifted off her neck and danced along a finger of breeze.

He teased her, hoping that she'd look at him. "Saved again in the nick of time. How'd you find me? You following me?"

She turned and looked back toward the water. "Yes."

"I don't know whether to be flattered or worried." Still teasing, he took a step toward her.

"Worried? Why?" When she looked at him, her amazing eyes had widened.

"I'm just not used to being stalked." He grinned at the thought of this girl stalking anybody.

She kept her gaze on him. He'd aroused her curiosity. "'Stalked'? What does 'stalked' mean?"

"Follow someone around a lot without him knowing it."

She tossed her head and the breeze caught her tangled hair and pulled it away from her face. "Now you know I'm following you. Maybe I'll stop." Here she stuck her hands in the pockets of her cargo shorts and turned away from him.

John darted forward and caught her arm before she could walk more than a step. Her skin and hair smelled salty. "No you don't. Your abrupt exits are unnerving. Besides, I know you're not stalking me. Stalkers don't usually act the part of guardian angel."

She didn't try to escape; if anything she shifted closer. "Guardian angel?"

"My protector. Please, stay for a while." He gestured to the tree where he'd been sitting and sat down. "No more peanut butter sandwiches, I promise."

She squatted on the sand, imitating his posture. "How's your diving?"

John realized that he hadn't stopped grinning. "Well, I passed my test so now I'm certified! You'll have to come up with another reason to follow me around."

She wrapped her arms around her knees and stared at the sand near her feet. She said nothing. His grin faded. Maybe he'd gone too far.

John took a long pull on his water bottle and changed the subject. "You know when the sea turtles start coming in to lay their eggs?"

Tamarind pushed a clump of hair behind her ear where it sprang immediately to freedom. "They come to land after the rain starts, perhaps in a week or two."

"You ever helped out with counting eggs or monitoring beach conditions?"

"No. But my family helps out whenever we see any on their way here."

"How d'you do that? You can't put out a beacon or anything, right? I thought lights distracted the turtles from finding their nesting spots."

She shrugged. "We do whatever we can. Turtles aren't very smart. They eat anything that looks like a jellyfish. You people dump a lot of garbage."

"You sound like a marine biologist." As he spoke, he idly traced her name in front of his toes with his fingertip.

Tamarind shifted so that she could bend her face nearer to the sand. Her elbows jutted out on either side of her torso and her hair fell over her face in riotous deluge as she studied the letters, the layer nearest her slender neck damp and smelling of the sea. For an instant, John thought he saw the iridescence of mother of pearl at the top of her spine, but when he squinted for a better look, her smooth skin was bare. She wore no jewelry at all.

"What's that?" She pointed at his tracing. "I've seen that before."

"I should hope so. It's your name." He touched each letter as he called it out. "T-a-m-a-r-i-n-d. Tamarind."

"It is?" She didn't look at him. Instead, she reached her forefinger out and drew over the letters. Under her breath she repeated their names. Then she traced the letters again under his, repeating them as she did so.

"You can't read?" He said this gently but surprise still colored his voice.

"No."

Something in the way that she hunched her shoulders told him not to ask anything else about the topic. She shifted back onto her buttocks and draped her arms around her bent knee. She hummed a bit, as though trying out a tune and then began in earnest. As abruptly as she began, she stopped.

"Did you come just to learn to dive?"

"Pretty much. I came to spend a couple of weeks getting used to the water for a research mission I'm going on next week. I got seasick once and needed to get my sea legs before I sail."

"Sea legs?" Then she laughed the same delightful burble that he'd heard when they first met. He hadn't realized that he'd wanted to hear it again until now. "*I* have sea legs and I want land legs!"

Turning to squint at the sky, he shaded his eyes with his hand. "I also came to spend some time away from a computer screen and cinderblock walls." It felt safe to let that out.

"So you aren't going to be here much longer?"

"Just another week. Then it's back to the salt mines."

"There's a lot of salt in the sea." She looked serious.

John whooped, a head-thrown-back, hand-slapping-thigh reaction. "That's priceless! I'll have to use that next time I want to take off when I should be working."

A sound in the bushes behind them caused John to turn around. A dark-haired, brown-skinned man wearing a khaki shirt and pants emerged from the path and stopped short when he saw them. He smiled, white teeth splitting his brown face. John guessed that he was a park ranger.

"*Hola.*"

"*Hola.*"

"*Hablás Español?*" When John shook his head, he went on. "This isn't the best beach for swimming, you know. The current here is very strong."

"No problem. We're just enjoying the view."

The man looked at Tamarind, who sat humming and tracing in the sand. He grinned again. "I see what you mean. It's especially lovely today."

John ignored the comment and he leaned closer to her. He almost put his arm around her but stopped himself. "I was wondering. You got all the volunteers you need this year to help count leatherback eggs?"

The ranger, who'd been rummaging through a large olive-green duffel, paused to think.

"Another pair of hands, they would make the work grow lighter." Another grin sent a sparkle to his eyes.

"Thanks." After the ranger walked away from them, John turned to Tamarind and smiled. "Maybe you should volunteer. I get the feeling you're going to need something to do after I'm gone."

"I can always find some other tourist to 'stalk.' You're not much different from sea turtles, you know."

Six

 og

ZOË ARRIVED ON CULEBRA the following Friday morning, an Amazon warrior barely civilized for life among unevolved men. John met her at the airport in a rented Suzuki Samurai and they drove to Tamarindo Estates to check in and drop off her gear. As Zoë dropped her duffel bag onto the queen-sized bed, she turned, lifted her arms and snaked them around John's neck.

"God, am I glad to be here. This trip has been one nightmare after another. First, some guy copped a feel outside the airport while I waited at the taxi stand. He wasn't even very subtle about it, just grabbed my ass as he walked by me on the sidewalk. The employees at the Marriott weren't much better. The man behind the counter slid the room key into my palm, rubbing his fingertips suggestively over my wrist. Then the bellhop just happened to caress my hand as he reached for my bag. What pigs."

"I doubt they would've pressed their attentions any more than that. If they did, you could've just kicked the shit out of them. Isn't that what you study for?" John said this as casually as he could, aware that he spoke for himself as much as some yokel in San Juan.

"That's hardly the point, John! I shouldn't have to depend on Tae Kwon Do when I'm traveling in the U.S. Puerto Rico isn't exactly the third world." She nuzzled the side of his neck. "Mmm. You smell good enough to eat, even if I *am* a vegetarian."

Her lips burned along the flesh of his neck, washing stillness down him as effectively as a fast-acting poison. He just managed to speak before the process was complete. It was a lame attempt to beg for forgiveness. "Where would the fun be if you didn't have some real jerks to deal with now and again? It's got to get pretty boring policing the misogynists at CMU."

"You're just thrilled that these guys make you look so good." She kissed him, pressing her whole torso against his. "It's been too long since we made love."

She pulled away long enough to close the curtains on the window overlooking the canal. Then she twined herself around him again as if she feared his escape, but she had nothing to fear. He was already paralyzed.

"Time to change that."

వావావ

Later, John drove her around the island, or as much of it as was accessible by road.

"Not much to see, really." They turned north toward Playa Flamenco. "The beach is world-class, of course, but nothing else is here."

"It's just because it's not built up, John. Some people would think that was a good thing, you know." She paused. "So whadya have planned for me this weekend, besides showing me how much you missed me?" At these words, she slid her left hand up his right thigh and into his crotch, squeezing gently.

John kept his eyes on the road.

"Actually, I wondered what you'd think about going out for some deep-sea fishing. There's a crusty old barnacle around here with a forty-three-foot yacht, the Sakitumi. That is, if battling big fish in the name of sport appeals to you." He held his breath. Given her rabid form of vegetarianism, he expected her to spit fire. He had no idea what had prompted him to antagonize her this way.

She stunned him with her answer. "How Hemingway. I'd love to go. Absolutely."

She leaned against the passenger door and looked out the open window. The breeze as they drove dared to lift her heavy hair and caress her neck. In her dark sunglasses and black camisole, she reminded John of a Hollywood starlet, exuding sex appeal as cloying as night-blooming jasmine.

"Maybe a little development wouldn't hurt," she said after a few moments as they drove south on 251 toward town. "Something that would help pay to clean this place up."

"What? You don't like having such an unobstructed view to the terraced dump?" John had forgotten the dump until it came into view and the sarcasm in his voice surprised him.

"Not in paradise I don't. They should plant some of those bright red flowers—what are they called?—in front of the trash."

"Bougainvillea. I think you're thinking of that. Or maybe hibiscus."

It took John only an hour to drive the circuit of the island's main roads. Perhaps it was Zoë's presence or the view from the driver's seat of the Samurai, but John surveyed all of Culebra's eyesores for the first time in two weeks. As they neared Dewey, they saw cramped cinderblock houses huddling along narrow streets. Boats rested on concrete blocks in the patches of land that constituted yards and everywhere they saw more trash: pipes, tires, and beer cans. Zoë wrinkled her nose and shifted away from the window. Even after they drove south past Dewey and left the houses behind, lines creased her forehead. Little existed on the southern and eastern arms of Culebra beyond a few side roads leading to homes that, from their vantage point, seemed to promise privacy to transplanted *gringos*. But for John, the trip away from Dewey reminded him of the serenity that he'd discovered while visiting the Enchanted Isle: every rise in the road brought views of the ocean, vivid against the sere brown and dusty green of the landscape.

Culebra exists only to draw the spirit to the sea around it. On the heels of this thought, Tamarind's ethereal blue eyes tantalized John's memory, but he shoved the image aside. Funny that he should think about a slip of a girl with crazy hair and incessant questions while Zoë's head rested on his shoulder—Zoë deserved better. He turned the Samurai onto the road to Tamarindo Estates.

"Wow, that was short and sweet. After a winter in Pittsburgh, this sun is a godsend, but I wouldn't want to live here." She hadn't moved even though he'd parked; instead, she ran her fingers along his forearm and the back of his hand.

John switched off the engine and looked down at her black hair, glossy and thick. She was too close; there wasn't enough room in the cabin of the Samurai to tell her the explosive news that he must tell her. So he settled for what he hoped was conciliatory humor. "Between the macho males and the roaming roosters, it's probably not the best place for you."

Lunch was larger and more gourmet than John had eaten for most of the past week; he'd hoarded his money and eaten only one meal out—a cheeseburger at Señorita's where he'd avoided seeing Raimunda, who managed to find him at the camp anyway. He had no idea why she kept seeking him out; more to the point, he couldn't understand the queer state that came over him whenever she appeared. He felt at the mercy of his lust, his rational thought subsumed to the white heat radiating from his groin. At these times, a shadow fell over his spirit that left him in a funk until he went to sleep; and then the dream returned and washed away the darkness as oil is washed from skin. He felt cleaner, but a vile residue still remained. And then Tamarind would arrive somewhere on his journeys about the shore or cays and her smile was the sun burning away the clinging mist of night.

He shook his head as Zoë addressed him while they waited for their Nuevo Caribbean chickpea stew. *Now* was not the time to think of either of these island women.

"I need to call the vet's before we go snorkeling. Stella had to have surgery on Wednesday and she's staying there while I'm away."

"I bet that's expensive." It was perfunctory; he and Zoë's cat had never gotten along and it was even harder to fake concern after two weeks away from the mercurial tortoiseshell.

"Yeah. It's got me thinking I should consider veterinary school after I finish my Ph.D." She paused. "So Heath Garrett's just been named as faculty researcher of the year. He won a two million grant from ARPA. But that's not all. The rumor's going around that he's sleeping with his administrative assistant and she's married with two kids."

"You sound shocked." His tone was casual; he kept his eyes on his flatware, the water glass, anything but Zoë's face.

92

He felt as though he'd been slung up on a meat hook, however, and his chest tightened.

"I am. The man's got no scruples. Can't he at least bang someone from another department?"

He had to defend Dr. Garrett although he couldn't stand the arrogant prick. Struggling around the feeling that his left lung had collapsed, he spoke in reasoned words. "C'mon, he's a geek, Zoë. He doesn't have any social skills and he's not meeting many women holed up in that lab of his. He's probably grateful to have the attentions of anything remotely female."

"Are you speaking from experience? If so, I'm not sure that's a compliment." Had he misheard? Was there menace in her voice?

He picked up his ice water, choked on a sip, and wiped his mouth with his napkin. Time to take the self-deprecating route, seasoned with truth. He forced himself to look at her. "Oh, please. You know damn well you're out've my league. That makes me an extra-grateful geek."

Zoë preened. "True, too true. I expect you'll show me how grateful later."

Beneath the table, John felt her bare foot on his calf. He thought of the crescent kicks she often whizzed past his cheeks as they walked around campus. Once, she'd misjudged the distance to his head and connected with a kick. His ears rang for the rest of the afternoon. She'd apologized and given him a thorough body massage later, but he still couldn't think of her feet without vestigial tinnitus.

"So you got your paper out, I take it?" John sipped at his Medalla.

"Thanks to yours truly, we not only got it out, but the data from the last-minute experiments actually got verified, graphed, and explained coherently. Not a single person on my project can write his way out of a wet paper sack without me."

"Good you know your own worth." Not that he'd ever doubted that she did, but he meant it: women computer scientists often had to be their own champions even in so-modern an era as the mid-1990s. It felt good to be genuine and straightforward.

Zoë picked up one of his hands with both of hers and rubbed his fingers with the pad of her thumbs. John wanted to take his hand away, to build on his slight honesty, but he couldn't.

"Okay, so that wasn't so modest," she said. "But I'm really speaking out of frustration. I hate to work so hard on research and have it documented by illiterate buffoons. Just because they can write an elegant piece of code or practically visualize where all the locks and keys go in a system doesn't mean they get a pass when it comes to explaining what they did."

"Not everyone's as well rounded as you. And take it from me, most people can't write their way out of a wet paper sack. You should see the Trench proposal. I had to annotate it heavily during the kick-off meeting. Luckily for me Dave Pendergrass speaks better than he writes or I'd be completely lost."

"Now you're really asking for something special." She wagged a finger at him. "I never said I expected these guys to explain their work to people outside the field. God, that's too much to ask for."

"That's why the most brilliant scientists—Hawking, Sagan, Wilson, Gould, Glieck, Feynman—" John freed his hand to tick them off on his fingers, "stand out. They bring science to the masses. Maybe it's your destiny to illuminate computer security issues for the average person. There certainly need to be more women science writers."

"Ugh. Forget it. I just want to win the Turing Award." She smiled a coquette's smile and John remembered their first meeting last September at an IC event for new grad students. She'd ignored Stefan's full frontal assault and bestowed all her dazzling, dark radiance on *him*. No matter what happened between them, he'd never forget the thrill of being her choice and the heady first days of their dating.

"Now *that* would be a glass ceiling worth breaking." He raised his Medalla and smiled, his empty hand dropped to his lap and freedom.

Zoë picked up her beer in toast. "Here's to the future. May it bring us many worthy research problems, outstanding recognition, and plenty of time to bask in the glory together."

John raised his beer and dipped his head, wondering if he'd promised something with his acquiescence that he couldn't honor.

❧❧❧

John woke the next day stiffer and more tired than he'd been after two weeks of sleeping on the ground, even after hiking. He'd dreamt odd fragments filled with wraiths and foreboding. In one, Tamarind floated in shallow water, her arms uplifted to the sky; instead of skinny legs, a scaly, muscular mermaid's tail undulated beneath her perky breasts. In another, Zoë crouched at the edge of a cliff overlooking the water, unblinking eyes staring at something, her black hair loose and tangled. When he tried to call out to her, she looked at him with zombie eyes, dark and devoid of life. At the same time, he saw Raimunda standing behind her, swaying and smirking. Then, as dreams tend to do, everything discernible dissolved, only to be replaced by fleeting snatches of color and emotion that left him feeling uneasy.

He found himself alone in bed. He lay along one edge, his right arm dangling and his pillow covering his head. Lifting his face, he studied Zoë's pillow. An irregular hollow wafted back a faint trace of spicy perfume. Her presence lingered there in some memory of density and form. He could not have relaxed into the expanse of the bed now any more than when she'd actually lain next to him. After a moment, he rolled onto his back and looked at the ceiling fan in the clear early light, restless until he realized that he couldn't hear the sound of surf or the sharp cries of seabirds. Releasing his breath at the thought, he pivoted on the bed and stood up. In the bathroom he took a piss, relishing the luxury of standing in a clean, lit bathroom first thing in the morning. He wanted to shave again—he'd already showered and shaved the night before—but he settled for brushing his teeth and washing his face. In the mirror, the dark stubble gave his face a haggard appearance.

Outside their cottage, Zoë practiced Tae Kwon Do on a bare patch near the main building. She'd pulled her hair back with a plain silver clip and wore a tank top—sans bra—and black Lycra bicycle shorts. Although her face was free of makeup, her bare feet revealed deep-red polish on the toenails. There was no mistaking her physical strength. As John leaned against the rough stucco wall watching, she put her well-trained body through its paces, gracefully and forcefully lifting her legs in a variety of kicks that he'd seen knock expert martial artists on their butts. She breathed heavily and her skin glistened. Several minutes passed before she noticed him. When she did, she bowed toward him before bending over to grab her sandals off the rocky ground.

John stayed against the safety of the wall. "Morning."

"Hey." She squinted at him, smiled. "Ready for breakfast?"

"Sure."

Together, they walked to the main building's lobby where a continental breakfast had been laid out on a long table. They chose several items and sat out on the patio where they could look out over the canal while they ate.

"It's nice to get yogurt and coffee for a change," John said as he sat down. "I don't mind sleeping at the beach, but I'm getting tired of eating peanut butter sandwiches or dry granola for breakfast."

"No wonder you're looking so skinny." Zoë put a hand under his t-shirt and rubbed his chest. "Do we have enough time before we need to be at the dock?" Her voice sounded husky.

"'Fraid not. It's the first time all week that a rooster didn't wake me and I slept in a bit. We need to get going, actually." He hoped that she couldn't hear the relief that threaded his voice.

"Too bad." She leaned over and nibbled his neck.

"Zoë, please." John pulled away from the fiery touch of her mouth, but he regretted the reflex at once. He put a conciliatory hand on her forearm. "Let's just eat and go, okay?"

She sat back and looked at him, frowning. His cover was blown, no doubt about it. "No problem, chief. I guess snagging a flailing fish is much more enticing than boning your girlfriend, who you haven't seen in two weeks." John winced at her crudity.

They ate in silence and Zoë, who finished first, stood up without waiting for John and cleared off her dishes. John finished his coffee without hurrying. He found Zoë a few minutes later waiting in the Samurai, her profile stormy. As if answering her mood, it rained as they drove into Dewey—enough to wet the pavement on the highway and lighten the air. During the brief shower, a single cloud paused as it glided overhead and then the sky was bright, without a trace of cumulous. Afterwards, there came renewed birdsong along the coast, vigorous and joyful after the storm's interruption. What had seemed dry and tired in their surroundings only moments before was simultaneously sharper and softer, more vivid.

By the time they'd reached the dock and boarded their fishing boat, Zoë appeared more relaxed than she had at the outset of their drive. John hoped that she'd let his insult go. Several damp strands of hair, not used to being confined for long, had escaped the silver clip and now softened the angles of her face. She asked John to rub some sun block on her shoulders and upper back, sitting patiently and relaxed while his hands worked it into her skin. He was required to wait upon her to redeem himself. If fortune smiled on him, no more would be asked of him on this outing.

It wasn't likely she'd handle his infidelity with such equanimity, however.

John watched half a dozen seabirds—dark filaments against a bright sky—fly high overhead. If he could escape into the heavens with them, would he? No. The gravity of his conscience anchored him here, with Zoë. Once he'd managed to tell her about Raimunda, adding the insult of an extended leave from grad school would probably suit her just fine.

They were met at the gangway by their captain, Captain Joe, who had the mien of a New England lobsterman: taciturn, angular, and tanned. He didn't look as though he belonged on a Caribbean island skippering a boat for green-gilled landlubbers out on a sporting cruise. John couldn't help wondering what had brought Captain Joe to Culebra—a cheating wife? a drinking habit? a lobster boat lost in a storm?—but he also didn't have any doubts that the silent skipper would take them straightaway to the best fishing available in the waters off the coast. Captain Joe, true to appearances, said little beyond the necessary once all the would-be anglers had boarded: life jackets were to be worn at all times, no one was going to risk his life trying to reel in a big one, and he, Captain Joe, was the sole arbiter of what was and wasn't safe on his vessel.

Two other couples joined them. After several minutes, it became clear to John and Zoë that these two couples had planned their vacations together—and that something was going on between two of them that the other two didn't know about. John wasn't tuned into such things, but shortly after they'd gotten underway Zoë poked him with her elbow and whispered in his ear to watch the furtive manner in which the man in the baseball cap touched the dark-haired woman's elbow, shoulder or hip. The first time it happened, John wondered why Zoë would think that such a small, light touch meant anything. Then he realized that the man wearing the baseball cap seemed to be obsessed: he touched the dark-haired woman so regularly that his actions resembled a reflex or a tic. Even still, that wouldn't have struck him as odd if the man hadn't been sitting most of the time with his arm draped around his wife's shoulders. Watching them, John wondered if unfaithfulness is always so obvious to outsiders.

To John's surprise, Captain Joe headed straight for Amberjack; he hadn't realized that amberjacks were a sport fish during his diving session there last week, and he said as much to Captain Joe.

The skipper squinted at him, his left eye nearly shut. "They ain't too flashy, not like a marlin or a shark, but they ain't too easy to catch, either. Any number of hotshot fishermen from the States come here and guffaw over what looks like an easy catch. But the jacks, they tax your tackle and your stamina like few other fish do. If you hook one, you'll have the fight of your life."

John's question had elicited more than Captain Joe's usual elliptical phrases and nonverbal grunts. He took this as a sign of the crusty old man's respect for the fish and not him, a "hotshot fishermen" by virtue of his origins. He didn't have a problem with this until Zoë, not he, won the fight with one of these *pez fuerte*, earning a high spot in Captain Joe's hierarchy of regard.

While they were still underway, but not more than five hundred yards from Amberjack, the captain baited a forty-pound test line off the stern of the Sakitumi with some squid. When one of the other passengers asked what he was doing, he said that the squid was leaving a downside scent, much like an erratic, wounded baitfish on the retrieve would. With any luck, he'd snag one of the jacks and then some of its comrades would follow it to the surface where they'd all have a better chance of catching them with their lighter tackle.

After he'd set anchor at the site, Captain Joe came around and helped them bait their rods with frozen chum, then demonstrated the appropriate way to hold a deep-sea rod and reel: the end of the rod placed under the left armpit while the right hand reeled in the line. Zoë, who was left-handed and used to reversing all instructions, slid her rod under her right armpit and waited for something to bite. It didn't take long. John immediately felt a tug on his line, but just as quickly he lost the jack without setting a hook. In the process, he himself was hooked. For a while, he wasn't aware of Zoë's efforts to handle her own tackle; it wasn't until he heard Captain Joe's sharp intake of breath and a muttered "take it easy" next to him that he realized that Zoë had managed to snag something big. When he turned to watch, his own rod loose in his hands, he discovered that Zoë had found a rather unorthodox method for setting a hook: she now held her rod between her thighs.

It turned out to be an extremely effective means for catching a twenty-pound amberjack. Zoë was able to choke up on the rod past the reel, gaining better leverage, and use her entire body weight to fight her fish. John was so entranced by her performance that he nearly lost his own rod overboard when another jack hooked onto his line. Together, they fought their individual catches, John simply trying to keep his line from crossing Zoë's, Zoë bent on bringing her fish to the surface to see it. His jack eventually got away, but not until after Zoë had hauled in her amazing catch.

Dripping and red-faced with exhaustion, she turned to John while Captain Joe, his foot on the line next to the jack, cut the still-quivering fish free.

"He put up a fight but in the end I was tougher."

Seven

ଔ

TAMARIND HOVERED JUST UNDER THE SURFACE of the water, watching John standing on the boat above her. She recognized the old man who stood behind and to the side of John—she'd tailed his boat countless times through the waters to the south and west of Culebra. When she'd first happened upon his boat, she grew excited at the prospect of observing a human outside of the forbidden shores of Culebra, but her excitement quickly evaporated. Many times he dropped anchor miles out from the harbor and sat on his deck alone, drinking something. Under his white hat, his face resembled the warped and weathered texture of an old tree branch that had drifted far from land, preserved from natural decay by the salt air. Even from a safe distance in the water, Tamarind could see that his eyes captured no light from the water's surface. She no longer studied him for clues about humans. She satisfied herself with racing his boat instead.

Today he walked between John and five other humans, each holding a long stick with a glittering lure hanging from it and into a cloud of large silver amberjacks. Dead Branch, as she thought of the old man, stopped behind the woman nearest John and touched her forearm. The woman didn't acknowledged Dead Branch's presence, engrossed instead in flinging the lure away from the boat. Once, her lure caught around John's and she scowled at him.

As if it's his fault!

For a while, Tamarind refrained from swimming closer to the fish as she usually did if she found humans trying to catch them. Stupid as they were, fish of all kinds reacted to diverse stimuli, from sight and pheromones to vibration and water pressure. They probably swarmed the water around the boat because one of their comrades had already been caught and they scented a meal. Yet if she swam at their periphery, they would scatter, ignoring the lure. She didn't do this. Instead, she wrapped the seal glamour around her and waited to see how this sport would progress.

One of the fish abruptly swerved and swallowed John's lure. He gave a shout and pulled up on the stick he held. Dead Branch and the woman near John, whom Tamarind had dubbed Black Urchin, both moved closer. The amberjack zipped away from the boat and Tamarind saw John struggle to maintain a hold on his stick. Black Urchin leaned closer and gestured to John, perhaps giving him advice. The frown on his face deepened, whether from the advice or the battle, Tamarind couldn't be sure. She flipped her tail and headed for the fish, trying to corral it so that she could lull it into submission with her humming, but after zigzagging against John's line in the time that it took her to change direction, the amberjack broke free. As she expected, it wandered a bit before sensing one of its cohort and rejoining the school.

Dead Branch and Black Urchin stood side by side now. The old man spoke into her ear and she nodded, but John seemed absorbed in fiddling with the base of his stick. He hooked another glittering lure onto a line and concentrated on launching this new lure over the side of the boat. Tamarind no longer waited.

Switching her glamour to mirror the water around her, she headed toward the school. The amberjacks dispersed, but they didn't swim far. The smell of squid and their dead comrade permeated the water in which the innocuous lures undulated. Tamarind hummed a bit and rolled, gathering up scent particles in the palm of her hands and rippling these diaphanous globes through the swells and away from the fishers. The amberjacks darted a hundred different directions as the globes burst their scents in new underwater pockets. Tamarind laughed and tugged on the nearest piece of squid. Someone at the top tugged back.

Humming and swaying on the currents, Tamarind yanked at every flashing lure within fifty feet of the boat. Several times she broke the lures off with enough line to tie them onto a necklace for herself. Then she had an idea. Swimming toward a small group of amberjacks, she hummed to keep them from leaving their safe haven. She grabbed one, which rested in her grasp without twitching, and raced back to the boat. It took her a moment, but she finally identified Black Urchin's lure. She hummed some more and brought the amberjack closer to the wicked barb. It opened its mouth docilely and swallowed. Tamarind clutched onto the fish and sped toward the open ocean. The line followed her for several long moments before Black Urchin managed to stop her run. That's when Tamarind swerved, diving deep and rolling right.

Laughing again, she zipped and dodged with the amberjack, which continued to lie calmly in her hands. Black Urchin struggled to slow her down, but Tamarind, who often played games with dolphins, could have swum all day if she'd wanted to do so. After a few dozen passes, she swam back to the boat, letting Black Urchin reel in her line bit by bit. When she'd gotten close enough to see John wrestling with his own amberjack, she gave one last tug on the fish in her hands and then let go. She could have broken the line at the last maneuver, but just knowing this satisfied her. Let Black Urchin think that she'd won.

Rolling toward John's line, Tamarind saw that it floated free without amberjack or lure. She looked around, but the school had moved on. Tucking her arms to her side, she glided to the surface where she watched Black Urchin and Dead Branch grappling with the still-quivering amberjack. The woman's wet face shone, but she exuded triumph. When Tamarind looked towards John's face, she saw admiration and something else. Something she couldn't name, but it made her uneasy nevertheless.

ے ے ے

On the trip back to shore, an animated Zoë talked with Captain Joe, asking numerous questions about bait, tackle, the difference between amberjacks and the showier sport fish—marlin, shark, mahi mahi. If John hadn't known better, he would believe that Zoë had softened her stance on eating any flesh, whether from a fowl, a fish, or a four-legged mammal. Scowling, he noticed how patiently Captain Joe answered her questions, how the old man offered her a soda without saying a word to the others. He saw Captain Joe's admiring glances at Zoë's full breasts, her damp tank top clinging to them.

The old goat. Like he has any hope of catching his own quivering trophy. His jealousy surprised and confused him. His anger, unfocused as it was, flared. He closed his eyes and breathed. Until this moment, he hadn't understood how

105

volatile his emotions had grown on the Island of the Snake. He wasn't sure he liked feeling so out of control.

John swiveled around in his chair and watched the bow of the boat as they neared Culebra. His eye caught a glimpse of something in the water near their boat, something dark, which disappeared just as he turned his head for a better look. Perhaps it was a harbor porpoise, or a seal—maybe even a small whale. Whatever it had been, it was larger than the amberjack that Zoë had hauled on board and had disappeared under the boat with incredible speed. He thought about asking Captain Joe what it might have been but then changed his mind when he saw that the other man was still engrossed in conversation with Zoë.

They got back into port about twelve-thirty. John waited while Zoë posed on-board for the requisite photo documenting her catch, and then he had to wait further while she got advice from Captain Joe about where to take the twenty-pounder to have it cleaned, filleted, flash frozen, and shipped. It wasn't right, she said, to waste something that other people would eat, startling John again. After eating a late lunch at the Dockside, they split up so that Zoë could shop in some of the little artisan boutiques that exist in the smallest tourist area, those tenacious barnacles hanging onto an uncertain livelihood derived from the whims of sporadic shoppers. John had already bought souvenirs—some earrings for Cassie, a hair clip for his mom, a fountain pen carved from driftwood for his dad, and a t-shirt for Stefan who was chauffeuring him to and from the airport. So he headed to Señorita's and drank several Medallas in a dark corner instead.

"*Hola, gringo.*" Raimunda had found him. She sat down at the table across from him. "Buy me a beer?" After the bright morning out to sea, the shadows of the restaurant turned her white blouse and brilliant-orange skirt lurid.

John nodded and raised his hand to flag down his waitress. After she left, he looked at Raimunda. "I'm afraid that this is the last beer I can buy you."

"Why?" She leaned forward to grab his hands where they lay on the table. The neck of her blouse hung open to reveal bare breasts like an offering. "Is today your last day on this fair island?"

"Almost. But that's not why. Remember my girlfriend? She's here now and she's not good with sharing." For the first time since falling under Raimunda's spell, John's lust churned with disgust. He felt sick. His head throbbed. Images of Zoë practicing crescent kicks merged with her triumphant smile after catching her trophy and the randy leer on Captain Joe's face.

Raimunda accepted the Medalla from the waitress and lifted it high, sucking half of it down in a single drink. She wiped the corners of her mouth with a delicate thumb and forefinger.

"Too bad," she said at last. "But all good things must end."

She leaned back and slung her right arm over the back of the chair before raising her feet to the chair next to John. Her skirt fell away to reveal her legs, brown and slender.

"I am a tolerant woman." She smiled. "If your girlfriend should bore you, I would be happy to meet you at Playa Melones for a private goodbye."

John smiled but refrained from caressing the calf that skimmed his left thigh. A wave of nausea swept through him at the thought.

"I must decline out of concern for your safety. And mine, I'm afraid." He tried to smile and grimaced instead. "My girlfriend has spent years learning how to kick the shit out of any bastard who tries to hurt her. I've already earned a serious ass-kicking as it is."

"Ah." Raimunda toyed with the label on her beer bottle. "Perhaps she's not the best woman for you, my friend."

John scowled and gulped too big a mouthful of beer. Choking a little on the effervescence, he felt tears prick the corners of his eyes. For the first time since he'd nearly drowned in the canal, he felt his environment shrink around him. Señorita's pastel-pink, green, and yellow walls loomed over him. Sweat slicked his palms, his shirt stuck to his armpits, and his face grew hot.

Raimunda squinted at him but said nothing. She swilled the remnants of her beer without taking her eyes off of him. After what seemed like half an hour but must have only been a minute, the walls receded and the breeze from the overhead fan dried John. A chill streaked up and down his spine and faded away. John leaned his forehead into his left hand, which was propped up by his elbow on the tabletop.

"You must be careful when you drink your beer."

"Yes. No. I mean, that was more than a careless swig. I felt like the walls had shrunk around me so much that I was suffocating. I couldn't breathe for a moment."

"Your girlfriend must have quite some hold on you, my friend." How had he never noticed how feral her grin seemed? Her teeth, small and sharp, gleamed in the dull restaurant.

John closed his eyes, willing her to go away. She didn't.

"Look, you don't know me. I'd rather not discuss my girlfriend with you."

Raimunda pulled her feet down from the chair and leaned forward until her face came within inches of his, still propped in his hand.

"I know what your mouth tastes like. I know what your hands feel like on my body. I know what you feel like inside me." She paused and held his gaze with her own. "I know what desperation feels like, *gringo*. Desperation and escape."

She stood up. "Don't worry. I'll leave you to your misery, my friend."

John watched as she turned, her hair thick on her shoulders. In the dim light of the restaurant, her skirt glowed. He couldn't take his eyes off her hips as they swayed up the stairs and out into the Culebra sunlight.

ৡৡৡ

Zoë's head ached after so much sun and wind on the Sakitumi and she suspected that her sun block had either worn off or that John had applied it haphazardly. After leaving him outside the Dockside, she headed straight for Mayte's supermarket—shaking her head at the generous use of the term "super"—to look for water, Tylenol, and Aloe Vera lotion. She bought a bottle of water, but after drinking some of it, she wished that she'd purchased a Diet Coke instead. Studying the label, she saw that it wasn't spring water at all but distilled water. It tasted awful, like salty dishwater.

She left Mayte's and headed southwest toward the ferry dock and the lowering sun. Along the way, she passed Dewey's two churches, one Methodist, the other Catholic. A red rooster bobbed ahead and across the street from her, proudly leading several smaller hens to some unfathomable destination downtown. As she got closer to the intersection with the road in front of the ferry dock, she noticed a brightly painted figure leaning against a tree. Not having seen any other local art, she paused and studied it. The figure's staring eyes unnerved her and she wondered if Culebra had any practitioners of Santeria or voodoo. On a nearby abandoned building someone had spray painted the words *Culebra para los Culebrenses*. Together, the figure and words presaged some eruption of cruelty or of violence against interlopers. She shivered and hurried away toward the bright plaza.

Zoë passed the island's tiny post office and a Chinese restaurant on her left. Both appeared deserted, exacerbating her foreboding. Ahead, the pink and gray concrete blazed. A solitary figure sat under a tree on the small plaza. As Zoë got closer, she saw that it was a wizened old woman who sat on a mat or blanket. Dozens of small bottles and bags lay in neat rows before her. The old woman's head nodded and her hands lay loose in her lap. Napping. Which made a lot of sense in this stultifying heat.

Ignoring the cool lure of the seawater near the dock, Zoë turned away from the withered form. A heat vise clamped around her forehead and temples. If she didn't find an open, air-conditioned shop along this stretch of downtown waterfront, she'd have to head to the liquor store at the far end of the street and hope that the owner wouldn't throw her out for loitering. A door opened ahead of her with a jingle and she drew close enough to see a line drawing of a mermaid and the words "The Mermaid's Purse" on a sign protruding from the storefront. Sighing, she picked up her pace and reached the door panting.

Inside, air conditioning took the edge off the swelter but disappointed Zoë's hopes. Scowling, she barely returned the owner's greeting and drifted over to the far corner of the shop to pretend to study the cotton batik dresses until her headache abated.

"You'd look good in the red or the blue," the owner, a deeply tanned, champagne blonde, called. "Although I think the red is more dramatic."

Zoë lifted the colorful fabric away from the hanger and studied it. "I don't know. I wear a lot of black."

The woman came out from behind her desk and walked over to the rack where she folded her arms and appraised Zoë.

"Black is good, but red is bold, especially this color of red. It's *flamboyan* red. You're too early to see the blossoms of the *flamboyan* tree, but they're unmistakable. Try it on and see how it makes you feel."

Zoë accepted the dress and headed to the single, closet-like dressing room in the back. She thanked her lucky stars that her skin had dried and didn't stick to the cotton. The material draped nicely along her hips and the camisole fit well, not too loose along the seams and not too tight across the bust. The dressing room lacked a mirror so she stepped out into the store. The woman waited for her.

"Sweet Mother! You look fantastic!"

Zoë smoothed the skirt. "You think so? Or are you just trying to sell me a dress?"

"Well, sure, I'm trying to sell you a dress. But I don't need to lie to you. I'd kill to look like that in one of those dresses. You buy that, and you'll be the best advertising I could get. Just to show you how happy I am to see someone look so good in one of my dresses, I'll take twenty-five percent off."

Zoë laughed. "Okay, okay! You sold me. I just hope you're not feeding me a line...."

She kept the dress on and paid for it along with three turquoise and lime t-shirts emblazoned with a mermaid. When she stepped out into the plaza again, she scarcely noticed the heat that accosted her. The solitary figure no longer napped on the plaza but stared at Zoë, who felt a tingle. Was it curiosity? Whatever it was, it compelled her toward the figure. As she approached, the woman's face clarified within her crazy white hair and crumpled skin. She peered at Zoë, who saw that a milky cloud swirled over her left iris. She was half-blind then, and harmless.

"What's all this?"

The woman shrugged. "Just some tinctures for stomachache or headache or diarrhea."

"Are you some kind of folk healer?"

The woman grinned, showing small, even teeth. "You might say so. Sometimes I heal other things, like broken hearts."

"Really?" Zoë stepped forward a single step and then stopped. "Good grief! What am I doing? The Caribbean sun must have fried my brains good." She turned to go.

"Ah, a skeptic. I just thought a woman who wore such a vivid color might take a chance for the right man."

Zoë turned back. She stood looking down at the herbal remedies, trying to discern whether any of the bottles or bags held any merit. Nothing appeared especially enticing to her inexpert eyes.

"Is he here on Culebra with you?"

"Who? Oh, yes. '*The right man.*' Yes, he's here."

"That dress is sure to get his attention."

"I sure hope so. Being away from me for two weeks sure hasn't whet his appetite any."

The old woman sat up and stared at Zoë, her blue eye intent. "Perhaps it's another woman."

Zoë, who had been idly rubbing a small glass bottle in front of her, blinked. "Another woman?"

"Here." The old woman picked up a green glass bottle in the shape of a tiny flask, slid it into Zoë's limp palm and pressed her fingers closed with both hands. "Just a drop of this will spike his lust for you and drive away all thoughts of other women."

Zoë murmured something without being sure whether she said thanks or if she muttered nonsense. A fierce headache swelled and the next few minutes grew confused. She didn't know whether a heat haze blurred her vision or whether sun block got into her eyes, creating a film over her sight. She clutched the bottle to her chest and whirled away from the old cretin. Scurrying across the street, she wasn't aware of her steps or her surroundings. A cloud passed overhead, dimming her vision. Her heartbeat fluttered against her ribs. Almost as quickly as the cloud appeared, it scuttled away again and Zoë plunged down the street away from the plaza. She no longer felt the old woman's piercing gaze on her back and her heart settled into its usual rhythm. She held her hand open in front of her.

"Fucking garbage."

She looked around for a trashcan but saw none nearby. For a moment she considered smashing the bottle against the side of the nearest building, but then she caught sight of the painted figure and realized that she hadn't paid for the promised aphrodisiac. Just thinking about returning to pay the creepy old witch made her shudder. She looked again at the innocuous little bottle and then hid it in the pocket of her skirt.

When she descended into Señorita's colorful cave, she stopped at the bottom of the stairs to let her eyes adjust. At first, she didn't see John because she thought he'd be waiting at the bar, but only Hemingway's double sat there drowsing over an empty pint glass. She finally saw John sitting at a table in a dark corner. He stared out toward the small canal on the far side of the restaurant and his forearms rested on the table. A full glass of beer stood untouched in front of him. When she walked over to stand at his side, he didn't stir.

"Is this seat taken?"

"What?" He looked at her. Catching her eye, he looked away quickly but not before she'd seen something there. Fear? Guilt? "Uh, no."

She slid into the seat. "You're on your fourth beer already? Drinking alone is a bad sign."

John refused to look at her. "I haven't even touched this one."

"I see that." Zoë picked it up and sipped it. "What is it?"

"A Heineken. They don't have any microbrews around here."

"Ugh. How can you drink so much of it?"

He shrugged. "It beats the water."

She sighed and stretched her legs under the table. "That's true. I bought a bottle of something euphemistically called water earlier and gagged on it."

Silence fell between them while the waitress came at last to collect the empty glasses and take Zoë's drink order.

"Did you get enough souvenirs?" John watched his hands playing with his Heineken bottle. As if nothing else mattered.

"Just a few t-shirts." She held up the bag. "And this fabulous dress." She winced at the bitterness in her voice. He still hadn't looked her in the eye. "John."

Now he looked up at her. His green eyes were opaque in the dim light.

"John, I–" She paused. "Is something wrong? You don't seem as relaxed as I expected for two weeks away from the gray skies of Pittsburgh and the dungeon we lovingly call our office building."

He seemed to struggle with focusing on her words. His lips worked a bit before he got an answer out. "There's nothing wrong. I'm just really wiped out from the boat ride. I can't believe you've got enough stamina to traipse around to gift shops after that struggle with the amberjack."

"I do feel like I'm hung over. Another reason to avoid this." She tipped the beer glass slightly, studying the amber liquid, which glowed in the dimness. She couldn't bring herself to push harder, not here. Not now. Maybe later, when they were alone.

"Well, tank up on some bottled spring water here and then let's head back to the room. Maybe a nap is in order. I've got just the island hangout for tonight."

Eight

☙

TAMARIND WAITED UNTIL BLACK URCHIN walked away from the old woman before she shifted her cloaking glamour to the aspect that she'd worn for John. When she felt certain that no one else ventured out during the heat of the afternoon, she sidled over to the woman, who busied herself with wrapping her sundry bottles and tins into the woven mat. Tamarind watched the efficient brown arms, little more than bone and sinew, as they scuttled around. She knew that the old woman kept her waiting.

"You're an idiot, young one." The old woman didn't raise her eyes from her task.

Tamarind flinched but said nothing.

"I told you to stay away from that man, that he's dangerous. His woman is on the island."

Tamarind's glamour wavered, but she clamped down on her control.

"His woman?"

Now the ancient woman did look at her. She put a hand-rolled clove cigarette into her mouth and then lit it. After a moment, fragrant smoke clouded the air between them. "The term is 'girlfriend.' That was her in the red dress."

Tamarind bit her lip. "That was his girlfriend?"

"Yup."

"She's as prickly as a long-spined urchin."

The old woman barked a laugh. "For one so foolish, your description's apt. Nevertheless, he's leaving the island with her."

Tamarind tossed her head. "No, he's not."

The old woman looked at her for a long moment. "Ah, you know something."

"Perhaps."

"He's coming back to Culebra, isn't he?"

The wind off the sound surged through the spirals of Tamarind's hair, blocking her vision in a tangle of fine copper.

"Yes. He says he wants to volunteer to count sea-turtle eggs."

"And you want to try winning his heart, don't you? It's not enough for you to sneak around on the island after I warned you. Now you want me to help you. Help you keep those lovely legs of yours?" The old woman blew scented smoke out of the corner of her mouth.

"Yes."

"There is a way to put off your tail. But it's dangerous and painful, not to be done on a whim. Your father won't let you do it if he finds out."

"He's not going to find out."

The old woman sucked on her clove cigarette again. Its scented smoke obscured her withered face, but Tamarind felt the sting of her barbed gaze.

"You'll put your tail off, but you don't really understand what it'll cost you." She paused but went on again before Tamarind could say anything. "It's a terrible transformation, young one. You may die or worse—you may live but be

117

horribly disfigured, neither mermaid nor human. Are you ready for that?"

A chill tickled Tamarind's chest, but she nodded.

"It won't be enough, you know. It takes more than legs. You've got to learn how to walk among humans. Are you really willing to give up all that being a mermaid means? For some man?"

"Yes."

The old woman threw the cigarette stub on the ground and pressed it into the earth with a calloused sole. "I don't think you've got it in you to make it as a human."

There was a long silence. Laughing gulls mocked them from the fringe of mangrove trees along the nearby coastline. Tamarind studied the birds.

"You won't help me then?"

The old woman sighed and then turned back to her bundle. "I've warned you, but you're the one who has to choose, not me. I'll help you, but my help doesn't come without a price."

"What do you want? Cone snails? Jellyfish? Sea anemone? "

"Ha! Those are hardly enough for my help. No. You've got to be my servant and work off the debt until the rainy season ends."

Before Tamarind could accept these terms, the old woman spoke one last time.

"And your legs disappear, too, unless you mate with this human. That's why I want you to search your heart to make sure he's worth all you're risking. If so, return to me after the first rain."

≈≈≈

Tamarind wandered as far inland as the power she drew from the sea allowed her. With each step, the air around her threatened to suck moisture from her core and out through her pores. Each breath she drew seared her throat and lungs. After only a few dozen steps her head ached and her thoughts swam inside her head. She collapsed on the sidewalk under a *flamboyan* tree, wondering how she ever thought that she could sustain herself long enough to find John. Culebra might be a small island for a mermaid to swim around, but it might as well be a trip to the other side of the world for her to cross by land.

She looked up into staring eyes in the *flamboyan* tree behind her. In the space between two breaths, she switched to her cloaking glamour. When her heart calmed down a bit, she realized that the eyes and face belonged to a painted figure. The resemblance to *mer* art left at particular underwater meeting places reassured her. While she rested, she examined the distinctive dot pattern and wide mouth, the sightless eyes. Just as she began to hum to herself—a low, even hum devoid of clicking—she realized that someone had passed her on the sidewalk on the way to the plaza. She turned her head in time to see John pause and look around him, his eyebrows drawn together under a cap. When his gaze swept past her and moved around to the other side of the street, she switched aspects again.

"John."

He jumped. "Good grief, Tamarind! How in the world do you keep sneaking up on me like that?" He sounded annoyed. And something else that she wasn't sure about.

"Lucky, I guess." She held her breath until he changed subjects.

"Well, it's a good thing you found me. I had no idea how to find you and I'm getting set to meet my research boat in an hour. I wanted to say good bye before I left."

"Is your girlfriend gone?" For some reason, her voice burned her on the way out.

John squinted and hefted his backpack up onto his shoulder. "My girlfriend?" He sounded startled.

Tamarind plucked some pebbles from the sidewalk and tossed them across the street. "I saw her walking with you a couple of days ago."

"Ah. Well." He cleared his throat and looked away. "She's not my girlfriend. Not anymore."

"Hmm." Tamarind kept her eyes down on the perfect legs that she projected, but she wanted to hum in ecstasy. She'd read him right after all; he *was* happy to see her. Almost as good, she'd been right about Black Urchin, and Ana had been wrong.

"Hey, I volunteered both of us to help with the sea turtles. The ranger seemed really happy to have extra volunteers." He paused for a moment. "Why are you sitting on the sidewalk anyway? Do you want to wait at the pier with me until my mates show up?"

"Maybe." Her heartbeat picked up again. "Maybe not. I think it's too hot here and I need a swim."

"C'mon, we'll go into the liquor store and get some cold drinks."

"Okay."

He waited for her to get up and together they walked around the corner to the plaza and on to the liquor store in the corner. He smelled strange, not dusty with the natural scent of his body in the sun. Out of the corner of her eye, she studied his profile. No coarse hairs darkened the smooth skin of his cheeks and his hair lay coiled neatly in a dark ponytail on his upper back. His skin had darkened so that he looked like a native of Culebra. Her glance drifted down to his feet, visible within the straps of his sandals, and up his legs again.

Fine dark hair softened their angles. A strong urge to stroke those curves, to press her fingertips into the hollow around his knee and down the ridge of shin, filled her.

She realized that John had said something. "What?"

"Let's stop in this shop here before we get drinks."

She looked up at the sign over the entranceway. A woman with a tail instead of legs floated on an unnatural blue sea. Tamarind recognized the markings next to her as letters—some of them appeared in the written version of the name that she'd adopted.

"What's in here?"

John, in the act of opening the door, looked at her. "You've never been inside this shop?"

Several strands of hair blew into her face as a breeze off the harbor rushed past her and into the open door. She pulled at them to clear her vision. "No. Should I have?"

"I guess not. It's a gift shop for tourists after all."

He held the door and waved her in. She held her head up and stepped inside, blinking in the dimmer light. Her diving membrane slid over her eyes where it stayed, momentarily beyond her ability to control it.

"Do you like this?" John held up a vivid blue item.

Tamarind turned away from him and headed toward a display of shells, blinking to raise the membrane. It stayed in place.

"Is something wrong?" John stood behind her so close she could feel heat rising from his torso, and his breath tickled the hair on her neck. "I didn't mean to offend you. I just wanted to get you a gift."

Tamarind began humming and clicking and turned away from him to head to the t-shirt rack. Despite her unsteady heartbeat, she knew that she had to calm down in order to raise the membrane. She had no ready excuse for John if he glimpsed the thin blue layer over her eyes. Near the t-shirt rack she saw the dark eye coverings that many people on Culebra wore and grabbed a pair to try on just as John halted behind her again.

"Tamarind."

She twirled around and looked at him through the dark layer.

"We don't have to look around. We can go on over and get something to drink."

"It's okay. I just had a little trouble seeing when we first came in, that's all."

John nodded, but a shadow remained around his eyes. He followed her as she walked through the racks but didn't say anything more about what they saw hanging there.

"How about this one?" A woman with hair the color of the sand on Playa Flamenco and skin nearly as brown as a tamarind pod stood next to the rack holding the same vivid blue piece that John had spotted. "It would look lovely next to that mass of wavy hair of yours."

Tamarind continued humming, low inside herself to keep her mental grasp on her glamour, and turned to face the woman. The color of the material captured the brilliance of the afternoon sky around Culebra. She reached out and traced a fingertip against it. It was smooth, soft.

"The dressing room's over there." The woman pointed to a door in the corner. When Tamarind didn't move, she lifted the hanger off of the rack and held out the item to her.

Tamarind noticed that the woman wore clothing that resembled the blue material in texture if not color. So she accepted the item and walked to the dressing room. Once inside she looked more closely at the shape of the clothing. It appeared to be identical to what the woman wore. She took the eyewear off, grateful that John wouldn't see the diving membrane, which still covered her eyes. She concentrated for a moment until the image of the t-shirt and shorts that she'd borrowed from John disappeared. Then she pulled the blue material over her head and stepped out of the dressing room.

"Wow! Don't you look fabulous! That dress looks like it was cut to your figure! I must be doing something right because you're the second woman in two days to put one of my pieces on who looks absolutely amazing."

"We'll take it." John pulled his wallet out of his backpack.

Tamarind turned to go back to the dressing room to change.

"No, leave it on."

"Yeah, you must wear that around for me," the woman said. "I'll give you a bag for your other things. And I'll give you the same discount I gave the other woman."

"Oh, and add in the sunglasses, too. Just don't put them on yet. The blue in the dress really draws out the blue of your eyes."

Tamarind gasped and felt her temples. She'd left the sunglasses in the dressing room.

John looked at her while the woman ran his credit card. "You look amazing." His eyes never left her face.

A bouncy hum filled her upper chest before she could stop it and she found herself trilling a string of clicks with her tongue. She looked away from John. The diving membrane slid behind her eyelids, but she let her hair cover her face anyway.

"Here's a bag."

Tamarind snatched it from the woman's hand and rushed into the dressing room. For a moment the small space suffocated her and then she reminded herself how to breathe air. She picked the sunglasses up from the bench where she'd left them and returned to the shop. John waited for her by the door, chatting with the woman.

"Thanks for the tip," he said as Tamarind joined them. "Ready to go get something to drink?"

"Sure."

They left the shop and continued down the sidewalk toward the liquor store. The heat radiated from the concrete and reflected back at them from the glass storefronts. Tamarind felt her pulse throb in her left temple and a sharp pain pierced her left eye. She had never felt so dry in her life, not even when she sunned herself on a nearby cay. When they stood in front of the coolers in the liquor store at last, she opened the door and let the cold air wash over her. The pain in her eye disappeared, but her body cried out for water.

"What'll you have?" John held a bottle of something dark in his hand.

"Water." She plucked a bottle out and opened it.

John laughed and went to pay for their drinks. While he stood in front of the register, she tipped the water up and let half the bottle flow down her throat without taking a breath.

"What are you drinking?"

"Coke."

"Can I try some?"

"You've never had Coke before? I thought it was the drink of millions. Here." He handed her the bottle and she tipped it up as she'd done with the water. The Coke burned its way down her throat and left a sharp pain in her upper chest. She coughed and choked.

"Hey, take it easy, okay?" John snatched the Coke from her hand and patted her bare upper back. Even in her distress, his fingertips raised starfish bumps.

Air pressure rolled its way from her chest to her throat, much as it had done when she was young and she'd surfaced too quickly from a great depth. She opened her mouth to cry out and a tremendous ripping sound emitted. For the first time since she'd come on land to look for John, she felt all right.

John looked at her, his eyes wide. Then he threw his head back and laughed the deep laugh that she loved, until he panted. His cap fell off his head, but he didn't seem to notice; he just put his thumb and his forefinger in the inside corners of his eyes and stretched the lower half of his face. Gradually, his breathing slowed to normal and his eyes cleared. He grinned at her, then bent down and retrieved his cap off the floor.

"Holy crap, girl! That was mighty impressive. If fishing doesn't pan out for you, you might want to challenge some frat boys to belching contests."

"It doesn't do that to you?" Her heartbeat tapped against her ribcage.

"Well, sure, if I tip it back like you just did. But I've had a little more experience with carbonation, I guess. Just sip it slowly."

He handed her the bottle again and this time she only took a mouthful. It fizzed inside her mouth as bubbles popped against her palate, but after she swallowed the pressure remained normal. On impulse, she tipped the bottle up again. The pressure rose a bit in her chest. Grinning, she parted her lips and urged the trapped air up with her diaphragm. A smaller belch sounded.

John grinned but reached out for the Coke bottle. "All right, enough of that. C'mon, walk me to the marina."

The walk from the liquor store tried her stamina, but the water she'd drunk kept the pains and parched sensation from returning. Once they arrived at the dock, she was close enough to draw on the power of the water to sustain her.

John dropped his backpack and sat down on the dock's edge. Tamarind sat next to him. Her lower half, dangling above the water in the harbor, sucked energy into itself.

"You look a lot better than you did a little while ago. I guess Coke revived you."

Tamarind pulled the sunglasses out of her bag and put them on. "It's like looking through Coke."

"That's one way to put it, I guess." He said nothing for a moment. "I'm looking forward to coming back here in a couple of weeks and counting turtle eggs with you. I don't know what I'm going to tell my thesis advisor, but I'm not ready to go back to Pittsburgh yet."

"Is that why she's not your girlfriend anymore?" She didn't look at him. Instead, she bit her lip and swung her lower half back and forth.

"Partly." He rushed on, his voice hurrying away from the subject. "Hey, listen, I've got something for you." He bent toward his backpack and rummaged inside it. "Remember I took the ferry to Fajardo last week? Well, I drove to San Juan and while I was there I got these books for you."

He held them out to her. She took them and looked at the drawings on the covers. They clearly depicted creatures of some sort, but while they had recognizable faces, arms, and legs, they looked like nothing that she'd seen, either underwater or on Culebra. The creatures reminded her a little of the outline of the woman with the fish's tail on the sign over the shop.

"They're all written by Dr. Seuss. *Green Eggs and Ham*, *The Cat in the Hat*, *Horton Hears a Who*, *Red Fish Blue Fish*. All the classics."

She squirmed and frowned at him. "I told you I don't know how to read."

"I know. I'm going to teach you."

Tamarind looked at the books with their brightly colored covers again. Her eyes stung behind the sunglasses.

"Did I say something wrong?" John sounded worried.

"No." She tossed her head and squeezed her eyelids until the stinging stopped. "No. I can't wait for you to teach me."

There was a shout from fifty feet out in the harbor and John stood up. Suddenly, it was time for him to go. Tamarind shoved the books into her bag, ready to cloak herself as soon as John boarded and no longer noticed her. After the crew of the ship tied off and lowered the gangplank, John turned and ruffled her hair.

"Don't stalk any other tourists while I'm gone." He ascended the narrow bridge from the dock to the ship.

She didn't change her aspect even though he never turned around to look at her again. Instead, she caressed his calves with her gaze and hugged the bag of books to her chest.

"I won't," she said to his retreating form.

᪥᪥᪥

Ana squatted on the shore at La Playa Tamarindo, peering at the stones, seaweed, and shells arranged there. Overhead, a darkening cloudbank obscured the morning sun and the ever-present chatter of birds had hushed to stillness; in moments, the season's first rain pelted her and disturbed the outlines of her question before Mother Sea. This by itself was an omen, one that foretold that Father Sky would mediate the outcome. Even before she'd come to the beach this morning, Ana's intuition had spoken to her about the violence of the upcoming season and the oracle had just confirmed her suspicions. The hurricanes that blew through the Caribbean every summer and fall would be especially numerous, and one would batter her little island late in the season after pummeling the islands further south.

While this prediction disturbed her, Ana wanted to know something entirely unrelated to the future weather. She wanted to know whether the mermaid would return and accept her conditions for help, and if so, how she would fare during the transformation. This latter was a question that she wouldn't have dared to ask in her youth, but she was growing more tired—and lonelier than she would have thought possible—and she was willing to risk Mother Sea's ire by asking it. When she'd first returned to Culebra and taken up her role as healer and diviner, she'd been reluctant to aid the occasional mermaid who called upon her; as the years passed, she began to realize that a time would come when she'd no longer be able to carry out her duties. Now, she feared that each opportunity to help a mermaid become human might also be her last to find a protégée.

Ana rearranged the artifacts on the shore before her, adding a few shells here, removing a few stones there. She asked Mother Sea what the mermaid's immediate fate would be and waited, scarcely breathing. After several moments, seawater fingered her code.

Rubbing between her brows, she sighed and sat back on her haunches. The unequivocal oracle had shown that the mermaid would return and accept the conditions of her metamorphosis; and, blessed be the Creator, she would not only survive but would indeed have put off her tail. This was as much as she could hope to learn today and she would not be allowed to ask any more questions regarding the mermaid for at least one cycle of the moon. But it wasn't enough to satisfy her, to assure her that all would turn out as she wished. It occurred to her that she could get at some of what she wanted to know by asking a question about the man who had captured the mermaid's heart.

She leaned forward onto her knees, eagerly rearranging her artifacts while the rain fell.

Mother, will this human take the mermaid away with him after the rains end?

The waves, which lapped at her arrangement even as she placed the items, surged and obliterated all but a few of them. Satisfied, Ana picked up the remaining shells and stones and placed them within a small canvas sack. The oracle had suggested that John would leave the island alone, but she had seen her own hand in it and knew that this wasn't a certainty, only a probability. She must take every opportunity to ensure that what the oracle said came to pass.

Nine

☙

TAMARIND WATCHED FROM THE SECURITY of mangrove
roots along the northern edge of the Luís Peña Canal as the
old woman stooped over a section of beach, frowning at
some detritus there. This was not the first time that the old
woman had spent long moments contemplating seaweed and
shells, yet Tamarind still had no insight into what she was
doing. After a few moments, the old woman leaned forward
and rearranged some of the items around her and then
Mother Sea flowed forward, the foamy edge of Her waves
caressing them. All at once, Tamarind understood that the
old woman was communicating with Mother Sea. *Mer*
people, living in symbiosis with Mother Sea, did not speak
with Her. She embraced them, gave them refuge, provided
power for them to draw upon to protect themselves, both
underwater and on shore. She never spoke to them.

The old woman leaned forward a second time, moving
bits of shell, seaweed, and stone. This time, Mother Sea
rushed forward before she'd finished, sucking most of her

items into the canal. Instead of appearing angry or upset, she appeared relieved. She gathered the remaining stones and shells and tucked them into a small bag, then rose and turned away from the shore.

Tamarind waited a moment. She had only to walk on borrowed power to the old woman's house. *What if reality is less wonderful than my vague fantasies? Will I wish I hadn't risked so much for so little?*

Closing her eyes and lifting her chin, she sent her thoughts out to the water around her to transform her tail into a pair of human legs; she would store some energy within her mind, doling it out along the short walk to the old woman's house. She swam until her new feet reached the bottom of the canal, then stood up and walked from the clinging grip of Mother Sea. As she walked, the rain tapered off and stopped altogether; by the time she reached the edge of La Playa Tamarindo, the sun shone overhead.

When Tamarind arrived at the old woman's squat cinderblock house, she was sitting in the doorway smoking a clove cigarette. Her good eye sparkled, alive in her shriveled features. She didn't smile. Tamarind's stomach churned and her glamour wavered. She came closer to the old woman, transfixed. Even though the sun was bright, she felt cold. For the first time that she could remember, the hum that always waited inside her core had fled, leaving her empty.

"I've been waiting for you, young one. You agree to my condition?"

"Ye—" Her dry throat trapped her voice. She cleared her throat forcefully. "Yes."

The old woman's eye flashed; she bent and smashed the stub of her clove cigarette into the ground. Smoke continued to drift up around her head, twining like ghostly seaweed. She unfurled herself and disappeared into her dark house.

Tamarind hesitated, unsure whether she should follow, but the old woman reappeared holding a clear container filled with a dark brown liquid, its surface faintly hissing.

"Here, drink this."

Tamarind took the container from the old woman's outstretched hand. As she did, she caught sight of a silvery sheen between the fingers and nearly dropped the smooth container. She steadied her hand and raised it to her lips. Its contents hissed, reminding her of John's Coke. She sucked in some of the liquid, tiny bubbles rising from its surface and popping on her cheeks. The liquid's heat slid furiously down her throat and consumed her. Her heart responded as wildly as a netted fish, flopping against her ribs. Just as she started to back away from the old woman, the heat subsided, leaving a strangely sweet taste.

"Drink all of it."

The old woman watched as Tamarind lifted the container again, choking on the first drops of liquid. She wanted to spit it out, to throw the container down and run away, but its heat rooted her and the old woman's eye compelled her to finish it. This time, the liquid lost some of its heat. Tamarind flushed, just as she did after an afternoon lying on a sheltered beach. Her thoughts loosened and swam away from her.

The old woman took the container before it could slip from her grasp. She was about to take a step on her borrowed legs when, to her surprise and horror, she found that her glamour had vanished and she lay on her side. She called for her father, but her mind's voice refused to escape her head.

"Don't bother. He can't hear you this far inland and the beer has dulled your mental energies." The old woman paused. "I didn't poison you. The beer will fortify you for your coming ordeal—it's all I have to help you, but it'll wear off soon enough."

Tamarind tried to latch onto the old woman's words, but they darted about like tiny fish among coral.

"Gather yourself and follow me." The old woman turned away from Tamarind and walked toward some low bushes.

Tamarind blinked. She hadn't moved when the old woman stopped by some guinea grass, coarse and thick, and turned her glittering eye onto her. Tamarind leaned over and put her forearms onto the ground and felt the familiar surge of energy into her upper body. Mustering her focus, she pulled her limp tail into the air where it hung suspended over her head and lurched across the ground on her hands. Panting, she dropped down near the guinea grass. The old woman stooped and parted two clumps with her hands until Tamarind saw a long cleft in the ground. Smaller ridges and fissures surrounded this narrow opening, which was almost entirely obscured once the grasses sprang back to their normal places. Tamarind scooted closer on her belly.

"You must enter this cave, young one. Not head first but with your tail."

Tamarind wasn't sure how she could fit inside the cleft, but she nodded and pushed herself sideways until her tail neared it. It was just wide enough to accommodate the muscles of her tail once she'd tilted her flippers and eased them into the opening. She grunted as she backed herself into the earth, which widened out after the lower half of her tail had disappeared inside it. The soil was warm, clinging to her skin, yielding and conforming to her. And then her flippers pushed against unyielding earth and her torso hung over the lip of the fissure, half in and half out.

"I can't go any further."

"You will, you will."

Before Tamarind could puzzle over her words, the old woman let go of the overhanging branches, concealing her with their leaves. She considered pushing her way out of this cave and through the branches, but her willpower drained away into the earth instead. The old woman returned and told her to drink something sweetish, slightly salty and viscous. She nearly retched, but the old woman held the cup to her lips and gripped her jaw until she'd swallowed it all. In moments, she felt dizzy and incoherent, alternately hot and cold.

The old woman left her alone for some time—Tamarind had no idea how long—only to return with a pot filled with a pungent salve. The old woman dipped a finger into the pot and traced it along Tamarind's forehead and cheekbones, all the while muttering. She set the pot onto the ground, grasped Tamarind's shoulders and, simultaneously lifting and pushing, slid her further back into the cave. Tamarind cried out as her tail bent against the rear wall and doubled underneath her. Her whole torso now fit inside, but her shoulders wedged at the entrance until the old woman twisted them into alignment; then the old woman leaned her whole weight into Tamarind until her head disappeared inside the lip of the cave.

Tamarind heard a sound and she realized that she was sobbing. The cave, which had initially conformed to her in a comforting way, now painfully immobilized her. She couldn't have escaped if she'd wanted to and, now sober, she knew that even the old woman could not pry her out. Blood pounded in her ears and she nearly lost consciousness, but she fought it and her tears. After a few moments, she mastered her breath and as it slowed she grew calm.

The cave was darker than the deepest cave she'd ever swum within, moist and almost airless. The pain in her tail was terrible, but now that she'd regained control of her thoughts, she believed that she could survive this ordeal. She had to stay focused. Neither it, nor the old woman, would get the best of her. A paroxysm of pain gripped her. It was in her midsection and it was everywhere, all at once. Her head arched away from her flippers, bringing her mouth toward the cave's opening. A scream ripped the air and she scarcely knew that it came from her. She had no idea how long the pain seized her, but at last it subsided and she panted in her airless space. From outside the cave came faint noises. In the suffocating stillness, the smell of the old woman's clove cigarette reached her.

Tamarind clung to the scent while the next pain squeezed her. She had no idea when it would quit wracking her body, but every time it ceased, she prayed that it was over. Still pain rose to overtake her and soon there were hardly two breaths between waves, hardly enough time for her to gasp out a plea.

"Please." And the next time the pain hit her, "I can't!" And then, "Oh, Mother," and she vomited into what little space she had.

After that, she said no more because she no longer had any thoughts. Each new round of pain rode upon the heels of the last so that she could no longer distinguish them as separate assaults even if she'd been capable of doing so. Time had no meaning for her and she couldn't have said if moments or days passed. Groans rolled over her lips with the immutability of waves. Yet long before her voice failed, the pain began to lessen.

She grew aware of her hands digging into the soft soil around her torso: they'd gouged deep holes in her agony. Pain still shuddered through her lower body, but she knew herself again. Before she could do more than note this return of awareness, she felt an indomitable urge to unfold herself.

"Wait, wait, young one!"

Tamarind had no idea what was happening to her, but she fought the urge to push against the constricting earth. She felt the old woman's fingers dig into the cleft and clamp onto her shoulders.

"Now."

A new insistence filled Tamarind and she gave into it; deep inside her she knew that this was the struggle that would free her. As she pushed, the old woman pulled her head clear of the cave wall and the pain in her lower body eased. The old woman let go of one shoulder and then quickly brushed loose soil and vomit from her eyes and out of her clogged nostrils. Tamarind sucked in air and laughed.

Another need to push gripped her. The old woman barely grasped her shoulders in time to twist them through the narrow cleft. With an odd *shlucking* sound Tamarind slid out onto the cool ground and lay not far from the cave's entrance. She closed her eyes, but not before she saw that it was night. She heard the old woman bustling around her, but she wanted only to sprawl on the ground. She lay there without moving until the old woman rolled her over onto her back, startling her with the light in her hand. Pushing up onto her elbows, she held one hand out; the other shielded her eyes.

"Leave me alone."

"Look at yourself."

Tamarind peered down her torso toward her tail. She was covered in mud and something else: in the light's glow, she caught sight of blood. Her blood. She was so shocked that at first she didn't register the oddness of her tail under all the obscuring muck. When she did, she saw that it was no longer gray but fish-belly white. It was no longer strong and muscular but atrophied and knobby. Where her strong flippers had been, she saw two stubs.

"Don't understand, do you?"

"Understand?"

"Perhaps this will help."

The old woman turned back toward the bushes, dark and indistinct against the lighter sky. Overhead, tiny pricks of white, scattered where Father Sky had thrown them, glittered. She knelt, setting her lamp on the ground and then leaned into what must be the cave's entrance. For a long moment all was silent and Tamarind began to shiver. The old woman sat back, something sagging and dark in her hands.

When she turned around, Tamarind's breath caught at the base of her throat. *My tail.*

Where it had been hard and convex, filled with muscle, bone and sinew, her tail was now hardly more than a shell. As she watched, the old woman spread it out for her so that she could see the inside lining. It was veined and knotted, quilted with blood-purple fat and long strips of shredded muscle and torn ligaments. At its center, strung like beads on a necklace, she could see oblong vertebrae spanning the length of the tail, disappearing at last among the cartilage of her flippers.

Tamarind tore her gaze from the remnants of her tail and looked again at herself. Now what she saw were unmistakably legs, thin and wobbly looking but legs nevertheless. She pushed herself up into a sitting position.

"I did it! I put off my tail!"

"That you did." The old woman had lit another clove cigarette and now took a long drag on it. "Help me bury it."

Tamarind blinked. She rolled onto her side, pausing to look at the night sky. After several moments, the old woman cleared her throat. It was a harsh, rattling noise like the sound of pebbles inside a desiccated crab shell. Gripping her lower lip with her teeth, Tamarind pulled herself along the ground to the spot where the old woman waited. Once she was there, the old woman knelt down and together they dug a shallow trench with their hands and lay her tail in it.

When Tamarind awoke later, the sun sailed overhead and hunger hollowed her to her new toes. She lay on a thick, rough cloth on the floor inside the old woman's house, which was filled with the scent of fish, among other odors that she didn't recognize. Blood and soil caked her skin and her lower body burned near where her new legs extended from her torso. She was about to call out for help when the old woman appeared in the doorway to her house.

"Awake are you? Lots of new sensations? Bet most of them aren't pleasant."

Tamarind nodded and licked her lips. She couldn't speak.

"First things first. Let's get you outside so you can empty your bladder. After, food, drink and a bath."

She came over and helped Tamarind sit upright; Tamarind's head spun and she clutched the old woman's arm.

"That's it, take it slowly."

Tamarind gathered her concentration from where it had scattered and pushed herself up onto her feet. If the old woman hadn't pulled at the same time and steadied her, she might not have made it. Twice she stumbled and once she actually fell, pulling the old woman down beside her. It took five minutes before they were both standing outside the house in the sunshine.

"Don't go far. Squat down here. I'll clean it up later."

The old woman never let go of her arm as she slunk down onto her new haunches. She sat there until the old woman told her to urinate.

"I don't know how."

"Yes you do. Focus on your functions. Remember what it felt like to empty your bladder in the sea."

Tamarind nodded and withdrew her thoughts into herself. At last, she could remember the feeling that came whenever she released her bladder. She triggered that release now. Hot urine shot out between her shins, splattering her. As it hit the ground, she saw a trickle of blood from between her legs. After the ache and burning from her over-full bladder had drained away, she felt her soreness as well.

"You'll bleed for awhile, maybe a whole moon. Then you'll bleed again, once each moon. All human women do."

As she stood up, Tamarind clutched the old woman's arm. "Will I always feel so tender in the place between my legs?"

The old woman removed the stub of her cigarette and tossed it onto the damp ground where it hissed and stopped burning.

"No, you'll heal. The only time you'll feel sore is if you copulate with a man."

The old woman steadied Tamarind against her side and led her back to the shade inside her dwelling.

"Do humans also have difficulty mating their minds?"

The old woman ignored the question and shuffled Tamarind to a far corner where she made her sit on something hard and round that was raised from the ground by several long sticks of wood.

"Don't mind how hard it is. I didn't want to get your blanket wet."

She turned to a flat surface that was raised higher than the one Tamarind sat on and pulled a shallow container of water towards her. In it was a small cloth, which she rung out before carefully wiping Tamarind's face. She hadn't forgotten Tamarind's question, however.

"Humans don't mate their minds. Sometimes two humans grow close. They appear to share a mind, but they can't mate the way *mer* do." The old woman bathed the rest of her with gentle hands. "For humans, mating is temporary and absurd. They try to make up for it by committing their will to each other. They call this 'marriage.' It's as flawed as humans are."

"Marriage." Tamarind tried the word out.

"I was married once. Didn't last more than ten rainy seasons. *Couldn't* have lasted much longer."

"What happened to your husband?"

"Don't know and don't care." The old woman's pincer-like fingers gripped Tamarind's thighs as she scrubbed the dirt away. "When it's dark, go to the resort not far from here and use the beach showers."

"Why do I have to go when it's dark?"

"They don't want you to use the showers, young one. Don't worry about why. Just don't let anyone see you." She dropped the filthy cloth behind her and stood up. "Time to get you some food."

The old woman walked over to the shiny vessel, which emitted a fish-scented cloud. Picking up a flat stick with an appendage that looked like a curled hand, she scooped up some of the liquid and poured it into a shallow container near her. This she set on the flat surface, simultaneously handing Tamarind a shiny object.

"What is it?" Tamarind held the object in her hand before waving it in front of her.

The old woman laughed. "Got a lot to learn, don't you? This," she said, touching the object in Tamarind's hand, "is a spoon. This is a bowl filled with fish broth." She mimed using the spoon to dip up the broth and bring it to her lips.

Tamarind wasted no time in tasting the broth. As she ate, the old woman pulled something out of an opening in the front of her clothes and tossed it next to the bowl.

"Crackers to eat with the broth. Dip them in." She paused. "Since we're naming things, I'm Ana."

Tamarind hardly paused in spooning in the broth; she grabbed crackers and dipped them into the bowl. Ana chortled so loudly that Tamarind looked up at her, the crackers halfway to her mouth.

"No, no, young one! Tear the plastic bag open to get the crackers!"

As Tamarind watched, Ana took the bag from her and pulled at one end of it until it split open like a skate's membrane. Out tumbled several white crackers. Ana laid the bag next to Tamarind's bowl and pursed her lips, her hands on her hips.

"What are we going to call you?"

"Tamarind," Tamarind told her between gulps of broth.

Ana looked surprised. Then she smiled, the first smile to curl the corner of her single eye and lift her whole face upward.

"Yes, Tamarind. That's what we'll call you."

Ten

✂

JOHN WAITED FOR TAMARIND in the gathering dark at the bottom of the hill next to the service road that led to Tamarindo Estates. Since returning to Culebra two weeks ago, he'd driven nightly to the same spot and waited for her silhouette to descend toward him, the last of the day's sunlight her aura. Tonight, he'd waited for twenty minutes and still she hadn't appeared. To the northwest, sooty terns streamed toward their nesting grounds on the tip of the Flamenco Peninsula, their black oblongs parting and merging in a fast flow against the lemon-orange layer of sky above the treetops.

He drummed his fingers along the steering wheel and then picked up his flashlight and checked it again to make sure the batteries still had enough juice. He popped the glove compartment and verified again that there were spare batteries. On the floorboard of the Samurai rested his backpack with water and soda bottles, chips, sandwiches, mosquito repellent and a copy of *The Lion, The Witch, and*

The Wardrobe. He switched on the radio, leaned against the driver's side door, and closed his eyes. A new guest had arrived mid-morning at Posada La Diosa where he'd rented a room since his return from the Trench mission and he'd been unable to sleep until nearly noon. If Tamarind didn't arrive soon, he might fall asleep.

Humming reached his ears before the sound of her feet on the pavement. Stirring, he sat and looked up the hill. As usual, she skipped barefoot toward him, her corkscrew hair jouncing with each little leap. She wore the mermaid t-shirt that he'd bought her from The Mermaid's Purse and a pair of shorts that were too big for her. Every fifth skip she stopped and hitched them up. When she reached him, he saw that she sucked on a Popsicle. Orange stained her upper lip and tongue.

"It's about time you got here. We're going to be late."

She shrugged. "So? The turtles won't get there until it's dark. We've got time."

She came around to the passenger side and got in. Hearing the music, she leaned forward and began pushing buttons on the radio.

"Please buckle up so I can go."

"Oh, yeah, right." She stuck what was left of the Popsicle into her mouth and reached around her right shoulder for the belt. After she'd clicked the belt into its slot, she reached for the radio again. When she found a station playing Lito Peña's *Yo Vivo Enamorado*, she stopped jabbing, turned the volume up and began singing along. John smiled to himself as she rocked in time with the music, the Popsicle dripping everywhere as her arm swung wide.

"I bet you'd be fun at Isla Encantada." He started the Samurai and u-turned south onto 251. An image of Tamarind dancing around the restaurant's worn floor teased his inner eye. All at once, he knew that he wanted to hold her. Would it feel as though he held a will o' the wisp? Or danced to the music of the spheres?

"Isla Encantada? What's that?"

"You don't get out much do you? Your father must keep you on a tight leash. It's a bar that has live music on the weekends."

"'Tight leash'? What's that mean?"

Mentioning her father made him squirm. He couldn't take Tamarind into his arms as he wanted if she was as young as he feared she was. "Never mind. It's just a figure of speech. But that reminds me. Are you twenty-one?"

"Twenty-one?"

"Twenty-one years old." An image of Zoë slithered into his thoughts, but he shoved it into oblivion. She'd tried to insist that they were taking a break, not breaking up. What would she think about him hitting on a girl who looked and acted younger than his sister?

"Oh, I'm way older than that. Why?"

"You have to be twenty-one to dance at Isla Encantada. Do you have some sort of ID?"

She stopped rocking. "ID? No, I don't have any ID." She sounded as if she didn't know what he was talking about, though.

"Don't worry." John patted her head, letting his fingers linger just long enough to feel the surprising softness of the tangles. "I've never seen them check. I just wanted to be sure for my own peace of mind."

"Piece of mind? Which piece of your mind needs to know how old I am?"

John laughed. "The biggest piece."

They drove along without speaking for a while, listening to more *boricua* jazz. John turned north after they reached

144

Laguna del Flamenco. The road ended short of Playa Resaca; they'd have to leave the car and hike over the same hilly terrain that John had first hiked over in late March. He turned the radio down before they reached the place where they'd park the Samurai.

"I brought a book that I want to read to you while we wait."

Tamarind looked at him. Even in the growing darkness, the blue of her eyes astounded him. Hair fell into her eyes, but she didn't seem to notice. "You brought a book? Where is it? Can I see it? What's it about?"

"Whoa, whoa! All in good time. Let's just say it's a classic of children's literature and I'm looking forward to reading it to you."

Tamarind hummed a bit and looked out the window. Without warning, she leaned over and kissed his right hand. "Thank you." Her voice sounded thick.

Fifteen minutes later they'd caught up with the four other volunteers and the National Wildlife Refuge park ranger who all sat as far inland as they could on blankets, talking quietly. All but Jesus smiled and waved John and Tamarind over to join them. When he'd found himself skewered by Jesus' hot glare the first night that they'd watched for leatherbacks, John braced himself for the inevitable angry confrontation. Jesus said nothing, however, about their first meeting and John stopped worrying about a destructive scuffle among the sea-turtle nests. Even so, he often caught the other man's eyes watching him.

In the deepening twilight, everyone brought out sandwiches and chips and listened to Pablo describe the time a nesting leatherback dug several holes before finally laying her eggs. When he finished, no one spoke for a while. The last of the sun's light faded from the horizon and the sky gradually deepened from a honeydew melon to pale blue and finally, deep blue. Stars extruded through the velvety backdrop of sky like diamond studs in a jeweler's display.

John snapped on his flashlight and pulled out *The Lion, The Witch, and The Wardrobe*. Although he read quietly to Tamarind, the other volunteers clearly listened in and refrained from speaking. He'd read only two sentences when she interrupted him.

"'War raids'? What are those?"

"This book is set during World War Two when the Germans bombed London, kind've like when the U.S. Navy used to bomb Culebra."

Next to him, she shivered. "I remember that."

John looked toward her, but the darkness obscured her features. Her wild hair appeared black against the royal sky, the stars crowning her with a glittering diadem. He laid his hand on top of hers where it rested on the blanket. "So I guess you can relate to the children in this book, huh?"

Tamarind shifted. "I guess." She spoke so quietly that John strained to hear her.

He waited, but she said nothing more and no one else spoke about the bombing or one of the former targets, an abandoned tank now rusting on Carlos Rosario—along with unexploded bombs amidst the island's largest nesting grounds. So he picked up the book and continued reading. After a while, he lost himself to the reading, to the story of the children playing hide and seek in the strange old country house to which they'd been sent. Underneath it rode the rhythmic wash of water on white sand and the taste of salt on the air. He'd read a third of the book when one of the other volunteers spoke in a low voice.

"Our first mother has arrived."

Everyone turned toward the beach, now illuminated only by moonlight. A leatherback—a large one, perhaps fifteen hundred pounds—emerged from the water and heaved herself across the sand toward them. They melted back into the tree line and waited until she found the spot she wanted and dug furiously at the sand. When she finished digging the tear-shaped egg cavity, Pablo came forward and lifted her rear flipper so that the rest of them had a clear view of the eggs as they dropped into the sand. Serena counted the large, fertile eggs and Inez counted the small, infertile ones. John and Tamarind measured the turtle after she'd finished laying her eggs. As she held the tape measure next to the leatherback's beak, Tamarind wiped the salty tears from the sea-turtle's eyes with reverent fingers. Jesus documented everything and took a picture of the leatherback—at six and a half feet from beak to tail, she was the largest seen on Culebra in several years.

The leatherback buried her eggs and turned toward the sea, throwing sand behind her to cover her tracks. They all watched her go. Tamarind stood away from John as she did every time a leatherback struggled back across the beach, her lips pursed and her eyes unfocused. She hummed faintly and the air around her seemed to vibrate slightly. When the sea turtle gained the wet edge of beach and seawater reached to embrace it, Tamarind sighed and relaxed her stance.

"She's safe again," she always said to anyone listening.

❁❁❁

Nightly turtle watch lasted through June. John picked Tamarind up every evening on 251 near Tamarindo Estates and dropped her off before dawn in the same place. Even though he urged her to let him walk her home, she always said no. The one time that he'd ignored her and followed her up the access road, she'd disappeared almost in front of his eyes. When he finally turned to head back down to the Samurai after calling for her for fifteen minutes, she jumped out of the scrub along the roadside, shouted, and laughed when he yelled out in surprise. Then she dashed up the road and out of sight still laughing. Tonight he just waited until she'd bounced up the hill like a schoolgirl and then followed a ways behind until he saw her approach a squat cinderblock building a hundred yards off the road to the southeast. It was an odd place for a house, so far from town where most of the Culebrenses lived. As far as John could tell, Tamarind's only neighbors besides the resort were wild horses and lizards. He never saw anyone greet her.

During their weeks watching for turtles, he finished reading *The Lion, The Witch, and The Wardrobe* and then the five successive books in the Narnia series. Pablo, Serena, and Inez huddled close, listening, but Jesus prowled along the edge of the beach as a panther paces near a water hole, waiting for quarry. While he read, John watched the flashlight beam that bounced among the acacia, wary at the other man's restless energy. As long it wasn't directed at him, he wouldn't worry.

Besides straining his eyes on dim text, John spent a small fortune on batteries for his flashlight over the course of their turtle watch. One night, when only a single turtle braved the trip from shallows to sandy beach, he drained two sets of spare batteries.

"I'll be glad when I can read to you during the day," he said after the flashlight dimmed so low that he had to shut it off or they'd be forced to wait for sunrise to walk back to the Samurai. "This is becoming expensive."

Tamarind sat so close to him that long spirals of her hair rested on his bare upper arm. The toes of her left foot, powdered with sand, brushed his whenever she dug them into the beach. She smelled salty and earthy at the same time.

"Don't you have to leave soon? I think maybe this is the last leatherback we'll see this season."

"I'm thinking about staying longer. I wrote a research paper based on my experience from the Trench mission. My advisor's okay with me staying as long as I keep getting work done." But Zoë was *not* okay with it. She'd found out where he was staying from Stefan and started leaving him phone messages with Valerie, the owner of the guesthouse where he'd rented a room. She'd written, too. He just couldn't bring himself to be as blunt with her as he should be.

"Oh."

"Still working on reading *Green Eggs and Ham*?"

She didn't answer right away. In the dark, John felt her swaying and guessed that she still traced her finger through the sand at her side.

"Yes," she said finally. "All the letters looked like bird scratching in sand for a while, but two days ago when I looked, the scratches rearranged themselves in front of my eyes. Some of the words look just like themselves now."

"You'll have to read to me then." He looked out toward the horizon, which lightened toward dawn. Fifteen feet away from them on the beach, the other volunteers sat talking quietly. "I haven't taken you dancing yet. The first Friday after the watch ends, I'll pick you up at the same time and we'll go grab some dinner first. How's that sound?"

Tamarind had grown still. "I've never gone dancing."

"Don't worry." He put his hand on her back. The heat from her skin warmed his palm through the cotton of her t-shirt. "I've seen you dance every day for the past six weeks and you'll put everyone else to shame."

"As long as I don't have to read to them."

A few days later, Teresa Jimenez, the refuge manager, called an end to the season's turtle watch. All the volunteers met at Señorita's at sunset that day to drink beer and poke fun at each other in the brighter lights of the restaurant. John had forgotten the burnish of Tamarind's hair, the peculiar blue of her eyes. For all that she drank only Coke—albeit several of them—her face flushed as the evening wore on. She even imitated birdcalls for their group with astounding accuracy.

He couldn't remember the last time that he'd been out with a group of people, chatting and drinking, and having such a good time. Probably last fall, around the time he and Zoë met. Even Jesus seemed relaxed, his sleepy eyelids minimizing his flat gaze and lending him a seductive air. John suspected that Jesus remained as alert as ever, however.

Half an hour later, Jesus proved John's suspicions right.

"Do you know what 'Culebra' means, Juanito?" He'd taken to calling John by the diminutive, but John knew that it had nothing to do with affection.

Everyone stopped talking to listen.

"Yes. 'Snake.'"

"Ah, *bueno*, good." Jesus toyed with the neck of his Medalla bottle. "There are no snakes on this island. Why is it 'snake island' then?"

"I dunno."

Inez spoke. Where she'd been red-faced and laughing only seconds before, she was very serious. "To remind us about the snake, the evil, that lives at the heart of paradise."

Serena picked up where Inez left off. "There cannot be an *isla encantada* without a *culebra*. Some say a great snake sleeps at the heart of the island, waiting for the end of the world when it will hunt again."

150

Jesus sneered. "These two, they are *virginal*. They do not understand, Juanito. *Pero tú comprendes, sí*? You want to show our little bird of paradise here the true meaning of *culebra*. You don't have it in you, though."

"What does that mean?" Tamarind's voice broke their locked gazes.

Pablo, who'd had too much to drink, slurred his words. "Means Jesus is jealous."

"Jealous? Why?" Tamarind looked at Jesus, puzzled.

"Not jealous. Just waiting. Waiting for you to fly from this spineless worm. When you do, *mi reina*, I will be ready."

The evening's mood soured after that. Inez and Serena, darting looks at Jesus, made excuses for leaving. Pablo, lurching to his feet, declared that he needed to get up early to go out on a dive and asked Jesus to walk him the five blocks to his apartment. Jesus finished his beer and dropped some cash on the table as he stood to go. He looked down on John and Tamarind but said nothing more. They watched him trail Pablo out Señorita's door, his posture sober and cocky. They didn't move or say a word until the waitress came five minutes later, and then John roused and said that it was time to head out.

As he drove Tamarind home, he reminded her of his promise.

"Looks like we're going dancing tomorrow."

"It's Friday?"

"Yup."

"Okay then." She looked out the window at the moon-washed road for several moments, but then a song on the radio caught her attention and she hummed along with it and tapped her fingers on the doorframe.

"Tamarind?" His voice had grown deep in seriousness.

She turned to look at him. "Yes?"

151

"Forget about Jesus. We've got bad blood between us, that's all. It isn't about you."

"'Bad blood'? Has he hurt you, John?" She'd sat up straight, her face in darkness against the moonlight.

"No, of course not. 'Bad blood' is just a saying. It means we've disagreed before."

"Oh."

Something in her voice, in its small uncertainty, caused him to reach out and push the hair from her face. Tendrils curled around his fingers almost as if they were alive. "See you around sunset, then?" He spoke gently.

She nodded. "I'll be here."

When John let her out at the bottom of the hill, he watched her silhouette shrink against the pricks of starlight until it winked out at the top. With her disappearance, the night diminished and became ordinary. Even the music on the radio sounded tinny and weak. He quickly turned and drove back south into town and bed.

Tamarind leaned against a palm tree waiting for him the following evening. She wore the blue dress that he'd bought her before he left the island in early April. For the first time since he'd known her, her hair looked combed and smooth curls lay sedately on her shoulders. Shell hair ornaments clipped long strands together in small bunches away from her face, and around her neck hung lures on transparent fishing line. But her feet were still bare.

She slid into her seat.

"You look great. You even make bare feet look dressed up."

Tamarind looked down at her feet as she pulled her door shut. "Should I have worn shoes then?"

"No, no. Wouldn't look natural on you, I think."

"Feet do?"

152

He glanced over as he pulled away and saw her looking down at her feet. Another glance told him that she wiggled her toes.

"I've never seen anyone whose feet look more natural on her than yours do on you." Out of the corner of his eye he sensed her looking at him. He grinned.

"We're going to the Dockside for dinner. Is that okay?"

"Sure."

They chatted about books during the ten minutes it took to get to the Dockside. John wanted her to take the ferry with him to San Juan and visit a bookstore.

"Really? You'd really take me with you?"

"Sure. You should get to help pick out the next books I read you. I also need to pick up some supplies, if you don't mind tagging along that is."

"Oh, no, I don't mind." She vibrated a low hum; a few soft clicks escaped her mouth.

"You know you hum and click all the time? I'm starting to be able to tell what all the different pitches, tempos, and volumes mean. I'm guessing you're being polite. Am I right?"

"No. I'm excited. And scared."

"Really?" He looked at her. "Well, I'll try not to disappoint you then."

The Dockside had few customers this hour in the off-season. The waitress led them to a two-person table looking out over the canal where they ordered *buñuelos de queso*, *mojo isleño*, and *tembleque*. John ordered a Medalla and watched with a smile as Tamarind ordered a Coke.

"How do you like your fish?"

Tamarind wrinkled her nose and sliced off a tiny wedge from the *mojo isleño*. "Not much. I can hardly taste the fish with all the other flavors. I like my fish fresher, too."

"How do you normally eat it? I thought this garlic sauce was popular in Puerto Rico."

"Oh. Well, we usually eat our fish raw."

"Like sushi?" At her puzzled look, he said, "That's what the Japanese call raw fish, seaweed, and rice. You'd probably like it."

"It sounds good. How do you like to eat fish?"

John sipped his beer. "I don't normally eat fish or animal flesh. I'm a vegetarian, but it's hard to stick with it here on the island so I've been eating fish." He figured that there was no need to mention his brief deviation into beef.

"No fish?" Tamarind sounded shocked. "Why not? I thought everybody ate fish."

"I guess there's a lot of reasons." John ticked off some of the issues that Zoë had given him when she insisted he become a vegetarian. They still seemed reasonable. "Mostly, it's not sustainable. I mean, huge fishing boats come along and trawl with their nets, scooping up whatever gets trapped in them. The fish can't possibly keep reproducing fast enough and sometimes other creatures die simply because they're caught in the net. Plus, I think it's healthier to cut out fish and meat."

"It's not because you don't like to eat fish?"

"No, actually, I love fish, especially sushi."

"But you don't want to kill them to eat them? Didn't you go fishing here?"

John squirmed a bit. "Yeah, but that's not what I find objectionable. It's kind've hard to explain, but it doesn't bother me if somebody catches a few fish using a rod and bait. That's just not how most people get fish in the U.S."

"Oh. Okay."

They fell silent. Tamarind continued to pick at her *mojo isleño*.

John decided to rescue her. "You don't have to finish that."

She sighed and pushed the fish aside. She dipped a tentative spoon into the coconut custard. "The *tembleque*'s good, though."

"Anyone who loves Coke as much as you do obviously has a sweet tooth."

Tamarind began rubbing the tip of her tongue over her teeth. "How do I know which one? None of them taste sweet."

John laughed. "Sorry! That just means you like to eat sweet things."

Tamarind frowned. "I always get it wrong."

He put his hand briefly on hers. "I love the way you get it. I feel like I'm looking at the world through fresh eyes when I'm with you. It's wonderful."

Tamarind blushed and dipped the spoon back into the *tembleque*.

They drove to Isla Encantada twenty minutes later and found the live music just getting going. Even in the dim lighting, John recognized Jesus in the far corner. To his surprise—and relief—he recognized Jesus' date as well. Raimunda's voluptuous curves and luxuriant hair were unmistakable. He didn't know what relieved him more: Jesus having a date or Raimunda's near-feral sexuality being contained. A small sound at his side made him look down to see Tamarind gazing at Jesus. John squeezed her hand and smiled.

Tamarind said nothing but sidled closer to John, who forgot all about Jesus at her nearness and led her onto the dance floor. She watched John and imitated his movements, but after John ordered a beer she drank half of it without taking a breath. She closed her eyes when she returned to the dance floor and appeared to listen to something in the music

155

audible only to her. John couldn't take his eyes from her, barely dancing. She looked like a poem set to music.

They might have danced minutes or hours. The heat of bodies, the dim interior and flashes of mirror and lights, the beat of drums and the sound of Spanish—all these cocooned John in a timeless world. At last Tamarind opened eyes in a flushed face and grabbed John's hand.

"Let's get out of here!" She pulled him to the door and outside into the cooler, though still warm, Caribbean night. "I need water."

"We can get something to drink inside."

"No, no. I need to swim."

The cocoon had split open and the night air touched a fingertip to John's damp forehead. The need for full immersion in water of any kind seized him after she spoke.

"Me too. Let's get out of here."

John headed north toward Playa Tamarindo, but Tamarind tugged on his arm when they approached the right onto 250. He turned as she directed and they headed east. He'd driven this route only one other time since coming to Culebra—the time that Zoë visited and they'd driven around the whole island. Even so, he'd kayaked and cruised the eastern shore and visited Culebrita and its hundred-year-old lighthouse so he knew the eastern shoreline. Since 250 ended at Playa Zoni, he thought he knew where Tamarind intended for them to go. However, not long after the road bore sharply to the north, she asked him to pull over.

"Here. I want to show you Puerto del Manglar."

After he'd parked the Samurai along the deserted two-lane road, they descended a rocky path toward the lagoon, which was bordered by a narrow muddy rim. A westerly breeze passed over the water and cooled their skin. Around them and along the shoreline of the lagoon, darker mangrove trees framed the night sky where stars lay scattered in brilliant disarray.

John tilted his face up to the dome of the night sky over them.

"I'm an explorer at the end of the world," he said. In the still night, his quiet voice seemed loud to him. "Thanks for showing me this place."

"Wait. There's something else you need to see." Tamarind bent down and picked something up from the ground. When she tossed whatever it was into the still waters, the incandescent filament of its plunge lit up the lagoon before his eyes. "There are tiny creatures that live in this water that react to movement by lighting up."

"Like underwater fireflies?"

John turned to Tamarind, but she'd already lifted her dress over her head and dropped it on the ground at her feet, sighing. She wore nothing under the dress. As he watched her stride into the phosphorescent water, thousands of the tiny creatures shimmered like blue-green fire along the surface of her skin and in the patch of hair between her legs. Around them, the *coquí* frog sang its distinctive refrain and mosquitoes hummed.

He took a step forward and then stopped. Tamarind swam in the obsidian water, her strokes luminous and eerie.

"I thought you were hot from dancing." Tamarind lay on her back fifty feet away looking at him, her torso elevated from the surface of the lagoon. Neon streaked the surrounding water as she stroked to stay afloat.

"I was."

"You're not now? Is something wrong?"

"No—yes. Sometimes I feel a little like I'm suffocating."

She swam closer, her eyes never leaving his face. "Is that how you felt the day I pulled you from the canal?"

"Yes."

"I know how you feel. Sometimes I find it hard to breathe when I'm out of water."

John remembered her swimming. "Coming from you, that makes perfect sense."

She stood up and walked to him, her small breasts high and their nipples taut. Seawater fell from her in a glowing sheet. When she reached him, she took his right hand in her left. He felt her vibrating hum through the skin of his palm.

"I'll take care of you." She lifted his t-shirt over his head while he stood there, shivering. "You're cold?" Her hands, normally cool and moist, felt warm against his shoulders.

She stepped closer and wrapped her arms around his torso, pressing against him. Her heat seeped into his skin and he shivered more. She laid her head against his chest and hummed louder. John closed his eyes and breathed. After a moment he realized that Tamarind breathed in unison with him and he felt warmer. Something inside his chest unlocked and his lungs expanded to let in air. Slowly he lifted his left hand and cupped the back of her head. She didn't move or halt her humming.

John shifted so that Tamarind looked up at him. In the dark he saw only starlight reflected in her eyes; her hair, so carefully clipped up earlier in the evening, curved around her face in damp clumps. He lowered his mouth to hers and tasted salt.

"Counting turtle eggs? You're so full of shit, John." Zoë's voice sliced through the night around them. "Care to introduce me to your naked friend?"

Eleven

ఔ

JOHN STOOD ON THE BERM between the road and the lagoon with the dripping woman shrinking beside him. He dipped his head and stepped sideways, blocking Zoë's view.

"Wha-what are you doing here?" He didn't look at her.

"Fuck if I know!" Her voice cracked on the last word and she clinched her hands at her side. "I believed you when you said you were sorry about fucking another woman, that you cared about me. I believed you when you said you just needed to get away from grad school for a while, spend some time in the surf and sand. I came down here to give you a second chance."

Her words flew at him. She almost wished that they were stilettos, and she didn't mean those ridiculous neck-breakers that Barbie dolls wore.

He turned and said something Zoë couldn't hear to his date. She scurried in the direction of the Samurai parked thirty feet from them.

"I didn't lie to you." John turned back to face her.

"So I'm supposed to believe that this–this—" She flung her arm in the direction of the Samurai. "That you haven't been fucking this island bitch all summer?"

The moon had risen over them, bringing John's features into sharp relief. Shadows underneath his eyes obscured their expression.

"You're supposed to believe that I never intended to hurt you." He raised his hand toward her—to ward off her next words or to console her, she didn't know which.

"My God! Even now you're dancing around the truth! You think you love her, don't you?"

John dropped his hand and said nothing.

"What is she to you? Someone not too educated to forget her place? You're an asshole, John, and I can't believe I've been tearing myself up over you. Let me show you what a real woman does when a man tries to make a fool out of her."

Before he could anticipate her or even protest, she lifted her right knee to her chest, rising onto the ball of her left foot. A fraction of a second later her right heel connected with his solar plexus, sending him flying away from her. He landed on the soft mud at the edge of Puerto del Manglar. She followed the kick up with a dash and a swing of her left leg that stopped short of his head; as she stood over him, panting, she knew he got the message: she could knock his block off if she chose. Then, after a long moment, she lowered her foot and turned away.

❧ ❧ ❧

Ana hunkered within the scant shade of her doorway, her good eye squinted against the mid-afternoon light. Smoke from her clove cigarette curled and wafted until it was snared within the strands of her coarse hair. On a grass mat before her was a mound of tamarind pods, nearly ten pounds, that she'd collected this morning after scouring the ground near the tamarind trees along the coast; it was the first of the season's fruit. She'd already washed each pod and now broke them into smaller pieces, leaving the outer shell and seeds with the pulp and tossing them into a large cast-iron pot at her right side. Reach, grasp, snap, snap, snap. Her body swayed and rocked as she worked, her movements efficient and easy; only the sounds of birds competed with her radio, now playing Latin salsa behind her.

After she'd finished breaking the tamarind pods, Ana built a fire under a cast-iron frame ten feet from her house. She hauled the pot to the frame and lifted it onto a hook over the flames. Next, she poured in twice as much spring water as fruit from her cache of bottled water and stirred the tamarind around in it, her left hand drifting to the stub of cigarette in her mouth before removing it; as she stirred, a spicy scent of tamarind fruit insinuated itself through the cloying smoke. She stirred until the water began to darken and the pulp separated from the shells and seeds. These she strained from the pot with a long-handled sieve and saved in a wooden bowl for later use in lotions and syrups for a wide range of ailments.

She let the water simmer for ten minutes or so before she tossed in a handful of cloves, allspice and black peppercorns, then slices of lime and ginger. She breathed the vapors rising from her brew and sighed before sinking down again on her heels under the shade of a nearby tree and waiting for the fruit and spices to flavor the water fully. A slight breeze stirred the air around her, drying the sweat from between her flaccid breasts and lifting the ends of her hair from her cheeks.

When she'd judged that the decoction was sufficiently spiced, she strained out the spices and fruit. Near the wooden bowl into which she deposited these spent flavorings sat two five-pound bags of palm sugar; she added these slowly to the pot, stirring until she had a thin syrup. She let this syrup boil for several minutes and then doused the fire under the pot. As the syrup cooled, she ladled it into a large glass bottle (which one of the Culebrenses had given her as payment for curing his diarrhea) filled with several gallons of purified water. Now the brew was cool enough for the yeast, which she'd already dissolved in warm water. Her task was nearly over: she would watch the fermentation over the next two weeks, adding sugar whenever it seemed to slow down. By the end of that time, it would be drinkable; in a month, it would be a spicy beer.

Ana had brewed a variety of other wines and beers from Culebra's fruits, but none tasted nearly as good as tamarind beer and she'd long since abandoned any other recipes that she'd tested. Even though she had no one but herself to please, she'd found that more than a few of the locals preferred her tamarind beer to commercial beers and she was able to sell a cup here and there for far more than that which a bottle of Medalla garnered.

She lifted the full bottle of fermenting brew into her decrepit refrigerator, its once-white exterior now chipped and pockmarked from a lifetime of use. It was one of the few modern conveniences that she'd grudgingly adopted from her previous life as a sailor's wife, but one which earned her respect for its ability to make her life more pleasant and pay for itself. It, a warming plate, and a radio were the only appliances that she owned.

Now that she'd finished brewing, she pulled out a smaller, two-and-a-half gallon bottle of finished beer from one of the higher shelves in the refrigerator and poured herself a cup. She took the cup and a fresh clove cigarette and returned to the doorway of her single room to wait for the rain that she smelled in the air.

A hush descended over the afternoon as the sun reached its zenith and all of the Creator's wildlife dozed in its heat. Even Ana grew sleepy in the still warmth, her head drooping over her cup and her hand holding the cigarette growing limp. Gentle fingers saved her from being burned and woke her with their cool touch. Struggling awake, Ana lifted her face. Seeing the mermaid, she shifted on her heels and brought her cup up to her mouth. It wouldn't do for the young one to guess that she'd been waiting for her. She drained the last of the tamarind beer, its fiery descent into her stomach bracing her, and set the cup down. She rose to face Tamarind, who still held her burning cigarette.

"I'll take that."

Tamarind handed it to her, her forehead puckered. The young one looked so much like Ana herself had before she'd married her sailor that a deep soreness settled in her chest, but this time there was no tamarind beer to fortify her nerves. Even if she had a mirror, Ana knew that Tamarind would not recognize her own innocence and vulnerability within it.

"You've been gone all night." She said, her voice gruff from the heartache, and took a drag. "Did you manage to win your legs by mating with that man?"

The muscles in Tamarind's face tightened. Ana noticed that her dress, originally brilliant blue, was dusty and torn in several places.

"Did he hurt you? Tell me and I'll brew him a special potion. Or I'll call on Mother Sea and curse him to the seventh generation!"

Tamarind sank into a squat and folded her arms across her chest. Her corkscrew hair concealed her face.

"He didn't hurt me the way you think. We went dancing last night and I took him to Puerto Manglar to show him the glowing ones. Then he kissed me."

She stopped, but Ana said nothing. Instead, she went inside and returned with a cup of the tamarind beer. She handed it to Tamarind, who gulped some of it and winced.

"His girlfriend appeared at just that moment. Her anger pulsed from her—it nearly overwhelmed my senses. John asked me to wait in his Samurai, but I could still hear them talking." She paused long enough to sip the tamarind beer. "Then she kicked him in the chest. He fell hard and she nearly kicked him in the head, but she didn't. I could tell she wanted to though."

Ana dropped her cigarette butt onto the hard ground and twisted her heel on it. "Ah. Did he plead with her?"

"No, he lay on the ground, clutching at his chest. I waited until she left to go to him, but he said nothing to me, just waved me back into the Samurai. When he finally got in, he said it was time for me to go home. He dropped me off at the bottom of the hill."

"Where've you been then?"

Tamarind looked into her cup as though she looked at it for the first time and didn't like what she saw. "Just wandering—and swimming. I couldn't sleep anyway."

Ana gripped Tamarind's chin and made her look up. "I warned you to stay away from him. He's not worth the pain you've already been through. Don't let him hurt you anymore."

"His girlfriend said he thinks he loves me."

"Bah! She said that in the heat of the moment. Even if she's right, he's not to be trusted. Look how he's hurt her. I doubt he knows what he wants. And as hurt and angry as she is, I bet you a colossal squid for dinner she'd take him back if he asked her to."

Tamarind stood up. "I need another swim."

"Go and have one. But keep in mind, young one: you win this man, you're not likely to live close to the ocean. You won't be able to swim whenever your heart troubles you."

Tamarind frowned. Without speaking, she turned toward the hidden path to Playa Tamarindo and trudged away.

Ana lit another clove cigarette and took a deep drag, her eyes all the while on Tamarind's hunched shoulders. After Tamarind disappeared over the rise, she smiled and exhaled smoke, which lingered around her face pleasantly.

∽∽∽

John's head ached. His head and torso felt as if they'd been hollowed out and then stuffed with a mix of sandpaper and wool. He groaned and rolled over onto his side, misjudging how close he was to the edge of the bed. He crashed against the floor hard, but the pain receded quickly as he realized that the air washing over his face was cool. Looking up to the clock on his bedside table, he read 4:08 p.m.

He lay there for a long time. The headache only grew sharper and his tongue, now swollen and hairy inside his mouth, commandeered his thoughts once he noticed its state. With willpower alone, he pushed himself into a seated position, wincing as an invisible pick plunged through his skull and out his left eye. He remembered enough to focus his energy on standing up and getting into the bathroom where water and ibuprofen awaited him. His legs had fallen asleep while he lay on the floor and prickles danced up and down his calves and out his toes as he hobbled across the room.

Every act of getting ready took much longer than it should have, but by dinnertime John had managed to shower, shave, and dress in clean clothes. He still felt tired, but his headache no longer plagued him and the gallon of water that he'd ingested one cup at a time had returned his tissues to their normal fullness. A residue clung to his tongue even though he'd brushed it with toothpaste.

He walked to Señorita's and asked for a table in the corner away from James, the ever-present double of Ernest Hemingway that he'd seen during his first stay on Culebra. James would happily buy him a hair of the dog, but John didn't feel like listening to his exploits or his complaints this evening. When Janelle came to take his order, she clucked and grasped his chin in her free hand to tilt his face toward the light.

"Sweetie! You look like someone mugged you! Are you all right?"

John shrugged and pulled away. "Just too much to drink, Janelle. I'll be fine tomorrow."

"I'll bring you a club soda with lemon. Order something healthy, too. No fries, hear?"

John sank back into his chair after Janelle brought him his drink and fussed over him. He kept his eyes on the tiled tabletop, but there was no one around to meet his gaze. Although the weekend beachgoers arrived on the ferry this morning, Playa Flamenco absorbed their numbers and town remained quiet. Very few tourists came to Culebra during the summer—that hot, dry hurricane season—and no one followed John into Señorita's for the next half an hour. After she delivered his food, Janelle retreated to a barstool next to James and across from Tim, the bartender, and the three of them gossiped in the otherwise empty restaurant. John cut up his fish and lifted food into his mouth, but every bite tasted like sawdust.

He heard laughter near the entranceway just as he finished eating as much of his dinner as he could swallow. Looking, he caught sight of Raimunda. Wearing a tight t-shirt and blue jeans, she stood gazing up at Pablo, whose right arm curled around her waist. So. She was a free agent, but he knew that, didn't he? Maybe he should renew their relationship. Same terms as before, even if he didn't have a girlfriend anymore. He didn't know how he felt about Zoë. Or Tamarind. He did know how he felt about Raimunda. It was lust, plain and simple. And he deserved the funk that swallowed him every time it came over him. John pushed his plate away from him without taking his eyes from her and put his feet up on the seat of the chair opposite him. When Janelle came to collect the plate, he put his hand on her wrist and ordered a Medalla.

"If you say so, honey," she said, but he only half heard.

John watched Raimunda as he sipped his beer. She never turned to look at him but kept her attention on Pablo and the bottle of beer Janelle brought her. When Pablo left Raimunda to head to the bathroom, John tipped his beer up and drained it before pushing his chair back with a loud squeak. At the sound, Raimunda turned to watch him, a smile twitching at the corners of her mouth.

"*Hola, gringo.*"

"*Buenas noches.*" He sat down in an empty chair. "I came to steal you away from Pablo."

She smirked and lifted her beer to her mouth. John watched her throat pulse as she swallowed. Above the collar of the t-shirt, a small shell pendant rested in the hollow at the base of her throat. She touched the tip of her tongue to her upper lip as she set the bottle down in front of her.

"Perhaps I don't wish to be stolen away, *mi amigo*."

John leaned forward and traced the inside of her upper arm with his index finger. "Perhaps I don't care what you want," he said into her ear.

Raimunda laughed and tossed her hair out of her face. "Oh, I think you care what I want all right."

John picked up her hand from where it rested on the table and pulled it into his lap. "I know what you want."

"John? *Qué pasa*?" Pablo materialized not far from them.

Raimunda slid her hand up and around her beer bottle before Pablo reached the table. John wondered if Pablo had seen.

"Not much, *amigo*. Just saying hello to Raimunda."

"John and I are old friends," she said as Pablo sat down. John saw her hand disappear under the table and he imagined it on Pablo's thigh. From the look on Pablo's face, he'd guessed right.

"Well, it was good to see you two, but I'll leave you alone to enjoy your dinner." John stood.

Pablo, whose eyes had fastened on Raimunda's ripe mouth, barely nodded. "*Hasta la vista*, John."

John walked around Dewey for the next hour, passing by Señorita's entrance a dozen times before Pablo and Raimunda finally left together. He watched Pablo weave down the sidewalk north toward his apartment. Raimunda propped him up as he chattered incomprehensibly next to her; she intermittently uttered soothing sounds in response to his commentary. After they'd gone fifty yards, John followed them. When they reached Pablo's apartment, Raimunda folded her arms and leaned against the wall of the building while Pablo tried to insert his key into the deadbolt. John waited until he'd caught her eye and pointed to Pablo, then shook his head and pointed to himself. Raimunda grinned and took Pablo's arm. Waving to John over her shoulder, she took the key from Pablo and unlocked the door. Pablo nearly fell into the building as she swung the door open and away from him.

John waited, his lips compressed. After only a few minutes, Raimunda reappeared in the doorway—alone. She scanned the far sidewalk and when her eyes met John's, she smiled and leaned again, this time onto the doorframe. John strode toward her; when he reached her, he gripped her elbows.

"Pablo can't hold his beer, can he?"

She shrugged. "He's sitting on his sofa muttering in front of his TV. Good thing he's got a satellite dish."

"Let's go find out if I know what you want."

Raimunda rose up on her toes and kissed him, hard. "I want exactly what you want, *gringo*."

She threaded her fingers through his and together they walked toward Posada La Diosa and his room there.

Twelve

ↂ

WET SAND CLUNG TO JOHN'S BARE FEET as he strolled along the strip of Isla Verde beach owned by the Ritz-Carlton's San Juan Hotel. He heard dozens of voices from other conference attendees as they spilled through the hotel's doors to the beachfront, chattering without seeing the beauty in front of them. He'd already presented the paper that he'd written about the difficulties in storing and accessing large amounts of digital video while onboard a marine research ship. He'd escaped the ongoing presentations and milling graduate students as soon as the last questioner scurried out of his particular conference room on the way to another talk. Somewhere inside, his advisor deftly worked his industry contacts, always looking for a way to turn a spark of interest into funding.

"Hey, man, you look like you should be combing the beach for loose change, the way you've got your pants rolled up like that," said a voice several feet behind him.

John whirled. His friend Stefan stood at the edge of the manicured lawn holding a wineglass and a notepad.

"And you look like Eddie Murphy in *Beverly Hills Cop* when he lied his way into the Beverly Hills Hotel. You ever think maybe a t-shirt and blue jeans weren't the best things to wear to the Ritz?" John walked over to where Stefan stood. "Have they put out lunch yet?"

Stefan nodded and raised the wineglass to his mouth. "The wine's actually pretty crappy. But I doubt too many of the others will notice. They're too wrapped up in debating optimal bit rates and lossless compression. They don't have our refined sensitivities."

"We'll just have to make do with the hotel buffet for lunch, but tonight I'll take you across the street to this Cuban place I know, *Metropole*. They have the best *moros y cristianos* in Puerto Rico. Their *pastelitos* are also very tasty. I eat there about once a week now."

They turned and made their way toward the Vista Mar Terrace where the largest number of graduate students, faculty members, and industry researchers now congregated around open bars and tables laden with crudités, cheese and crackers, and fresh fruit. When they'd managed to fill their small plates and gotten full glasses of wine, they positioned themselves in a corner furthest from the building and chatted between bites.

"So I met Elí Arroyo López from Polytech last night at the reception. He's very excited to have an 'exchange' student as he puts it for the summer. He told me he's been working for some time to create a real department instead of offering a single EE degree."

John popped a water cracker laden with Brie into his mouth, chewed and swallowed. "Elí's a good guy with a lot of ambitions for his beloved PUPR. Who knows? Maybe he's prescient about the need for high-tech degrees in Puerto Rico. A lot of people are talking about India these days, but Elí thinks there's a large pool of talent closer to home."

"You getting a lot of work done here? I read your paper in the proceedings and it looks like you might have yourself a thesis topic percolating in there."

"Actually, I've been working on another research paper for the Video IR Symposium in October. It's amazing how much work you can get done when you don't really know anyone."

"No? I thought maybe there were one or two women in this tropical paradise."

John shrugged and looked down at his plate. "I've been spending weekends on Culebra where I have some friends. Some of them happen to be women."

"That explains why Zoë's been a regular storm cloud around the CS department. You two still together?"

"No." John didn't elaborate.

"Ah. Well, no wonder you're in no hurry to get back to Pittsburgh." Stefan grinned, his Cheshire-cat grin. It irritated John. "Let me know if you need a place to stay when you get back."

"I'm in no hurry to get back to Pittsburgh because I needed a break, Stefan." John set his empty wineglass down on the terrace wall a little harder than he intended. A passing waiter glared at him as he rescued it. "My time away from CMU hasn't been wasted. I've seen endangered leatherback turtles struggle onto dark beaches where they exhaust themselves digging pits for their eggs, which they leave, trusting that the next generation will survive the greediness and stupidity of people. I've also spent a lot of time teaching an illiterate woman how to read. Compared to those two activities, worrying about which RAID scheme works best for video storage seems a tad inconsequential."

"So what's the answer then? Chuck it all and live on a Caribbean island?"

John looked out over the horizon. "If I figure out a way to do it, I just might."

Later that night, John left the window looking out on La Isla Verde open. The moon illuminated his suite so well that he found himself unable to sleep until long after he lay down on the Egyptian cotton sheets. He slept without knowing he slept, or so he came to believe. In the vivid light, he saw Tamarind standing framed in the window. She wore the blue batik dress that she'd worn the night that they went dancing and even in the shadows around her head he could see the hue of her eyes. Pearls studded her hair, which flowed as smooth as water around her head; abalone and obsidian ornaments dangled from her ears and neck. She studied his face without smiling, but her eyes hinted at mirth. After a moment, she hummed and clicked until John lost the dream and sank into sleep.

❧❧❧

Ana trod barefoot over the dusty path toward Playa Tamarindo, her calloused feet insensitive to the hard stones and uneven ground. The dry heat burned her lungs as it had done for more years than she cared to remember, but she knew that she had long passed the point where she could choose a different home, a better life. Above her, her favorite laughing gull hovered protectively and occasionally dropped down to her shoulder and chuckled reprovingly in her ear.

She stopped just as the path began to descend again toward the shore and peered down through the opening in the thorny scrub ahead of her to Tamarind's scraggly-haired silhouette embossed against the night sky. Around the motionless form emanated an aura like a grease slick on wet pavement. Seeing it, Ana's breath quickened and she bit her lower lip. Half the rainy season had already passed and still the mermaid pined for the weak, lustful man that she'd saved from a watery death. Ana could no longer wait for Tamarind to abandon her mad hope for something more to happen with John. She must entice her with a powerful alternative.

છ ઊ ઊ

Shifting her buttocks a little, Tamarind shoved her feet against the stones in front of her and lifted her face into the breeze, her eyes closed. The fan-leafed palms and tamarind trees lining the beach's edge whispered as the breeze tickled their leaves and the ocean *shush-shushed* them; otherwise, the reverent night was silent beneath the moon overhead. She felt the strength of the trees rooting down into the ground and she leaned into their strength, wanting to draw it into herself and keep it there.

"So. I find you here." A raspy voice and the scent of cloves came from behind her.

Tamarind didn't answer; she only closed her eyes.

"T'won't do you any good to sit here and moon over that idiot."

"What business is it of yours what I'm doing?" She didn't look at the old woman.

For a moment she heard nothing; then she felt Ana's presence next to her on the stones.

"None of my business, that's what. I'm neither kin nor friend to you. But I speak from experience, young one." She paused. "I was once a mermaid like you and also fell in love with a human man."

Tamarind stared at Ana. "What happened?"

Ana shrugged and sucked hard on her clove cigarette without looking from the distant horizon. The sound of burning paper and her harsh exhale mingled with the rich scent of clove. "Not important what happened. All you need to know is I put off my tail for love. Long after I left this island behind, I found myself alone. Came back here and begged the island midwife to undo what she'd done, to send me back to the waves. She said it was impossible for me. I was no longer the same person; I might die trying to put a tail on again. I insisted anyway, saying I was as likely to die from grief."

She turned to look at Tamarind. Both opaque eyes appeared blind in the starlight.

"Obviously didn't work. But it wasn't a complete failure. Instead of dying, I lost only the sight in my eye. If you'd been paying attention, you'd've seen the *mer* in me. I still hear *mer* speech, though not like I once did. Along my flanks are pores for sensing movement underwater." She smoothed the side of her shirt. "Mine no longer work. Only give the Culebrenses something to gossip about."

Tamarind studied Ana in the brilliant moonlight. She thought that she must always have known. Signs of the *mer* showed clearly on the old woman: she had a bit of webbing between her fingers, almost indiscernible now from the loose skin of old age, and her eye, piercing as it was, was the changeable blue of Mother Sea.

"Why are you telling me all this?"

"Because, unlike you, I didn't really have a choice. I tried to force my way back, but it wasn't my fate. You gotta choice."

"What choice? When the rainy season ends, I'll revert back to being *mer*. You said I couldn't remain human unless I consummated my love with John."

"Yeah, I did say that. But you can keep your legs if you copulate with any human male while you're transformed."

Tamarind started to speak, but Ana cut her off. "I'm getting old and need an apprentice, Tamarind. There's always been a midwife. She tells the *dragos* what she can about the humans on her island. She casts and keeps glamours. Sometimes she helps a *mer* put off a tail. Took me a while to see I'd been chosen, but I came to accept my fate."

Her last words hung, heavy as ripe tamarind pods on slender branches, over them.

"You're offering me the choice of becoming a midwife, like you? To remain human?" Tamarind paused, shaking her head. "I don't want to be human if I can't be with John."

Ana squinted her eye before pushing the stub of her clove cigarette into the stones at her side. She exhaled smoke in twin streams from her nostrils. It writhed and expanded in front of her face. "Don't have to decide now. You still have time before the rains end. Think over my offer. That's all I ask, young one."

Tamarind noticed the book that lay on the ground near Ana like a dark smudge in the moonlight. Thick, with a dirty cloth cover that was torn and water-stained, its yellowed pages exuded age—and *power*. She'd seen Ana consulting this book numerous times, but Ana had always guarded it and said that it was for no one's eyes but her own.

"You can't read," Ana said the first time that Tamarind asked about it. "What's the point in looking at a book when you don't have any idea what it says?"

At the time, Tamarind shrugged and said nothing. Now it lay between them like a promise. Ana saw where her gaze fell and she put withered fingers on it.

"Intrigued by my book?"

Tamarind looked at the old woman's face. Ana gazed back at her with a mild expression. So she picked the book up with reverent fingers and pulled it into her lap. Her eyes, used to the dimmer underwater world, had no difficulty distinguishing details, faint as they were. Turning pages as fragile as dried seaweed, she glimpsed lists of herbs, spices, sea creatures and underwater plants—many items were words that she didn't recognize from her short reading experience. Underneath the lists, she saw directions for preparing the items and instructions for keeping and administering the final preparations. In the margins, there were handwritten notes and occasional drawings.

"I'll teach you to read it."

Tamarind nearly responded that she already knew how to read before something stopped her short; she blinked instead and recalled that Ana had tempted her a long time with the key to human learning.

"Why should I believe that you'd teach me how to read?"

"Because it's the midwife's book. If you're gonna take my place one day, you have to be able to read it."

Tamarind bit her lower lip. "I haven't said I'll take your place."

"True." Ana nodded, the clove cigarette clamped between her first two fingers where it dangled in front of her. "When you do, you'll find many, many useful recipes and spells. The method for helping a *mer* put off her tail—and the method for putting it on again—to name a few. Become my apprentice and I'll show you how to do lots of amazing things."

Tamarind continued to turn the pages and to run her fingertips over the contents. On a page two-thirds of the way through the book she squinted at instructions for transforming someone into a temporary copy of another, living or dead. As long as the caster had some item that belonged to the person being copied, something taken from the body, then an elaborate potion could be brewed and distilled that transformed the caster for one turn of the day. She frowned.

"Tell me, young one. Where is it your father thinks you've been all this time?"

Tamarind's frown deepened. "I let him think that I went to the Hidden Caves of Camuy for training with the *mer* elders."

"Ah." Ana rummaged in the small pouch she wore on a long strap around her neck. After a moment, she pulled out another clove cigarette and a small object that glistened in the moonlight. Muttering something that might have been a spell, she raised the disc to one end of the cigarette and sucked on the other until a thin plume of smoke appeared near the disc. "So your father intends for you to be a *dragos*. He sees the same qualities in you I do. We just don't have the same ideas about how best to help the *mer*."

She smoked the cigarette in silence while Tamarind continued turning pages in the book. A laughing gull flew over their heads, a dark speck that spiraled around them until it had descended low enough to land on Ana's shoulder. Tamarind had never seen a bird flying at this time of night before. She watched the bird nuzzle Ana's cheek and appear to whisper in her ear. When the laughing gull cocked its head and turned a bright eye on Tamarind, she thought it studied her coldly. It again whispered in Ana's ear and the old woman laughed. Tamarind ignored them and struggled to read more spells in the waning moonlight.

"What's he gonna think when he finds out you spent the rainy season with me?"

"I don't know."

"Yes you do. You just don't know why he hates humans so much. I do. It's because of your mother."

Tamarind sat up straighter. "What do you know about my mother?"

"Enough. She was the first mermaid I tried to help put off her tail."

"What? What lie are you telling me, old woman?" She'd never spoken to Ana so rudely before; she'd caught a residue of thought from the former *mer* and responded to its flash of visceral ugliness.

"No lie." The gull laughed at them and launched itself into the air above their heads. "Just like you, she mooned about wherever she could see humans: beaches, boats, cays. And, just like you, she fixated on one, a boat captain. And one day, she came to me and asked me to help her put off her tail."

"But how did she know you could help her? I didn't know about you before we met. I certainly didn't know *mer* could put off their tails."

"Ah, that's because your father drowned the knowledge among your community. If any remember, he's forbidden them from sharing it among the others."

"But—but Mother was a mermaid! I was very young, it's true, but I still remember her. If she'd been human, how could she and my father have mated, let alone had six daughters?"

"Yeah, she was a mermaid when she died." Ana picked up a clove cigarette. Her lined face seemed to shrivel even more and her eye no longer blazed. "Her tail never came off. I remember the sound she made when I eased her out of the ground. Like a baby seal mewing. Her tail bruised and bloodied, one tip broken and limp—it still haunts me.

"Something in her mind died that day. Her thoughts frothed and foamed. Your father loved her before she came to me, though she never returned his love. He took her, poor wounded thing, and mated with her. His strength kept her safe for a while and you and your sisters were born. But she couldn't stay away from humans and kept wandering toward them."

Here Ana stopped and sucked on her cigarette so long that Tamarind thought that the story must be done. She was about to ask Ana why she had told her all this about her mother, when Ana began to speak again.

"I've thought about that spell of transforming over and over. I just can't be sure it wasn't my fault it failed."

Tamarind hesitated a moment. "Is that why Father kept us from knowing about your powers?"

"No." Ana looked away. "Putting off the tail has always been dangerous for *mer*. He didn't blame me for that. No, he didn't want any of you to know how to become human because he despises humans."

"Because Mother was so fascinated by them?"

"That's partly why, young one." Ana brought her eye to Tamarind's face with visible effort. "But it has more to do with the fact a human killed her and very nearly killed him, too."

Thirteen

ANA STUDIED THE SMOKING STUB between her fingers without meeting Tamarind's eyes. After it had burned almost to her fingertips, she leaned forward and sunk it into the seawater caressing the stones around their feet. It hissed briefly. She flicked the remains into the tree line behind them. Time to wield the truth like a shark's tooth.

"It's more than ten rainy seasons since I found your father on Luís Peña. Back then I could still swim. Swam over there to look for birds' eggs. That day, I finished gathering all the eggs I could carry and went up to the beach to look for seaweed. That's when I came across your father, bleeding his life into the sand.

"Took all my strength to wrestle him onto his back so I could clean his wound and get a better look. Can't tell you, young one, how scary that terrible hole in his shoulder was—never seen anything like it! Worse, I never cared for anyone so badly hurt. Whatever had done it was still in him and I had to get it out, and get it out quick. But everything was on Culebra, all my healing salves, all my infusions and tinctures, all my tools—not to mention my book.

"Fear turned me into rigid coral. I couldn't act. My thoughts swam. I cried out to Mother Sea but blood pounded in my head. Breath stuck in my throat. Couldn't hear Her answer. Then I remembered what my teacher had told me: listen to the sound of the waves and breathe with them. I closed my eyes until I had their rhythm, until I *became* their rhythm.

"I knew what to do when I opened my eyes. Couldn't swim over here and back in time, let alone bring everything. Had to bring him around, no matter how dazed he'd be, and then reach into his mind and direct it. Your father has a very strong mind—*very strong*. I knew it would take everything I had to save him. I reached into my pouch for the eggs, cracked them with my thumb and forefinger like so"—Ana demonstrated with a quick motion of her hand—"and sucked them all down.

"I entered his mind like a thief and pried my fingers into his wound. He groaned, a horrible sound like the rending of wood in fierce water, and his eyes fluttered. I kept poking until I found it.

"Couldn't tell what it was, just that it was very hard and warm—and sharp. It moved a little as I prodded but didn't come loose. It reached deep into his shoulder. I was so absorbed I forgot your father and kept jiggling it back and forth to dislodge it. While I was busy, he groaned again and then his pain stung me.

"'Do you seek to kill me, you who are chosen as healer?' he asked.

"'If I did, oh *dragos*, first and foremost among *mer*, I would've left you to die where I found you,' I answered.

"I ignored his rigid body and harsh breathing because I sensed he was going to slip away from me. I tightened my grip on his mind instead.

"*Come here*, I ordered using *mer* speech.

"He fought me. I kept my wits and drew upon the power of the water. He didn't fight long before I found myself looking through his eyes as well as my own. Pain rolled over me. I vomited and almost let go, but I expected this. Focused on breathing to shut off awareness of that part of his mind. In, out, in, out, in, out—until I felt nothing else.

"I threw a glamour around us and pushed against the power of the cay. Mother Sea pulled us down quicker than I expected, and saltwater slapped us hard. It stung your father's wound. I struggled to master both of us. Then, slowly, we moved around Luís Peña and on to Playa Tamarindo. It was excruciating, but I kept breathing and continued to draw strength from Mother Sea.

"We reached Playa Tamarindo finally. I was nearly beyond my limit. Got your father behind some scrub before I had to let his mind go. Got enough energy back to throw a glamour on him while I was gone. I reached home, clumsy and slow, dizzy and sick to my stomach, but I managed to find my book. Then I filled my pouch with a small knife, a candle and matches, some seaweed and a needle, and tamarind paste.

"I stumbled back. He was still unconscious and so pale he might have been bleached coral. The blood on his shoulder had congealed into a sticky black mass. I sank down on my knees and dumped my pouch out onto the rocks next to him. My fingers trembled as I lit the candle. Then I held the knife blade in the flame until it glowed. I let it cool a little before I started probing the wound with its tip. Your father didn't stir or make a sound. Scared me more than anything else. I decided to slice the wound a little deeper and probe some more. This time the object moved! Got the blade's point under it and managed to pry it up. It was the broken tip of a harpoon.

"Know what a harpoon looks like?" She didn't give the stunned mermaid a chance to respond. "I didn't spend too much time looking at it. I dropped it and heated the end of my needle. Then I threaded some seaweed into it and sewed the wound closed. It bled again, making my fingers sticky and the work hard, but I pressed the heel of my hand against your father's shoulder until he stopped bleeding. I washed the wound, spread some of the tamarind paste over the stitches, and wrapped some clean rags over it.

"After that, I collapsed. We must've lain there for most of a day and no human found us, thank the Creator. When I woke, I saw your father was also awake. He was in great pain, but he didn't have a fever. That's when he told me what happened to your mother."

Here Ana reached out and took Tamarind's hand. Its clammy skin was firm and smooth against her veined and wrinkled one. She ignored the spark of sympathy it engendered and her voice grew gruffer. Time for the climax of her story.

"Your mother was swimming alone near the cay the humans call Cayo Lobo, away from Culebra and towards the Hidden Caves. She saw a boat there, and not having any shred of sense, swam up to it. Your father had asked your eldest sister to keep watch over her, so as soon as your sister saw what your mother was doing, she called for him. He wasn't close by because he thought the outer cays safe enough. Didn't know anything about drug runners."

"Drug runners?"

"Men who sneak around with pills and powders and herbs outlawed by some humans because they're so powerful and dangerous, for the mind and the body. Drug runners are nothing more than bottom feeders—violent and mad. They saw your mother and dragged her out of the water, probably thinking she was spying on them. When they saw her tail, they dropped her back into the water and started throwing things off the boat at her but she didn't leave. Your father got there just as one of the drug runners picked up a harpoon. He grabbed your mother and dove underwater, swimming as fast as he could with her to Luís Peña. When he came up, he realized two things: the harpoon had caught him as he dove and your mother was dead. She had a large black hole in her cheek, but he didn't know how or when it got there."

Tamarind pulled her hand from Ana's grasp, leaned over her legs and dropped her face into the tent of her hands. She didn't move or say anything as Ana finished her story.

"Your father hid on Playa Tamarindo until he got strong enough to swim back to a hidden cove on the far side of Luís Peña where your mother's body lay. He took her to an underwater cave far east of Culebra and entombed her on a ledge under piles of sea rocks and bits of coral. I hadn't wanted him to swim so far so soon, but I didn't bother saying anything to him. He came to see me only once afterwards so I could check the scar on his shoulder. I gave him an infusion to help him heal faster and get his strength back.

"I haven't seen or spoken to him since."

≈≈≈

At the bottom of the service road to Tamarindo Estates, John slowed the Samurai and stopped, his foot resting on the brake while he looked up the hill through the dusty windshield. Finding Tamarind in the tangle of thorn acacia, stunted tamarind trees, and cactuses posed no real difficulty, but still he hesitated. For the first time since he'd found an apartment in San Juan and traveled back to Culebra for long weekends, Tamarind had not waited for him at the ferry dock when he arrived. He drove on to Posada La Diosa where Valerie sat in her kitchen sipping lemonade and crafting wire jewelry for sale at The Mermaid's Purse. Since he'd left for San Juan, Tamarind sometimes hung out talking with Valerie and learned how to shape and twist wire into jewelry from her. She'd created some unique pieces after only a few lessons that Valerie sold for her in San Juan and as far away as New York, and Valerie helped her spend the money on clothes and hair accessories. Valerie had only the neighborhood stray cat with her today, however.

"Seen Tamarind?"

"Nope. Come to think of it, I haven't seen her all week."

"Huh." John set his backpack and travel bag down on the floor next to the table. "It's not like her to miss the ferry."

"Maybe she's tired of waiting for you, John." Valerie clipped the end off of a piece of wire and looked up at him.

John refused to meet her eyes. Instead, he walked to the cabinet where Valerie kept drinking glasses and took one out. He poured some lemonade and sat down.

"That's pretty cool." He pointed to the piece she worked on. "What is it? A pregnant woman?"

Valerie slipped a long strand of her graying-blond hair behind a delicate ear and picked up her lemonade, which she sipped. "Well, yes, she is. But not just any pregnant woman, John. She's the Goddess, the Divine Mother, that many cultures worshipped before the Judeo-Christian patriarchy tried to eradicate Her. She's always shown with a large belly and breasts because She symbolizes fertility, of the mind and spirit as well as the body."

"Does something like that sell well?"

"Oh, I can't make Her fast enough for the two shops I supply in New York. Chuck's always telling me I have to return and open my own shop, but I told him he doesn't get it. I need to be here on Culebra to channel the Goddess. In New York, I only channel lots of cappuccinos while running from meeting to stressful meeting."

"You don't ever look like you get stressed."

"Oh, don't let my serene appearance fool you. I spent a dozen years as an aggressive media buyer in New York. I *lived* on stress until I realized it was making me sick."

"Is Chuck still moving here in September?"

Valerie sighed and shrugged. "Apparently, he hasn't quite topped off his retirement funds as he'd like. I keep telling him that he won't want much once he gets here, but he's not ready to give up the game yet. Whatever. I'm not going anywhere."

She set her lemonade down and returned to the Goddess figure. "I did see Ana, the old woman who sells herbal remedies in town, a couple of days ago. I showed her one of the pieces of jewelry that Tamarind made and she knew somehow that I hadn't made it. She got very excited and practically gave me some of her most expensive remedies to buy it. When I asked her if she knew Tamarind, she told me that Tamarind is her apprentice and has been staying with her all summer."

"Funny, Tamarind never mentioned her. I thought all this time she lived at home with her father and sisters. Does this Ana live out near Tamarindo Estates?"

"Yeah, not far west of 251. You can't really miss it. It's a one-room cinderblock house with a dirt front porch and a chicken coop out back. The wild horses and laughing gulls really love her and she brews this wicked ale from a mash made from tamarind pods."

"Wait a second. Do you mean that scary-looking old woman who sits on the plaza selling herbal remedies?" John frowned. He'd gotten the distinct impression that Tamarind avoided Ana. He knew that *he* did. "Tamarind's staying with her and learning her arts?"

Valerie nodded. "That's what Ana said anyway. Why don't you go out there and talk to Tamarind yourself? You look about as forlorn as a puppy sitting in the rain while his owner doesn't see him from the kitchen window."

"Whatever that means." John stood up and rubbed the stray cat's head where it lay on the table among Valerie's jewelry-making supplies. "Don't worry about me for dinner. I'll grab something to eat at Isla Encantada."

Ten minutes later, he waited at the bottom of the hill leading to Ana's house in the growing heat of afternoon. Tamarind didn't magically appear to save him the trip so he slipped the gearshift into drive and eased the gas pedal down. At the top of the hill, he parked the Samurai and walked the rest of the way on foot toward the cinderblock house to which he'd followed Tamarind nightly in June. A few brown hens meandered through the dirt patch beaten in front of the low-gray building, but no one sat in the rusty aluminum chairs outside the front door.

He knocked on the door, but when no one answered, he walked around to the back where the chicken coop and what looked like an apartment building for birds stood. To his surprise, several laughing gulls poked their heads out of the holes in the stacked wooded compartments and eyed him curiously. A rooster strutted around the side of the low cinderblock wall and crowed when he saw John. John jumped a bit and relaxed. The spicy warmth of clove insinuated itself in his nostrils as he stood there facing the vigilant rooster.

"She's not here," rasped a woman behind him.

John turned to face Ana. He hadn't been this close to her since March. Her white hair wove a fine mesh around her miniature features. The drooping lid of one eye lent her a sinister air. She stood with her arms crossed loosely over her chest, a hand-rolled cigarette smoking in one upraised hand.

"How do you know who I'm looking for?"

"Don't sound so belligerent, *gringo*. Would you believe I can tell the future?" She laughed at his response. "Okay. Scratch that. I saw you and Tamarind in town more than once. And she told me you might come looking for her."

"She did? Where is she?"

Ana narrowed her eye and took a drag on the clove cigarette. "I'm not sure she wants to see you." The words issued forth in an effluence of hot smoke.

"Why not? Why can't she tell me herself?"

Ana dropped her cigarette arm and walked a few feet away from him. Several laughing gulls fluttered out of their nests and hovered around her head. Reaching into her apron, she tossed bits of something into the air around her. The birds lunged and snapped for them. One bird, bigger and faster than the others, managed to shoulder aside another gull and snatch its catch away from it. This bird landed on Ana's shoulder, looked directly at John and laughed, and then began to preen itself.

"This is a small island, *mi amigo*. Some have seen you here and there. Sometimes you are with Tamarind, sometimes you are with another woman. Perhaps you understand how people in such a small place as this love to gossip."

"Where is she?" He gritted his teeth as he spoke.

"Carlos Rosario, not far from the nesting grounds on the peninsula, gathering seaweed and bird dung." Just as John started to turn and go she called out to him. "From what Tamarind told me about your fight with your girlfriend, it sounds like you have quite a way with women, *gringo*." Her laugh rang in his ears.

He said nothing but returned to his Samurai and drove to the parking lot next to Playa Flamenco. He hadn't visited this beach since his first weeks in Culebra, but it took him only moments to find the head of the trail leading to the beach locals called Impact Beach. He walked the narrow dirt trail among dusty, drooping plants while overhead terns and brown boobies patrolled the skies where Navy bombers once descended upon decoy targets. The effulgent sun scorched his vision and parched him until his forehead ached and his crown burned. At last the trail ended at Carlos Rosario.

The beach appeared deserted. Then John recognized Tamarind's shape on the far side where she kneeled among the tall grasses. He halted on the beach and watched her as she searched, tendrils of her unmistakable hair floating on invisible air currents around her head. When she looked up and saw him, he smiled and waved. She didn't wave back.

John trotted over to where she waited, her face never leaving his and her arms still.

"Hey." He stood close enough to see the blue of her eyes.

"Hello."

"You weren't at the dock today."

"No." She turned back to combing through the grasses near her.

"I brought you a book. *Grimm's Fairy Tales*. I enjoyed it when I learned to read to myself." He held the book out, but she didn't turn back to him. After a moment, he slid it back into his backpack.

"Is something wrong, Tamarind?" His voice caught on her name. "That old woman you're living with—Ana—she said you didn't want to see me. Can I ask why?"

Tamarind sighed and sat up. She pulled out a small bottle of something and poured it into her left palm before rubbing her hands together. After a moment she lifted a bottle of what looked like water from the ground near her left knee and poured it over her hands. When she finished, she wiped them dry on her shorts and then she pushed her hair out of her eyes, only to have the wind send it fluttering into them again.

"It's been a long week, John. I have a lot of things to do and you shouldn't expect to see me at the dock any more when you come to Culebra." She stood up and pulled the burlap tote next to her feet up onto her shoulder.

John fell into step beside her as she walked across the beach toward the path. "No problem, I understand. So, dinner at Isla Encantada and then I'll read some of these fairy tales to you?"

Tamarind stopped and looked at him. "Actually, I have a date to go dancing with Jesus tonight." She started walking again. "Maybe we'll see you there later with Raimunda."

John said nothing until she reached the head of the trail. "Yeah, sure."

Tamarind waved over her shoulder without slowing down. "You can keep the book. I've got plenty to read right now. Thanks anyway." Her last words drifted back to him as she disappeared around a turn in the path.

Overhead, a seagull laughed as it bobbed and glided away toward the south.

Fourteen
cs

TAMARIND WAITED UNTIL ANA LEFT for Dewey with her bag full of remedies, love potions, charms, and the secret cache of poisons that she didn't know Tamarind had discovered. Although Ana had already spent the morning in town waiting for weekend vacationers from the ferry, she'd returned because a wealthy patron from San Juan had arrived unexpectedly with a special request. Tamarind had grown used to Ana's frequent absences to treat wealthy locals and so she bided her time until Ana had gone from sight. When the old woman disappeared over the hill on the path toward the road, Tamarind shut the door and headed toward the shore.

Not far from the water she stopped on the path and crouched down. Moving several rocks and chanting under her breath, Tamarind released the cloaking spell that she'd used to hide her clothes and hair ornaments. She hummed for the first time all week, clicking through several octaves in a complex melody familiar to every *mer*. She checked over her growing collection of items and then stood up, removed her shorts and dirty t-shirt, and walked into the water until it was over her head. She lay back on the buoyant saltwater and stared above her where terns and brown-footed boobies played games in the cerulean sky. Around her, the water mirrored their antics. If she closed her vestigial earflaps against the water and wove a glamour between herself and the edges of her vision, she could imagine that she drifted on air currents with the sea birds. When one landed on the surface of the water not far from her, she shifted her head and studied it.

After a long time, Tamarind released the glamour. The horizon and the uneven outline of Culebra's plant life disturbed her soak so she rolled onto her stomach and kicked toward the shore. Walking from the water on her own legs almost made up for the struggle to move against the inherent power of the lagoon.

She noticed that the lapping waves had deposited several shells and strands of seaweed near where she emerged. She stopped to look at them. Their resting places suggested that they'd been placed there by design, but she had no idea what they meant. In a moment a wave fingered the closest shell, lifting it a bit and sliding it into the design further. All at once, Tamarind understood that Mother Sea sought to tell her something. Sinking down, she cracked her knees on the slippery stones, plunged her hands into the water, and closed her eyes.

Mother, I don't understand. What are you trying to tell me?

Her thoughts flowed from her fingertips into the current and for a moment she felt tension fill her and something powerful surged around her mind, but the meaning was lost.

A residue of fear and warning remained as the power drained out of her.

Tamarind slapped the stones with both palms and stood up, water dripping from her hair and shoulders. She closed her eyes again and let out an audible breath. After a moment she hummed softly and gestured. Her fingers pulled continuous warm air strands over her body and hair. When her hair and skin had dried she uttered a single word and sliced the air in front of her with her right hand. The air calmed.

She returned to the hoard of clothes and searched around until she found the patterned halter dress that Valerie had helped her find on her first shopping expedition to San Juan two weeks ago. Even as she picked it up from the bundle and slipped it over her head, the memory of that trip played itself before her mind's eye. Gray asphalt ribbons hosted multitudes of cars like speeding schools of amberjack while concrete and glass buildings hemmed them all around. Her chest tightened at the images and she remembered John's words about having difficulty breathing sometimes.

After she tied the halter around her neck, she stepped into a pair of panties. She'd lingered in the lingerie store where the feel of silk on her fingertips engrossed her so long that Valerie laughed at her and strode around the store to pluck pairs from tables without a second glance. If she hadn't spent so long gazing at the tern earlier, she might have scattered the panties around her on the warm stones and tried them on one by one. Should she live to be half the age of a *mer* elder, she would never grow accustomed to the feel of silk rubbing against her crotch as she walked, the way the elastic encircled her upper thighs and the material hugged her buttocks. As she repacked her clothes, she shoved the red wisp of material that Valerie called a thong deep into the bottom of the bag. The power suggested in that triangle made her heart beat faster.

She extracted the smaller bag that Valerie had given her along with a variety of barrettes, hair bands, and hair clips. None of the manmade items worked half as well as her shell ornaments, but the sticky, thick liquids and foams that Valerie showed her how to use tamed her hair so well that the fragile things sufficed. Even so, the colors and patterns of the plastic pieces rivaled the beauty of her former underwater home and the crystals had no equal in her experience, except for the reflection of stars on the night sea.

At last she found the large flat barrette crusted with sparkling cabochons. She laid it alongside her thigh while she squirted a mound of fragrant foam into her palm. She distributed the foam between her hands and then worked it through her hair. She plucked through her curls with the long tines of a comb and then gathered a handful from either side and clasped the barrette around it. The mirror in her small bag reflected the tiny stones in her hair when she glanced at the stranger that she'd become within in its hard edges.

Done transforming herself, Tamarind stowed all of her human possessions back beneath the stones and reset the protective glamour. No prying eyes could discern where she'd hidden them. She glanced at the late afternoon sky and stuck her tongue out to taste the relative humidity of the air because her skin always felt dry since she'd put off her tail. Slowly she headed back to Ana's where she waited to walk the twenty minutes to Isla Encantada. Once the sun kissed the horizon, she set off barefoot toward the access road.

Jesus sat outside the restaurant on the curb talking to some of his friends. When he happened to look up and see her fifty feet away, a grin split his dark face and he leaped up. His deep brown eyes gleamed.

195

"Look at you, *mi chica linda*! We're going to make everyone else look like clumsy beasts tonight." He took her hands in his and held her arms up so that he could look at her. "Ah, I have dreamed of this all summer."

Still holding her left hand, he turned to face his friends. "I told you. I am the luckiest man on Culebra. Come, *cariño*, let's go get something to drink."

They went in and found a table not far from the bar. As she sat down, Tamarind felt a prickling along her flanks and the sides of her neck where *mer* sensory pores still pocked her skin. She looked around and saw John sitting in a far corner, staring at her. Their gazes met, and for the few seconds that they held, Tamarind felt shock rise up her spine and electricity pulse in her brain. Then, as in her brief contact with Mother Sea, the charge flowed away. This time, her arms and legs trembled.

She turned back to Jesus and slapped the table with an open palm. "Where's my drink?"

He startled, then grinned. "Only tell me what you'd like to drink and it's yours, *mi corazón*."

"Beer. I'd like to have a beer."

ঞ ঞ ঞ

John ordered another Tom Collins even before finishing his first. In the dark of Isla Encantada he could see only indistinct shapes where Tamarind and Jesus sat, but he'd recognize her profile under a burqa. Tamarind sat sideways to him so that he glimpsed little flashes from the barrette she wore as it caught what ambient light existed. When she leaned over to speak to Jesus, he saw in the candlelight that her tame curls cascaded across her shoulders and framed her face. As she laughed, candlelight caressed a reflective pendant at her collarbone. She laughed a lot—especially after drinking from the dark bottle Jesus brought her from the bar. After their earlier eye contact, she never came over to say hi or even turned in his direction. The snub hurt more than he could have imagined.

John scowled and sipped from his Tom Collins. He glanced at the door, but Raimunda didn't saunter through it wearing a clinging white shirt and ruffled skirt. Several Culebrenses came in and settled down at neighboring tables while the band fiddled with keyboard and drums before their set. The smell of fried food reached his nose as a waitress emerged from the kitchen with a plate of yellowtail snapper and plantains. He'd skipped dinner and should have been hungry, but his stomach only tumbled.

He switched to drinking *coquitos* on his third drink and the coconut and rum congealed in his knotted gut. Then the band began playing and the din tunneled into his brain unopposed. He leaned his face into his raised hands and massaged his temples with his thumbs. When he looked up, he saw Tamarind and Jesus dancing. She had eyes only for Jesus, who led her in the peculiar rolling gait of the salsa; his arm wrapped around her waist and his stomach pressed against hers. The small triangle of chest above her dress shone and the dim light glittered off the pendant and the stones in her barrette as they danced. Her delicate feet, as bare as always, lifted and settled on the tiled floor.

"*Hola*, *gringo*," said Raimunda at his side. "She's a tasty bit, that one is, isn't she?" She leaned over and kissed him, long and hard. "But I'm a full meal, *mi amigo*."

John said nothing as she sat down on his left side and held up her hand to signal the waitress. While she waited for her beer, Raimunda leaned closer to him, her hand on his inner thigh. She nuzzled his neck and nibbled his ear. John lifted his *coquito* and drained it.

"Let's dance," he said and stood up, his chair scraping loudly.

He pulled Raimunda to her feet. She grabbed her Medalla, tilted it at her mouth, and gulped half of it down as he strode to the dance floor ahead of her. When John pulled her into his arms, she laughed and clutched the half-full bottle between them. As they danced, John closed his eyes and focused on the music. Raimunda sinuated about him, her full breasts brushing now against his upper arm, now against his chest.

John abruptly lurched from the dance floor and out through the entrance. Bending over, he braced his hands against his thighs and breathed in.

"Too much to drink?" Raimunda leaned against the doorway, her arms crossed.

John breathed in and out several times before standing up. "No, I'm fine. Let's go back in."

They walked back into the stuffy restaurant, Raimunda's arm entwined in his and her hip rubbing his thigh. John's gaze traveled to the dance floor where Tamarind and Jesus still rocked and swayed to the loud Latin music.

"I'm going to the toilet."

"No problem, *mi amigo*. I'll just wait at the table and order another Medalla, on you." She smiled and dipped her eyelashes.

John went to the men's room and gripped the white porcelain rim of the pedestal sink. In the harsh fluorescence, he stared at his reflection in the mirror. He looked like a madman: strands of hair had escaped his ponytail holder, darkly misting the outlines of his pale face; his wide eyes suggested that he'd just witnessed his mother being raped and his father shot. Closing his eyes for a moment, he leaned his head back and expelled his breath. Then he turned on the cold water and splashed handfuls over his face. When his eyes had relaxed and his breathing had evened out, he turned off the water, dried his hands, and made his way to the bar. Raimunda sat looking toward the dance floor, a bottle cradled in her hands.

"You know that guy over there?" John gestured with his chin toward the dance floor.

Tomás, who'd been talking to the bartender, looked up and out at Jesus. "*Sí*, Señor Juan." He shrugged. "He's well known around Culebra, especially by the women."

"What's that supposed to mean?"

"He's, how you say it? A ladies' man? Most of the ladies like him."

"Most? What's that mean?"

"Some say he isn't always sensitive about whether a *mujer* wants to be with him or not."

"Are you talking about date rape?"

Tomás shrugged again. "Who am I to say? Me, I think women always find something to complain about. If it's not the way they look, it's how much money we spend on them."

"I believe in the old adage 'where there's smoke there's fire.'" John stared at the couple. "Some women just don't know they're going to get burnt."

He looked at Tomás until the older Culebrense looked away. Then Tomás nodded and turned back to the bartender. John left the bar and headed toward Tamarind and Jesus. When he reached them, Jesus saw him first and swung Tamarind out and away before embracing her. Jesus smiled at John over Tamarind's head.

"Look, *mi dulcinea*, it's John. Hey, *amigo*, what's up?" His grin didn't reach his eyes, as flat and malevolent as ever. "This time, I get the bird of paradise, no?"

"No." John turned toward Tamarind. "Tamarind, dance with me."

Jesus spoke for her. "She's with me. *Comprende*?"

Tamarind, her smooth curls already frizzing from heat and sweat, lifted her chin and looked at Jesus. "Don't worry, Jesus. It's just a dance. I'll be right back."

Jesus slipped his arm around her waist, tight. "Just one dance, *cariño*. I am—how you say *un amante celoso*? A jealous lover." He turned to John. "Take good care of her, *amigo*, or you'll answer to me."

Jesus nuzzled Tamarind's neck before kissing it, his eyes on John. She tolerated the kiss but looked embarrassed. Jesus sauntered back to their table and grabbed his beer. When he turned to watch John and Tamarind dancing, he crossed one arm over his stomach while the other kept the bottle within easy reach of his mouth. John didn't look at Raimunda.

He placed one hand around Tamarind's waist and took her hand with the other. He glanced over at Jesus and smiled as if he meant it. As they danced, he spoke through his teeth; he found it difficult to take his eyes off of the small Culebrense waiting for Tamarind at the edge of the dance floor. "Tamarind, you need to be careful with Jesus."

"Why?" Heat from her seeped through his t-shirt and the front of his pants. She smelled salty and like something else—like a mix of seaweed, sand, and sunshine. She smelled like freedom.

"Because he's got a reputation for liking women. A lot of women."

"So? You seem to like a lot of women yourself."

A different heat scalded his neck and seeped out his palms. "That may be true, but I never force myself on anyone."

"Force yourself on anyone?" Tamarind screwed up her brows. "I don't know what you're talking about, John. I really must get back to Jesus. I think Raimunda—that's her, isn't it?—is waiting for you."

The song still played but Tamarind halted and disengaged herself from John's grip. Slipping out of his arms, she skipped over to where Jesus sat and held her hands out to him.

John didn't remain on the dance floor to see Tamarind and Jesus dancing again. Instead, he returned to his table and leaned over Raimunda. Her dark hair smelled faintly of cloves and musk. He'd tried, and it hurt like hell.

"What was that about a meal? I'm hungry."

She smiled and slid the neck of the bottle suggestively into her hollowed mouth before sipping. Then she licked the rim without taking her eyes from his face. "Let's go where we can discuss this in private."

John helped her to her feet and they walked out of Isla Encantada holding hands. He'd left the Samurai at Posada La Diosa so they walked south along 251 toward town. Here and there a few people sat on their patios in the dark, talking and listening to music. Sometimes the glow of cigarettes and the clink of glass joined the sounds of voices and Latin jazz energized the low-key gatherings, but the parties remained contained.

Valerie's light still glowed in her room, but darkness shrouded the rest of the guesthouse. A black shape darted in front of John's feet as he reached the front stoop and he nearly tripped over the stray cat that had adopted Valerie. It growled when he stepped on its tail and hissed as he stumbled away. Raimunda laughed, but the cat refused to come near her when she bent down and reached out a hand for it. John pulled out his key and turned to the side so that the moon illuminated the lock. While he fumbled to insert the key, Raimunda—still bent over—ran her hand along his calf.

They moved without speaking down the hall toward John's room. John left the light off and pulled Raimunda in after him, groaning before kissing her and shutting the door. They tore at shirts, John pushing aside the low neckline of Raimunda's peasant blouse and grasping her full breast. He pulled his face from hers, rolling her nipple between his thumb and forefinger and then descended upon the hardened flesh with a hot mouth.

Raimunda raked fingers through his hair and then tugged at her skirt. Together, they worked at the button at his waistband and struggled to lower his shorts to a safe enough distance for him to climb out of them. Then they stumbled nearer to his bed before launching themselves at it. Now John clawed, kneaded, pinched, and sucked at every inch of flesh beneath him while Raimunda's long hair cloaked him in clove and something spicy sweet. Grasping a handful, he wound it around his hand and pulled her face closer to his.

"Tamarind."

"I'll be whoever you want me to be, *amigo*. Just fuck me."

John's chest seized and his breath stopped. The airless room encapsulated him and he couldn't move, couldn't think—couldn't see in the suffocating black. Collapsing, he trapped Raimunda under him. She responded by squirming and kicking until she'd managed to roll him off of her and onto the bed.

"What the hell is wrong with you, *gringo*? You're as hard as obsidian one moment and limp as seaweed the next—and you nearly crush me!" She sat up and pushed him away from her.

John opened his mouth, but nothing came in or out. Pricks of light danced in front of his vision. His blood roared in his ears. He felt Raimunda get off the bed and sensed rather than heard her search on the floor for her blouse and skirt. He tried to remember the sound of Tamarind's humming, to feel her arms around him again as she promised to take care of him, but he couldn't snag the memory and he felt the darkness winning. As he lost consciousness, he heard the door to his room click shut.

જ જ જ

Ana scurried into the plaza near the ferry dock, her bag slung over her shoulder. She didn't have much time. She laid the bag on a concrete table and pulled out the wire-wrapped Goddess that she'd bartered from Valerie, the hair that she'd taken from Tamarind's sleeping mat, and the potion that she'd brewed using both items. Next came a copy of the destroyed blue batik dress, the one that John had bought for Tamarind weeks ago and that she'd worn the night they'd gone dancing. Muttering and turning, she waved her right hand in the air until the cloaking glamour reflected the night plaza seamlessly around her. Should anyone wander into the plaza, he'd see only empty tables next to the dock.

Stepping out of her skirt and blouse, Ana lifted the batik dress over her head and let it drop down over her shoulders. She squinted down at her discarded clothes and frowned. Muttering again, she wove both of her hands in the air above them. Now a small pile of paper cups and wrappers littered the pavement.

She lifted the bottle from the table and hefted it in her palm. So small, yet so crucial. She slid her thumbnail into and around the wax seal and then pushed the stopper out. A minute pop issued and she felt infinitesimal droplets as pockets of gas burst against the skin on the back of her hand.

She waited until the bottle grew warm in her palm and then she tipped it up and let it slide down her throat in one breathless gulp. She coughed and wiped her lips with the back of her hand. Her book said that the potion needed time to spread throughout her body, trailing change with it, but she had been a midwife a long time and had developed her own techniques, ones that improved upon the original.

She grasped the wire Goddess and rubbed the beads that Tamarind had so carefully bound there. Tamarind had also bound some of her own essence as well and Ana sought it now. Closing her eyes and whispering a chant, she drew upon the charm to speed her transformation. After only a few breaths, she opened her eyes again. It was done.

Fifteen

CB

JOHN CAME TO WITH A SENSE OF URGENCY. The room around him vibrated with the aftereffects of sound and he waited, certain an alarm or clap of thunder would rend the air. He heard nothing but the harsh rasp of his own breathing in the stifling dark. Sitting up, heart pounding, he tried to think. He glanced at the clock and saw that Isla Encantada had closed an hour ago. He groaned and twisted on the bed until his feet touched the floor and the clothes he'd left there. Without searching for the light first, he found his t-shirt and shorts and put them on. His sandals still lay just inside the door where he'd kicked them earlier and he slid them on, fumbling with the straps.

The stray cat passed him in the hallway, this time rubbing against his calves and purring. John ignored her and walked quietly past Valerie's door. Once outside, he glanced toward her window and saw that it was dark. He hurried down the sidewalk. Everyone had long since gone to sleep in town; no streetlights lit his way. Only the sound of water lapping at the canal and the squeak of his sandals on pavement broke the utter silence.

He didn't know where he planned to go, but he walked north on 250. At this hour in Isla Verde in San Juan, people wandered streets laughing and chatting while cars cruised along the *avenida*. Casinos and restaurants catered to restless tourists and young lovers, but here on Culebra, only wind and water spirits kept him company. After a few minutes, he heard voices and he picked up his pace. A young couple—he sat on the stoop and she stood between his bent knees with his hands on her hips—talked in the shadows of a doorway. John recognized the young man's tennis shoes and his date's ponytail. They were college students from the U.S. who'd bought a *Let's Go! Puerto Rico* and had arrived on Culebra a week ago. Hearing his footsteps, they stopped talking and glanced in his direction. John waved. They waved back and he kept on walking.

As he'd already known it would, Isla Encantada stood dark and empty when he came up to its entrance. He sat down on the curb outside the restaurant and propped his head in his hands. Darkness enveloped him like an old friend, its soothing arm laid across his shoulders. He smelled the dust from the sun-baked pavement around him, stale beer and cigarettes, old cooking oil, salt air and something else—a thin tang of green life holding out against the strength of the ocean on one side and the indifferent crush of humanity on the other.

Looking up, he studied the sky. It loomed impassively above, innumerable tiny twinkles mocking him. Culebra was a tiny island and he was just a speck on it. He sat still, staring at this yawning chasm, waiting for it to swallow him and blot out everything. Eventually the mosquitoes hummed so loudly in his ears that they compelled him to his feet in search of a better place to loiter. He shuffled onto 250 where not even the shadows had voices any more, his gaze polishing the rough pavement just a couple of feet in front of his sandals. He'd reached the fork in the road where 250 split into one-way streets, but just as he thought to stay on the left and continue toward Posada La Diosa, he spied something gleaming on the sidewalk at the fork. Bending down, he saw that it was one of Valerie's wire-wrapped Goddesses. He picked it up, tossing it lightly in his palm and then absentmindedly rubbing the largest stone in its globular belly with his thumb.

An urge struck him to take the other fork before heading west and then north again toward Playa Melones. He hadn't been to Playa Melones since April when Raimunda had led him there for the first time. The soft squeak of his sandals' rubber soles sounded eerily loud in the still street where obsidian storefronts glimmered darkly at his passage. He needed to reach Playa Melones and the waves that whispered along its slight expanse.

Ten minutes later, John left the low buildings of Dewey behind and his sandals crunched on the thin gravel lining the path to the beach. He'd walked so quickly from town after finding the Goddess that a flush warmed him. He scowled at his pace but didn't slow down until he'd reached the water's edge. He gripped the wire figure in his hand so hard that it bit into his flesh. He scarcely noticed this, however, until it began to burn as if it contained a heating element. Yelping, John dropped the Goddess.

"What the fuck!" He sucked on his palm.

That's when he heard a low sound, a moan of pain, from a mound of vegetation not far north from where he stood. Forgetting his own pain for the moment, he went to investigate. There was a break in the shrubbery and he crept up near it, not willing to barge in without seeing who and what lay before him. As he knelt down, he shot a glance around the deserted beach, suddenly aware of his isolation. He saw no one else.

Shivering, John held his burnt palm off of the stony ground and leaned closer to the opening in the thick vegetation. When he caught sight of the forms writhing on the ground in front of him, John stifled a laugh. He started to rise cautiously from his knees until the sound of his rising caught the attention of the woman lying sprawled beneath the frantic man. In the sharp-edged moonlight, there was no mistaking Tamarind. Their eyes met and she smiled, a wide smile that reflected the light.

For a moment, John's throat constricted so painfully that he thought that he might be suffering an anaphylactic reaction. Swallowing hard, he nodded slightly at her and stood up without any more effort to quiet his movements. He took a step or two backwards and then swiveled on his left heel. Even though he could no longer see her face, John felt the strength of Tamarind's gaze on his back as he lurched back across the sand and the path leading to town. As he passed by the spot where the wire Goddess lay after searing him, the stone in its belly glowed as if mocking him.

John squeezed his lips together and pushed his shoulders back. He walked faster and faster until he was running and panting and he didn't stop until he'd reached Posada La Diosa. Even then, even as he struggled with the finicky lock on the front door and tiptoed down the main hall towards his room, his body quivered with the need for running. As he lay back onto his empty bed, his chest heaved. He gave himself over to the feeling of running, running as if he flew, running as if his legs would never tire. He fell asleep running on an infinite route through the clouds.

The next morning, the sun woke John early. His upper back ached, his forehead ached, and fine sandpaper lined his throat. Blinking and squinting against the glare that accosted him through the wide-planked shades, he groaned and eased himself onto his side. After several more moments pinned to the mattress by an implacable bar of sunlight, he groaned again and swung his legs over the side. Dead weights that they were, his legs dropped to the floor, but his upper body refused to comply with their pull and remained leaning against the mattress. His whole body felt like a punching bag the day after the heavyweight champion pummeled it, and for a long time the strain on his waist from the awkward twisting of his upper and lower halves failed to compare.

At last his bladder chimed in with its burning fullness and he had to ignore the stabbing pain through his left eye and the wave of nausea that rose up as he leveraged his upper body away from the bed with his hands. He managed to piss into the toilet before the nausea overwhelmed him and then he collapsed onto his knees, clutching at the cool porcelain bowl as he threw up hot fermented *coquitos* into it. The sour tang of bile and partially digested coconut milk clashed with the acid of his urine, causing him to heave until the spasms echoed in his abdomen reflexively.

He gripped the edge of the bowl for a moment before pushing the handle down and standing up on trembling legs. His reflection grimaced at him as he gulped a mouthful of water and swished it around his nasty mouth. Although it helped, he couldn't rid himself of the taste until he'd brushed his teeth and tongue.

Still weak, he managed to return to his room and find a pair of shorts and t-shirt on the floor of the closet that didn't look too rumpled and smelled faintly of salt water. He pulled these on, buckled his sandals onto his feet and slid his sunglasses over his fragile eyes. Then he set out for the only *mercado* open at this hour, Mayte's. He needed Tylenol and whatever liquid that his queasy stomach would tolerate. Later, when he returned to Posada La Diosa, he would try drinking coffee, but he doubted that he'd eat much.

"Stefan would laugh at me, getting hung over on only three drinks."

Only the stray cat lying on the sun-warmed stoop heard him and she simply purred in response. Small yellow-and-black bananaquits squeaked nearby as they fluttered between several messy, globe-shaped nests and the bowls of sugar that Valerie left along the canal for them. John watched the bits of wild brightness dart for several moments, and then he sighed and headed into the morning sun toward Mayte's. When he got there a handful of Culebrenses shopped for necessities—eggs, bread, rice, beans—and a couple of them leaned against the counter, chatting with the dour owner, Luisa. They ignored John as he toured the aisles looking for Seven-Up and Tylenol. He'd just found the over-the-counter drugs when Sister Maria Margarita from La Virgen Del Mar entered the aisle from the other end.

"*Buenos días*, John." She stopped, holding a basket over her right forearm, and looked him up and down. "You don't look so good. Too much sun and sand or too much Medalla?"

"Neither." John grimaced. "Look, Sister, I won't be coming to Mass any more. I've decided it's time to return to Pittsburgh and get back to work on my research."

She nodded, pursing her lips. "There is a time for everything, as the wise man says. It is for you to judge when is your time to leave us, though I am sorry to see you go."

"Being here has done me a lot of good, Sister. I used to sit on one of the *playas* sometimes and just stare out at the endless blue without thinking anything at all, just listening to my own breathing. I can really breathe here."

"You can always breathe, John. You just need to remember how. God will remind you, you must trust in that."

She placed her free hand briefly on his forearm and squeezed. She smiled a little and walked on down the aisle. John watched her for a moment and then he returned to his immediate search for pain medication.

᪣᪣᪣

Tamarind waited outside Ana's house on the plot of bare earth that served as a porch, her feet curled under her on the aluminum chair. She watched the sooty terns take to the sky as the sun diluted it to pale saffron tinged with a deeper salmon along the horizon. In a stunted tamarind tree not far from where she sat, a laughing gull perched on a lower branch, its head half-tucked under a wing and a single bright eye watching her. She wondered if it was Ana's favorite and whether Ana had set it to spy on her.

Ana still slept inside. She hadn't come home until nearly dawn. Tamarind had returned last night from Isla Encantada to find the cinderblock house dark and empty. At first, she'd been relieved that Ana wasn't there to catch her in her clothes and makeup, but she'd managed to hide them away and scrub her face with saltwater and still Ana hadn't returned. She sat for a while in the moonlit doorway studying the constellations that John had taught her. *Mer* folk also had names for the stars, but they'd grouped them differently and identified these groups with way stations undersea. There was the Great Coral Passage, the Deep Blue Hole, and the Cave of the Ancestors. Viewing them last night had brought saltwater to her eyes.

Humming, she studied her bare feet. Over the past few weeks, calluses had grown on the balls of her toes and her

211

heels. Even though she continued to find the ground rough and the pavement painfully hot, she still couldn't tolerate wearing shoes. John had often teased her about looking like an urchin and when she'd finally asked him how bare feet made her look like the prickly sea creature, he'd only laughed.

"No, not that kind of urchin, silly. I mean a child who lives on the street without anyone to care for her."

So that's how John saw her: an unloved orphan.

After another couple of hours, Tamarind decided to go inside to get something to eat. She brought out some plantain chips and a jar of peanut butter with a spoon. John had also laughed at her craving for salty snacks and asked her if she smoked pot. When she got upset after learning that pot was a name for an illegal plant that some people smoked, he quit teasing her.

She'd finished the bag of plantain chips when she heard a throat being cleared behind her and smelled a familiar scent of clove.

"You were out late last night." Tamarind didn't look around at Ana.

"Uh-huh." Ana sat down next to her. "It happens. How'd your date with Jesus go?"

Tamarind shrugged. "Fine. It was fine."

"That doesn't sound so positive."

"I don't know if I can do this, Ana. The best part of the evening was when John watched us dance together. After he left, I spent all my time keeping Jesus' hands away from me. He's like an octopus. It was exhausting."

Ana bit her thumb, her clove cigarette balanced between her first two fingers. Smoke caressed her forehead. "You only have to put up with him once, young one. Then you're free of all men."

Tamarind opened the jar of peanut butter but eschewed the spoon that she'd brought. Sticking her forefinger into the jar, she scooped out a large dollop and licked neatly at it.

"Raimunda reminded me of someone."

Ana dragged on her cigarette. "Oh, yeah?" Smoke streamed along with the words.

"Yeah, but I don't know who." Tamarind twisted the lid back on the jar and looked at Ana for a moment. "John looked like thunder when they left together. I don't think he's with her anymore."

"And you think maybe he'll come to his senses and be with you now?" Ana laughed. It was a choppy, rough sound. "I wouldn't bet my legs on it, young one. The sooner you forget him, the better off you'll be. Mark my words."

Tamarind shrugged again and stood up. "I'm going for a swim. My throat's as dry as a piece of driftwood this morning."

Ana watched Tamarind trudge up the path toward the beach. She wore only a white t-shirt and shorts. After being briefly tamed the night before, the long kinks of her copper hair reveled at the sun's familiar touch. Her legs, where they showed below the fabric of her shorts, had grown as gracefully muscular as a dancer's. She watched until Tamarind had disappeared from sight and then she smiled.

Tamarind continued on down toward the playa, but she had no intention of swimming beyond a quick sustaining dunk. After wetting herself completely, she shook out her hair and then dried most of the saltwater from her skin and hair. Already, she felt less parched and stiff. She pulled John's t-shirt back over her head and stepped into the shorts. She glanced toward the secret path to see if Ana had followed her, but the old woman had not. After a moment, she knelt down and arranged several rocks on the shore at the outlet of the

213

path, humming a bit while scooping handfuls of seawater over them. If Ana should happen to walk this way, she would forget why she'd come to the playa and have a strong urge to return to her house. It was the best Tamarind could do on Ana's own turf.

She got up then and hurried toward Tamarindo Estates and the road toward 251. By the time she reached Posada La Diosa, she felt dry and worn out even though it was only mid-morning. Her feet and calves ached from her haste.

Valerie sat outside on her patio next to the canal, drinking coffee and twisting wire jewelry. Behind her, a yellow and black bananaquit fluttered around the feeder that Valerie kept filled with sugar water. On the pavers at her feet, a black cat lay on its side licking its front paws in the sunshine. Tamarind watched the tiny bird for a moment and the ache in her legs disappeared. Then, drawing on the water in the canal to restore her further, she hummed a purr to the cat, which stopped licking and looked at her. It blinked once and purred back.

"That's a pretty amazing trick you have. You're a pretty amazing girl, aren't you?" When she looked at Tamarind that way, Tamarind thought Valerie knew her secret. "Want to help make some pieces today?"

"Yeah, sure."

Tamarind sat down and began gathering necessary bits and tools. Valerie had plenty of wire, but her store of polished stones had grown low and nothing appealed to Tamarind. She picked up some wire and began twisting a figure anyway. She could add a stone later.

"Do you know someone named Raimunda?"

Valerie snipped a bit of wire before answering. "No, can't say that I do. Why, should I?"

Tamarind bit her lower lip and twisted a tight spiral. "Well, I thought you might if John's been bringing her around here."

"Ah, that's what this is about." Valerie put her piece down and took a sip from her coffee. "Last night, he brought someone home but I heard her screaming at him not long after they got here. I don't think she stayed long."

She watched Tamarind deftly twist two arms and a head for her Goddess.

"There aren't any good stones here." She fingered the pile in front of her. "Of course, some might tell you to go ahead and put in any old stone you find and what you've got will be good enough. I say you have to wait for the right stone for your Goddess to be polished and set carefully into Her form. The love and care you take will be nothing short of pure magic. But I think you know that, don't you, Tamarind?"

She held up the Goddess that she'd been working on. In its belly was an inferior stone, dull and pockmarked.

"See? This one doesn't have any power with the wrong stone. Now take this stone here." She picked up a dull blue one. "This stone looks rather unimpressive in its current state. But I can tell by its shape and color that it's actually rather rare. It's a blue moonstone. Blue moonstone symbolizes the water signs in the zodiac. It's supposed to make wearers more receptive so they recognize the truth and to bring them dreams. It's also said to calm emotions so two lovers can see their future together without fear or pain."

She paused and looked steadily at Tamarind.

"You know, I think you should have this one, Tamarind. If you're patient and wait for it to be polished, you may find that this moonstone is exactly the right stone for your Goddess."

Valerie slipped the milky-blue stone into Tamarind's palm and closed her fingers around it. "Just take care of it, Tamarind. Something this rare won't come across your path again. I know it."

Tamarind looked into Valerie's eyes. Swallowing hard against a dry throat, she nodded and squeezed the blue moonstone even tighter. She would keep the promise of this stone against her heart as long as necessary.

Sixteen
ᘓ

JOHN FELT THE SOLID PRESENCE of the hills between the Pittsburgh airport and the Fort Pitt Tunnel as his friend Stefan's car climbed and plunged. Once through the tunnel, his gaze embraced downtown—"dahntahn" in the vernacular—and the point where the Allegheny and the Monongahela Rivers met to form the Ohio. As they passed over the Monongahela, he could see the dark bulk of Three Rivers Stadium across from the Point State Park. He'd missed so many of the Pirates' summer home games.

The drive from the airport to Stefan's place in Squirrel Hill took only half an hour; Stefan asked no questions and John volunteered nothing. They chatted about inconsequential things, the latest gossip in the CS department, the incoming first years, the big grant won for a robotics project. They headed to the Squirrel Cage where Stefan's favorite waitress, the one John used to tease him was his soul mate, brought them hand-formed hamburgers and black-and-tans. Pittsburgh residents and grad students filled the booths of the dark bar, their cigarettes and chatter comforting to John. He'd had no idea how fond that he'd grown of this former steel town or how much he'd missed its coffee houses and bagel shops. When they'd finished dinner, he urged Stefan to cross over Murray Avenue to the Eat'n Park for dessert.

Stefan's last roommate had graduated in May and he hadn't yet found a new one. John viewed the available bedroom, which was still furnished in low-budget melamine from the popular Swedish furniture store, and thanked Stefan for letting Zoë dump his clothes and books there. He'd get the rest of his stuff from storage later, after he'd had time to get back into the groove at school. Dropping his bags near the door, he went over to the window facing the street and opened it wide to the muggy August evening. He stood inhaling the mingled smells of exhaust and baked motor oil and listening to the sounds from Murray Avenue where people laughed and talked at outdoor tables or walked between restaurants and shops. Underneath it all the sound of cars washed like the waves on Culebra's beaches. He'd returned to the place he belonged, but he'd left his soul behind.

When he lay down on the bed's bare mattress, no dreams graced his sleep.

❧ ❧ ❧

As soon as John walked onto the Carnegie Mellon campus, he saw his advisor. Steve appeared surprised to see his errant graduate student—and exceptionally happy. His surprise at seeing John lasted about two minutes, long enough for John to cross the quad to the main entrance to Wean Hall.

"Hey, John! You have impeccable timing," he said when John got within five feet of him. "I've been working on a funding application for ARPA and it would really help our cause if you update your Web site with the digital stills and video from the mission."

As nearly all his colleagues did, Steve constantly sought sources of funding and the Defense Department's Advance Research Projects Agency proved to be one of the best.

"Yeah, no problem. What's the timeframe like?"

"Paul Stoddard is visiting next Monday so you don't have much time, John, but I think you could get something decent together by then. We don't have to show Paul much—he's got the capacity to make a leap or two, if we can just show him the outlines of what you've been working on. I had this idea just yesterday after I poked around your Pitt-Woods Hole site and I wanted to talk with you about it."

"Go ahead." John trailed Steve through the lobby of Wean. "Oh, hey, wait. I've got to get a cup of coffee here. It's been months since I've had a good cup of Joe."

Steve kept talking while John ordered. "You've got a lot of great images from the Puerto Rican Trench, John, but they don't give a big picture of the place. I mean, this trench is five miles below sea level and what you've got is a view from a few hundred feet above it."

"So what're you proposing? I'm not sure how my expertise in networked RAID and streaming video is very useful for presenting the image data."

Steve ordered a decaf latte from the cart. "Well, no, you don't have the expertise—yet. But I think you should go talk with Ken Abel in the computer-vision group. What I'm thinking is that your image data might be the source for a modeling program that puts it all together into bigger segments."

John sipped his coffee carefully; it burned his tongue nonetheless. "This sounds like a helluva lot of work. What happened to the work I was planning to do on my proposal?"

Steve gripped his own coffee and looked squarely at John. "Look, John, I'm not one to give anyone advice on how to live his life—what's done is done. But let's face it: you've been gone for nearly five months and now you've got to do a little extra to redeem yourself. Six months ago, I could've let you stick with your original plan. But now, I think you'd do well to labor on something a little more glamorous, if you know what I mean."

John adjusted his backpack higher onto his shoulder. He could feel his chest tightening, his esophagus narrowing. What Steve was suggesting—no, ordering—was that he write a less evolutionary research plan and jump into a riskier technical challenge, one that might not result in a feasible working solution in the end. He said nothing for a few moments, instead focusing on breathing. A faint humming echoed in his memory and his chest released. When he and Steve made it to the Networking and Storage Lab, he spoke.

"Okay, you're the boss. There's a faint chance that I could actually write a proposal before Black Friday."

"That's the ticket." Steve opened the lab door. "Nothing like a high-stakes deadline to get the old adrenaline pumping and the mental juices flowing. I'll ping you in a few days to see how it's going."

A week later, John, ensconced in his office in the bowels of Wean Hall, had begun tackling the new thesis proposal when his friend Puneet poked his head into the lab.

"So it's true—you *have* returned from paradise! They say all good things must come to an end and here you are slaving in the dungeon already."

John grinned. "You know Steve, Puneet. He can drive a slave with the best of 'em. Besides, there's a corollary to your saying: eventually, you have to pay the piper. And that's what I'm doing."

Puneet walked into the lab and stood next to John's chair where he could see John's monitor. "Yikes! Don't tell me you're working on a proposal."

"Okay, I won't tell you. But don't act surprised when Catherine posts the date for my proposal talk before the end of the semester."

"So soon? Man, you're setting a bad standard for the rest of us. How long have you been here, anyway?"

"This will be my fourth year."

"What's your rush? Don't you have another semester or two before you're really under pressure to propose?"

"Not after taking a five-month vacation—at least, that's how it's perceived around here."

"Oh." Puneet drew out the sound as if it were a three-syllable word. "Look, I know you're busy, but maybe you could come up out of your underground dwelling and go to lunch with me. It's a glorious day outside and you don't see too many of those in Pittsburgh."

"No, you don't. Where should we go?"

"Mad Mex."

They walked into Oakland and spent most of lunch talking at length about what it was like to run away from research for a while.

"I don't know what happened to me, Puneet. There was something about Culebra—I don't know what exactly. I just found myself sitting for long hours staring at the surreal blue ocean. I even wondered if I could open up a microbrewery there and turn the local soda, el Tamarindo, into a wicked Snake Island Ale. Still sounds like a good idea, actually."

Puneet grinned. "No doubt, John, no doubt. That idea is definitely enticing." He toyed with his fork, tilting it this way and that so that it threw light shards onto the ceiling. "Especially when code won't flow. Or you despair that you've chosen a topic that's just another math problem, one only pointy-eared geeks care about."

"You're not afraid of that, are you?" John let his voice register his incredulity. For all his surface levity, Puneet was one of the most focused, most disciplined, graduate students he knew. "Don't be. What you're working on will protect our country's most important secrets."

"Me? I'm just building a more elegant lock for network security. That's enough to make me want to take up auto mechanics sometimes." Puneet laid the fork next to his plate and looked at John. His dark eyes, usually dancing with humor, were direct and sober. "John, you don't have to run away to an island in shame and frustration. You're going to help advance what science understands about the oceans. That's monumental, if you ask me." He paused. "So, tell me, what are you planning to propose?"

Puneet listened as John described the raw data he'd collected in the Puerto Rico Trench and his original plans to write special algorithms for storing and retrieving it over a high-speed network. When he heard Steve's revised standard for what constituted proposal-level work his eyes widened, but he said nothing until John had outlined the problem and described how he'd solve it.

"That's good, John. You sound like you're jumping in with both feet. But I think you've got a bigger technical problem than how to build a system that enables both quick-and-dirty analysis on-board ship and more detailed analysis after the survey is over. Those are really two sides of the same issue. No, the problem is more fundamental than that. I'm not a geologist and I don't know what the current state of knowledge is on the seabed, but I wouldn't bet that a generic algorithm is going to allow you to filter out all the noise from your video so that you can cleanly model the Trench landscape."

John frowned and pushed his plate away from him. "I guess that is a naive approach to take. But I should think the geologists have a pretty good idea what most of the noises are so all I have to do is pick Dave Gibbons' brain and write a few more algorithms. I'm not saying it'll be a piece of cake, but I'm not worried it's impossible."

Puneet nodded. "You're probably right. Still, I'd be prepared, if I were you, for a few surprises along the way. The oceans are the last great, uncharted territory on Earth. I don't think we know a tenth there is to know about them. That's why what you're doing is so valuable."

John said nothing, but he kept thinking about Puneet's remarks all the way back to campus. He was so engrossed that he didn't see Zoë until he'd almost bumped into her as she stood chatting with a group of friends outside Wean. As soon as they made eye contact, the chatter died down among her friends and one by one they all drifted away, though most stayed just out of earshot. Puneet murmured something polite and continued into Wean, leaving John alone with his ex-girlfriend.

"So." Zoë eyed him. "Back at last? Bring any mermaids back with you? Or have you grown up after dallying so long in the tropical sun?"

John winced and broke eye contact first.

"Ah." He could have shaved with her tone. "You came to your senses then? Playing Pygmalion isn't your strong suit?"

John expelled his breath, but little air returned to fill the void. "Listen, Zoë, I'm sorry you're still upset with me. But I think it's in both our interests if we agree to a truce right here and now—CMU just isn't a big enough campus for us to be at each other's throats."

Zoë squared her shoulders and stood straighter, her book bag falling down her right arm unnoticed. She appeared to consider his words. For the first time, he noticed that her dark hair had been cut level with her chin, swinging at an angle to the back of her head. Her makeup, always minimal—foundation and powder to cover less-than-perfect skin—was now a bit more obvious, though applied with a light touch. Her nails were still short and unpolished so he suspected that she hadn't abandoned her Tae Kwon Do or sports. The style of her clothes remained clearly in the black-is-artsy-and-cool realm—her Doc Marten boots added a good two inches to her five-nine height—but they were less secondhand-store chic and more mall-hip. Zoë had always drawn attention wherever she went, but now she demanded it.

"I don't see why not." She shrugged. "It's not as though I've gone to pieces over our breakup—I've moved on. You just gave me a shock, that's all."

John nodded and felt his chest ease. He was about to offer to buy her a coffee sometime when a rather tall man dressed in black jeans, red t-shirt, and black leather jacket came up behind Zoë from the direction of the fine arts building and put his hand familiarly on Zoë's forearm.

"Hey, Zoë." When she turned to face him, he gave her a kiss. "I've finished fixing the problems with the design of the gallery for the new student union and I thought I'd come and take you to Buns'n Udders for coffee."

Zoë caught John's eye, smirking. "Sure, Greg. I was just saying goodbye to my friend John here. John, this is Greg Moreland; he's a prof in the architecture department."

Greg barely glanced toward John. "Hey, nice to meet you."

"Nice to meet you, too."

John watched them head into Wean Hall, presumably to take the elevator to the first floor where they could take the shortcut through the parking lot behind Wean to Forbes Avenue. Zoë threaded her arm through Greg's as they walked, never glancing back at him.

೩ ೩ ೩

A month later, John biked into CMU in an early-morning shower that left him drenched; in a few weeks, he'd be forced to drive again to campus to avoid the cold, but today it was still warm enough for biking while wet. A few leaves had fallen already and wet clumps of them clung to the edges of Schenley Drive and Frew Street and to the sidewalks. Students and staff alike, indistinguishable from each other in their yellow rain slickers and backpacks, hurried to shelter wherever he looked. When he came up to the fourth floor of Wean later in the afternoon for a cup of coffee, he saw that the day remained gray and overcast, bathing the lobby in its steely light.

After he'd grabbed his coffee, he planned to go up to Steve's office on the sixth floor and drop off his latest chapter, the first one not rehashing old material. He had a surprise for Steve: instead of proposing to pursue a limited number of algorithms for recognizing underwater objects in order to model the environment captured in his Trench video, he planned to design a genetic algorithm that learned as it filtered out common noises. He'd already toyed with some basic genetic algorithms for fun when he'd gotten tired of working on networking problems for Steve and had set up a Web page of genetic haikus that "evolved" as visitors voted on lines that they liked best. It hadn't been anything fancy, but he'd gotten some notice and inspired a few other grad students to write more advanced algorithms.

If Steve didn't keep him too long glancing over his proposal's new direction, John planned to take a break for a couple of hours and drop in on a talk by some guys from Pixar over in Porter Hall, one of whom was James Wilson, a former member of the graphics group. Half an hour later, he and Steve were headed over to Porter, laughing about the current crop of first years, who were both a tad too uptight and a little too business-oriented, when Zoë fell into step at his side. He managed to say hi in an even voice and to keep talking as the three of them walked together. Zoë said little, her long legs easily keeping stride with them, her arms swinging slightly and her hair pushed behind her ear. A spicy scent warmed the autumn air between them and enveloped her in a soft, invisible cocoon.

"So you think they're gonna show some outtakes from *Toy Story*?" Zoë asked as if her presence wasn't explosive.

"Absolutely." Steve eyed them but said nothing.

"You planning to see it when it comes out?" John thought that he knew Zoë's answer.

"Sure—are you asking me to go?" She swiveled her head and leveled her gaze on him.

John blinked. "Yeah, why not?"

The conversation halted as they reached the door to Porter and another group of CS grad students came up behind them. Members of the combined group conjectured about how much Disney had influenced the work of the Pixar animators and storytellers, but Zoë said nothing more. She remained at John's side, however, and when he sat down next to Steve, she took the seat at his left. He became preternaturally aware of her forearm brushing against his, the swell of her breasts beneath her red camisole, the smell of her perfume.

When did she start wearing perfume?

Without bidding, images of Zoë, naked and sweaty above him, haunted his thoughts, overriding texture algorithms and rendering pipelines.

He didn't remember much of the talk afterwards and later told Steve that he'd been too consumed with his proposal to focus on what was being said. Zoë chose to take her leave outside Porter, murmuring something about an appointment on the other side of campus and then she was gone with the crowd spilling from the auditorium. John watched her go, her hair swinging confidently about her face and her lovely legs encased in black tights under a black-and-white checked mini-skirt. He remembered them wrapped around his torso.

"That's one cool customer." Steve's voice broke his reverie.

"What?"

"Nothing, John, nothing at all." Steve grinned.

Slowly, John walked back to his office. When he got there, Stefan half sat on the long table next to his desk, one leg on the floor and the other bent in front of him, chatting with John's office mate, Patrick. Stefan gestured for some time with his long fingers as he talked, his long face animated and his dark eyes gleaming underneath the overhang of his choppy brown hair. John sat down and began to type.

"Oy, it looks like John hasn't got the time o'day for you."

Stefan's hands stilled in mid-air as he turned his face toward John.

"Hey, man! What's up with you? You look like you just ate some unmarked leftovers in the lounge refrigerator. Steve ridin' you hard these days?"

John stopped typing and leaned back in his chair. He stomach roiled.

"No more than I deserve." He pinched the bridge of his nose between his thumb and forefinger. "What's up? Going to tonight's IC at Gilgenoff's house?"

Stefan grinned. "Absolutely. You have to ask? Have you seen that new first year? Astrid? She's smokin'."

"No, I got better things to do these days."

"Once burned? Anyway, that's not why I'm here, actually. I just saw CNN in the student center and there's another tropical storm developing in the Caribbean. They're already talking about naming it Marilyn. With all the hurricanes coming through these days, I guess you got outta there in the nick of time, man."

John blinked rapidly and frowned. "No shit?"

"Would I lie to you?"

John rubbed his palms along the sides of his head and rocked around in his chair. "Dewey's got one of the safest harbors in the Caribbean," he said, more to himself than to Stefan and Patrick. "It's been a really busy season, but nothing's come close to Culebra, not even Luis. I'm sure they're in no danger."

"You look more than a little worried, my man. Don't tell me you forgot to love 'em and leave 'em."

John, who sat staring at a pile of tech reports next to Stefan on the table, missed this last remark. "What?"

"Nothing, nothing. Hey, wanna come with me tonight to Gilgenoff's?"

John heard Stefan, but he still had difficulty processing his words. "Uh, what? Oh, yeah, sure. I'll be here until you come and get me. Loads to do."

"Okay, I'll swing by at 6:30. But, hey, John, do me a favor and find another ride if I happen to hit it off with Astrid, okay?"

"Sure, sure." John waved Stefan away.

He sat immobile long after Stefan had gone whistling down the hall. He didn't move, in fact, until Patrick rolled his own chair over and very gently pushed John around to face his workstation and put his fingers on the keys.

⁋⁋⁋

Tamarind stood outside Ana's house frowning at the sky, her hands on her hips and her hair teased by the wind. Yesterday, she'd heard the news on Ana's radio that a ferocious storm terrified the humans living on the islands south and west of Culebra and she knew, even without Ana's oyster-tight lips, that this storm would scour Culebra long before it blew itself out. Among the *mer*, it was said that these devastating winds and waves were the result of angry quarrels between Mother Sea and Father Sky and, until these two elements made peace, the *mer* sought refuge in the Hidden Caves. Without a doubt they swam there now, her father's mind urging her family and community to swim faster while his strength bolstered the flagging energies of the older *mer* and his will compelled the youngest to stay on task. When they arrived, he would discover her deceit.

She studied the sky, gauged the feel of the air on her skin, and tested the humidity with her tongue. Each hour the air pressure dropped further. Her experience and her instinct told her that they must find shelter before the storm hit in two days. While she stood there, Ana squatted at the shore, arranging shells, pebbles, and seaweed into an elaborate and inexplicable design. Tamarind had no idea what more Ana hoped to learn from Mother Sea. She dug hard fingertips into her hipbones and waited.

A laughing gull glided silently over the spot where Ana stood. Tamarind frowned at it before turning on her heel. She flopped down into an aluminum chair outside Ana's front door and nudged a big toe around the basket that Ana had packed that morning. It reminded her of the first-aid kit that the park rangers brought along for their turtle watches. She didn't recognize all of the vials and baggies, but Ana had included tamarind-and-lemon syrup for an antiseptic, a diluted cone-snail extract for numbing a small area, and a plankton tincture spiked with turtle grass and algae as a sedative.

She reached into her pocket and pulled out the moonstone that Valerie had given her. Just this week they'd traveled to San Juan and a jeweler that Valerie knew there. The jeweler had studied the gem for some time before lifting her eyepiece and smiling at them.

"Valerie, this is a beautiful specimen. Where'd you get it?"

Valerie shrugged. "I have a friend in New York who keeps a lookout for me. Cabochon cut, do you think?"

The jeweler rolled the moonstone between her fingers before answering. "No, I wouldn't. This one needs to become a bead. Then I can polish it on my wheel for you, but it will take some time."

"No, that won't be necessary. We'll polish it by hand."

The jeweler nodded and pulled her eyepiece down again. "So what are you going to use it for? It's so fine. You could make it the centerpiece of a pendant. Make a lot of money on it, too."

"It's not for sale. It's a gift for a friend." At her words, Valerie smiled at Tamarind.

When they picked the moonstone up later, all its knobby edges had been sheared away and it shimmered expectantly.

Tamarind held the bead in her palm and raised it to the light. For the first time, she understood that transforming power existed outside of the sea. Even after she'd slid the moonstone into her pocket, its light called to her fingers and she rubbed it without being aware that she did.

Today while she waited for Ana to return from communing with Mother Sea, she polished the moonstone as she'd done every free moment since their return from San Juan. Valerie had given her a strip of clean felt and a small jar of tin oxide paste.

"A wheel would polish it faster but not better. Besides, I rather believe in the lore around this gem. By polishing it yourself, you make it your own. Just remember to keep the tin oxide moist."

"How will I know when it's done?"

A smile lifted the corners of Valerie's mouth. "I imagine you'll know."

Smooth and cool, the bead disappeared beneath the white paste. Wrapping a corner of the felt around it, she rubbed it against her palm and hummed. She thought of John, who had left Culebra weeks before without saying good-bye and she wondered if he still worked in San Juan. For the season that she'd known him, Mother Sea and Father Sky had quarreled frequently. Valerie told her that the summer storms this year had destroyed homes and businesses on islands all around them. Now, as the time that she had human legs drew to a close, it seemed that Culebra too would suffer.

Tamarind stopped humming and rubbing the moonstone. She brought her eyes back from buffing the sky and looked at her hands. The tin oxide paste rimed the felt dangling between her fingers but a thin layer still lay upon the moonstone like dust, or heartbreak. She lifted the bead up on a flat palm to her mouth and exhaled warm breath over it. Then, with a delicate fingertip, she wiped away the last of the paste. The moonstone gleamed, aloof and invincible, against her grimy palm. It was time to set it into the womb of the Goddess.

Seventeen
❦

ANA FELT THE AIR LESSENING AROUND HER by incremental degrees even as she knelt on the wet stones quizzing Mother Sea. The storm she sensed had started far off to the east a week before and it gained power as it headed their way. The Culebrenses might not even sense the danger yet—it had been a long time since a hurricane had blown through their harbor. She would do what she could to warn and protect them, but strength no longer surged through her when she called on Mother Sea. Instead, she hoped for a generous upwelling to sustain her through the trial ahead of her.

"What's this?" She fingered the seaweed and coral laid out before her that Mother Sea had licked. She sat back on her haunches.

Mother Sea swept them into a pile beside her.

Ana moved several palm-sized stones aside and buried a horseshoe-crab shell into the resulting depression. Around this, she rimmed seaweed topped with oyster shells and the carcass of a sea star. Ocean lapped at the structure until it had filled in all crevices and nothing remained but a salty pool. Ana closed her good eye and stuck the fingers of her right hand into this water. An image of Tamarind's father filled her mind's eye.

"Ah, of course."

She made to draw her hand out of the water when another image replaced the first. This time, she saw Tamarind. The mermaid's lower half wavered as if distorted by water and a tail, dark gray like a manatee's, appeared under her transparent legs. Even though the rainy season had weeks to go, she understood at once from this image that Tamarind's transformation would be decided one way or another by the coming storm.

Pulling her hand out at last, Ana sat back and sighed. She plucked the dead sea star and several shells from the ground around her and slid them into the small sack propped against a rock behind her. She unfolded her legs and stood upright. Her knees ached from being bent so long.

A laughing gull surfed the air in front of her face, its wings tipping to control its descent until it landed on the rock next to her sack. On its foot, twine secured a roll of paper.

"Thank you, Ai, my love." She snipped the twine with her scissors and absentmindedly pulled some tamarind pulp from her apron for the gull. It had been a long time since she'd received a written message.

The midwife who lived on Guadaloupe had sent this one. She had read the signs of the brewing storm and tracked it as it came closer to the islands. Now a hurricane that the humans called Marilyn, it had passed southwest of her island on a course for the U.S. Virgin Islands. Its current trajectory put it on a path to cross over the eastern coast of Puerto Rico and Culebra. She estimated its arrival in less than two days.

Ana looked up as the gull wobbled into the sky.

"Hey, Ai!" She threw it another, larger, bit of tamarind pulp. The bird snatched it from the air, flapped once around Ana's head laughing softly, and then headed back to its home. It would have to hurry to miss the rising winds.

❧❧❧

John woke in the early dawn on September 15th, its pale glow filtering through the blinds in the northern wall of his guestroom in Culebra. Something was wrong, but it took him several minutes to realize that the morning was eerily silent. Every weekend for nearly five months, he'd awakened daily to the cries of thousands of brown boobies, laughing gulls, and a variety of terns at their nesting grounds on Flamenco Peninsula and, in the nearby lagoons, competing calls from brown pelicans, Bahamas pintails, masked ducks, and ruddy ducks. Then he remembered that Hurricane Marilyn appeared to be headed straight for Culebra, and he knew why the birds were silent.

Late last night when he arrived back on the island after taking a charter flight with a pilot, who made no secret that he thought John had lost his marbles, he went straight to Posada La Diosa. Valerie sat listening to her radio in her kitchen. When she caught sight of him, she jumped up from her chair, threw her arms around his neck and squeezed him hard.

"You're a welcome sight! I've been pretty nonchalant this season, even though Luís gave everyone else a scare. But after what Hugo did to us, I'm not sure I can weather Marilyn by myself."

"I don't know what help I'll be." He looked down at Valerie's jewelry-making supplies and the wire-wrapped pieces laying there. "Is Tamarind still making jewelry with you?"

Valerie went to the refrigerator and pulled out a pitcher of lemonade, which she poured into two glasses.

"Here." She handed him one. "While we still have electricity, we should enjoy cold drinks. Yeah, I see Tamarind a few times a week. We've been going to San Juan every now and then. She's never been off this island so I've made it my duty to educate her a bit, take her to museums, shopping, whatever."

John nodded once and sipped his lemonade.

Valerie sat down at her table and studied him. "But that's not what you wanted to know is it? She's not seeing anyone. I think she's still stuck on you."

"Is she still staying with that old hag, Ana?"

"John! That's a horrible thing to say! Ana's rough around the edges, I'll give you that, but she does a lot of good for the folks around here."

"I'm not a big fan of herbal lore and witchcraft."

"Don't knock what you don't understand, John. To paraphrase Shakespeare, there are more things in heaven and earth than you dream of, my boy. And, yes, Tamarind still lives with Ana."

"Do you think she'll be safe there?"

"I think Ana's one tough cookie who's weathered a lot. I think she'll know when to run for cover. But if you're so worried about Tamarind, why don't you go find her?"

John hadn't left town to look for her this morning, even though the hurricane watch had been upgraded around midnight to a warning. Instead, he'd gone to the ferry dock with Valerie to help unload a shipment of plywood, nails, and water. Everyone's mouths remained in tight lines, even the people that John knew and greeted. Today, everyone would be consumed with boarding up windows and buying supplies. And then they'd wait.

Somewhere in the small guesthouse, he heard a door slam and then low voices. Luís had already spooked most of the guests away from Culebra, and only one other of Posada La Diosa's guests planned to stay through the coming storm. He got out of bed, dressed hastily and went into the bathroom to piss and brush his teeth. He'd borrowed Stefan's cell phone so that he could call his parents before the storm hit—thank God he'd be able to reach them if the power went out. After he'd grabbed a bagel or something like it, he'd head over to the Sunken Reef Dive Shop and help Chris secure his boat in the marina and finish boarding up the windows in the shop. After that, he'd make sure that Valerie had gotten enough bottled water and groceries to last for a few days.

He arrived at the dive shop to find Chris already hammering at the piece of three-quarter-inch plywood he held over his front door; the larger sheet for the front window lay propped against the side of the shop. Chris said only "hey" when he saw John and handed him the bucket of nails to hold. Together, they finished boarding up all the glass surfaces for the shop before heading to the marina to add a few more lines from the dive boat to its mooring at the dock. As they worked, John paused frequently to stare at the southern horizon, which seemed a little darker to his searching eyes; even though the weather was still mostly sunny, the wind had picked up considerably. By the time they'd finished at the marina, it was mid-morning.

John wished Chris good luck, then almost ran all the way back to Posada La Diosa where he came across Valerie trying to herd the stray cat from the neighborhood into her door with her foot, her hands filled with grocery bags. The stupid animal refused to enter the half-opened screen door, instead insisting on winding itself around Valerie's ankles until she nearly tripped. Bending down, John swooped the cat through

237

the door and left it in the entranceway where it stood mewling in outrage. Valerie, clucking, urged John to grab the bag of cat food just outside the door and feed the cat to make up for its rough handling. John held the cat back with one hand while he reached through the half-open door for the food, and then squatted down to feed the stray, which purred vociferously. John laughed at how greedily, yet delicately, it ate its meal.

"Hey, Johnny. I have a couple cases of bottled water in the back of my Jeep. Can you bring them in for me?"

"Sure, no problem."

She came out with him to unload still more bags. John hiked the box of bottled water onto his shoulder and followed Valerie into Posada La Diosa. Valerie had already set the other remaining guest to boarding up the windows to his room, and his hammering blended with the hammering echoing up and down the street. She took the bottled water from John and directed him to the back porch where there were sheets of plywood propped against the guesthouse wall, an open paper bag of nails, and a couple of hammers. Grabbing a handful of nails, he tucked them into a front pocket of his shorts, slid the hammer's claws into his waistband, and then lifted a piece of plywood before heading toward the northwest end of the guesthouse and the window to his room. On this side of the guesthouse, which was less sheltered by the surrounding buildings, the gusts of wind were strong enough to whip his ponytail into his face and eyes. Still, he managed to nail the plywood securely in place without too much struggle and he prayed silently that all their efforts would be unnecessary.

When he returned to the back porch, Valerie was waiting for him.

"Why don't you come in and grab a sandwich? It might be a long couple of days and you don't need to start skipping meals now."

Valerie made hummus sandwiches and poured lemonade for both of them. They sat at the kitchen island eating and listening to Latin pop on the radio. Before they'd finished, reports from Miami aired. Although Marilyn currently moved toward St. Croix at more than 70 miles per hour, forecasters didn't expect her to strengthen beyond category one once she passed St. Croix. Still, she would reach Culebra before midnight.

"Dear God, why do they have to use the term 'strengthen'? It sounds so positive, like what you do for someone who has a bad back or weak immune system." Valerie licked the tip of her index finger and pressed it against the crumbs on the counter. She was about to stand up when John spoke again.

"Do you remember what you said about Shakespeare last night? You know, about more things in heaven and earth than I dream of?"

"Yes." She pushed her empty plate and glass away from her and bent her head in an attitude of listening with all her attention.

"Well, I've had some pretty vivid dreams in the last six months, nearly all of them on Culebra. For most of the time I was back in Pittsburgh, I didn't have any dreams—it was like I slept in a coma while I was there. And then two nights ago, I dreamt again about Tamarind."

"Again?"

"Yeah. One time, when I was in San Juan, I dreamt she'd come into my room and, you know, did that humming thing she does. But she looked and sounded so real I nearly reached out and touched her. A couple of nights ago, I dreamt

239

that she was in my apartment with me and she looked frightened. She asked me to come back to Culebra before the storm hit."

Valerie squinted her eyes before standing up to get a cup of coffee. "Dreams are powerful messengers."

"This was more than my subconscious trying to tell me something, Val. Look, I know this sounds crazy, but I think Tamarind really came to me somehow, that she needs me."

"You must not believe too seriously or you'd have gone to find her before now."

John stuck his fingertips into his hair, pulling out long strands from his once-neat ponytail. "I believe it, but I also don't believe it. I believed it enough to get on a plane and come here, but now that I'm here all these doubts crowd in my head and I can't bring myself to face her."

Valerie sipped her coffee and Latin pop filled the silence around them. After a moment, she spoke as if measuring out each syllable.

"John, did you happen to hear the phrase *del mar* while you were here this summer?"

John scowled and stared at his empty plate. "Yeah, I did. From Tomás and Chris. They suggested the woman who saved me from drowning back when I first got here was *del mar*. I thought Tomás was mocking me. And Chris? I just thought Chris had a lunatic edge."

Valerie looked at him, her lips pursed. She tapped the counter with her fingertips and then sighed noisily. "Look, this will probably sound nuttier to you than your theory about Tamarind achieving astral projection, but I think Tamarind is a mermaid."

John choked on the swallow of lemonade he'd just attempted. "Wha-at?"

"Okay, I know you're a rational, science-type of guy, Johnny, but hear me out. Mermaids have been a part of the mythology of any number of peoples around the world—from India, China and Japan to Native America. Maybe there's some basis for these myths."

"Mermaids are about as real as leviathans."

Valerie played with her napkin. "Actually, some scientists have proposed that leviathans might be a prehistoric ancestor to modern snakes."

"But that just means that mermaids are really dolphins or–or manatees. Not some half-person, half-fish."

"Once I read this book. I think it was called *The Aquatic Ape*. Anyway, the author hypothesized that if marine life crawled out of the primordial oceans and adapted to land, what's to say that some of the primates that evolved didn't go back into the ocean?"

John said nothing. He remembered thinking about what motivated sea turtles to split their time between land and sea. On the face of it, the idea of a primate heading for the ocean and adapting to it wasn't so outrageous.

"I guess." He laid his hands on the counter and studied them. "But why hasn't anyone confirmed this theory? Why are mermaids still just myths? Beyond a cheesy Tom Hanks movie and kitsch in resort towns, no one has ever seen a mermaid."

"That's not true. Why do you think the Culebrenses talk about the *gente del mar*? In fact, many natives of the Caribbean whisper about them. They say they walk in human form among us, that they protect the sea turtles and reefs, and that they bring vital sea life to help heal humans. They even say some of the *mer* folk fall in love with humans and leave the sea to be with their chosen loves.

"Besides, if you were a merman, would you willingly swim up to a human and announce what you were? If it were me, I'd probably stay as far from shore as I could. But Tamarind isn't me, is she?"

"No, she's not. So, what do you propose I do? Ask her outright?"

"Sure? Why not? Can't be any worse than asking her if her spirit leaves her body behind and travels to visit you, can it?"

"No, I guess not."

"Astral projection couldn't work for her anyway. Mermaids don't have spirits."

Eighteen
❧

RAIMUNDA SAT AT THE BAR OF ISLA ENCANTADA watching Tomás and the bartender, Enrique, nailing plywood over the bar's windows. She sipped her Medalla and nibbled on the stale *surullitos* resting on a small platter near her right hand. Every few moments her eyes slid to the door, which remained closed despite her vigilance. After a while, she pulled a packet of cigarette papers from the bag that hung at her waist and a handful of her special tobacco mix. Sprinkling a pinch onto a paper, she rolled a tapered tube, licked the edge of the paper, and lit it. As she sucked the sweet, spicy smoke into her mouth, she heard the door creak behind her.

She kept her face forward, the hand holding the cigarette propped up on an elbow next to her on the bar. Her lips curved at the corners. She set the cigarette into the ashtray next to her and picked up the Medalla.

"*Mi sirenita.*" Jesus kissed the back of her neck. "Somehow I knew I'd find you here, when everyone else is working so hard to save themselves."

She shrugged. "Why work when I don't have to?"

He sat on the barstool next to her. "Ah, yes, *mi alma dulce.* You live in a cave, don't you?"

"Always trying to find out where I live, *mi guapetón*? Let's just say that my home *es inexpugnable. Comprende?*"

"Well, not every woman is as *agradable* as you, *mi reina.* Sometimes I need some loving arms to welcome me."

"*Necesitas no más que llamarme buscarme.*" She sipped her beer. "Was it not a few weeks ago I saw you here, *mi amigo*, with that *chica deliciosa*? *Cómo se llama*? Tamarind?"

Enrique interrupted them to ask Jesus what he wanted to drink. After the bartender left to get another Medalla, Jesus picked up a *surullito* and broke it between his thumb and forefinger. Cornmeal crumbs powdered the counter in front of him.

"*Sí*, we were together that night. She was very coy and left here alone, only to show up later and drag me away, begging me to fuck her. *Pero no la he visto en mucho tiempo.* It's as though she doesn't want me to see her."

"I've seen her." Raimunda pulled on her cigarette, her lips making a slight smacking noise as they clasped and released it. "She was at the *norteamericano* bar, the Dockside, a few days later. She complained she hadn't had a good lay *todo el verano.*"

"*Es la verdad?*"

"*Sí. Te mentiría?* I was very surprised, *mi amigo*, very surprised. I listened while she told *todas las mujeres* about how small the cock was on her last fuck, smaller than that of the *norteamericano.*"

Enrique clanked Jesus' Medalla onto the bar. Raimunda saw his eyes flicker at her last words, but he said nothing, only took Jesus' money and returned to his inventory in the back.

"*Esa bruja! Le voy a demostrar mi miembre*! How do I find this bitch?"

"She's known to stay with *la mujer vieja* Ana."

Jesus swigged his entire beer in one breath and slammed the empty bottle down. "*Perdóname, mi preciosa*. I must go find *este puta joven* and teach her a lesson *no olvidará nunca*."

"What's your hurry, *mi amor*? Stay with me and have another *cerveza. Ahora no es el tiempo*."

"Wrong, *cariño*. Now *es el tiempo perfecto*. Once the hurricane hits Culebra, only those with a death wish will venture from the safety of their houses. We will have *mucho tiempo estar solos juntos*. Tamarind will think again before complaining to *los gringos*. "

"*Ah, ya veo. Buena suerte, mi amigo. Buena suerte.*"

Raimunda watched as Jesus dropped out of his barstool and loped away to the entrance. In the dim light from the boarded-up windows on either side of the door, she recognized the appetite of the man scorned, the single-minded focus of the predator.

≈≈≈

Even above the noise of the wind, Tamarind heard the sound of a car motor on the hill road from town and her heart leapt. But when she saw the battered old Pontiac through a gap in the scrub, she knew that it wasn't John and turned to look toward the canal so that the stranger wouldn't see the disappointment in her gaze. The car rattled to a stop not far from her and a man in a red shirt blooming with hibiscus and gray polyester slacks jumped out, the car's engine idling loudly.

"Señorita, dónde está Señora Ana? Mi esposa necesita ayuda ahora, por favor."

By now, Tamarind was used to people driving, walking, and riding horses or bikes to Ana's door at all hours of the day, although they had rarely shown such urgency. None of the Culebrenses had seemed very surprised to see Tamarind and she sometimes wondered if they attributed her presence to the power of Ana's magic—for all they knew, Ana had conjured her up from lifeless dust. Shrugging, she accepted their conclusions—they weren't entirely wrong anyway—and did nothing that would cause them to think differently. The Creator had allowed her to remain unknown among these humans and she must be careful not to invite suspicion to herself.

Without a word, she gestured for this latest supplicant to wait before sprinting away toward the beach, reveling in the feel of her toes pounding on the stony ground and the wind in her hair. At the edge of the beach, Ana waited for Tamarind, her knees under her chin as she squatted, her single eye glinting even though the sun no longer shone. She unfurled herself and stood up. Together, they hurried back up the hidden path toward the man, whose anxiety manifested itself in rapid, unceasing Spanish.

"Señora Ana! Señora Ana!" The man shouted even before he saw them. *"Es el tiémpo. El bebé va nacer pronto. Vengate con migo, por favor."*

Ana smiled widely when she came out onto the hill. "I've been expecting you, Jaime. Only Carme would have the bad luck to have a baby in a hurricane."

Jaime crossed himself. *"Madre de Diós! Digáme si ellos estén bien."*

"You think you're having a son? *'Ellas' estén bien, muy bien*, if we leave now. Tamarind, you must come with me and help."

Tamarind, who stared beyond the Pontiac where the road disappeared over a hill, started at Ana's command and looked at them with narrowed eyes. "Me? What do you mean?"

Ana swiveled on her haunches to look up at Tamarind; her hands flitted in the air around her. "Look, young one, there's a mother about to give birth. She's in a lot of pain and needs my help. And I need yours. So stop thinking about yourself and go back to my place. We're going to need a few things."

Tamarind's mouth opened, but she shut it again. Nodding, she listened as Ana told her exactly what to get before returning to the house on heavy feet. Inside, Ana's chickens chuckled nervously from a temporary roost in one corner. She finished gathering the midwife's book, some scissors, and the medicine basket when she remembered the moonstone Goddess that she'd hidden down on Playa Tamarindo along with all of her other belongings. Wrapping a cloaking glamour around herself, she slipped out of the door while Ana and Jaime secured a tarp over the chicken coop and the wooden seagull house. Ana had sent all of the seagulls away days ago to nesting areas on the Puerto Rico mainland. After the storm hit, they would fly over the islands and return to her with news from other midwives.

Tamarind reached Playa Tamarindo and quickly released the cloaking spell guarding her horde of human artifacts. She ignored the pile of clothes and hair ornaments carefully tucked inside and snatched the moonstone Goddess up. There wasn't much time and she had no idea if she'd mastered the necessary spell from the midwife's book.

247

Clutching it to her chest, she closed her eyes and murmured. She squatted, still murmuring and touched the seawater that surged restlessly toward her. A thrill ran through her fingers. On impulse, she popped up and hurried over to the scrub along the edge of the shore. Squatting again, she dug away at the roots of the closest low-growing bush and stuck her fingertips into the earth. Again she murmured. A new power tasted her skin and tickled her hand, unfamiliar and rich. When it flowed through her veins, it had none of the wild impatience of Mother Sea. Rather, it filled her with the dark, steady scent of the cavern where she'd gained her legs.

This new power stayed with her while she climbed away from the beach, her calf muscles straining against the incline and the soles of her feet aching from the stones and uneven ground. In the cavern of her fist, the moonstone glowed as if lit from within and the wires embossed themselves on her palm. She hummed a bit, deep and low, and several clicks skittered across her palate. Overhead, the flat gray sky waited, impervious and implacable. As she crested the top of the hill behind Ana's house, rising winds waylaid her, nearly knocking her off her feet and back down the hidden path.

Her hair fluttered into her face and then two arms wrapped around her, one around her mouth and the other around her torso. She dropped the Goddess. Fingers from the hand over her mouth pressed hard into her nostrils, asphyxiating her. From somewhere off to her right, she heard a hoarse shout and then the pulsating of her blood drowned out all other sounds. She squirmed and kicked a heel into flesh and bone. A kaleidoscope of vivid colors whirled across her vision before disappearing into soft, soundless charcoal.

When her senses returned, she found her arms wrenched behind her and her wrists tied tightly together. Her ankles too were tied together and she lay on her side in the back of a moving vehicle. A gag bit the corners of her mouth and choked her dry tongue; some rough cloth covered her eyes. Beneath her, unidentifiable objects dug into her side and the reek of old fried foods, the bitter tang of stale beer, and the slightly sweetish scent of something else mingled together and assailed her. A sharp ache threatened to split her forehead and nausea burbled in her gut. In her current condition, so far from sea and unable even to manipulate the fine drops of water in the air around her with her fingers, she had no hope of calling on any magic, let alone producing a cloaking spell for herself.

Gusts of wind rocked the vehicle and a male voice swore in Spanish. The voice sounded familiar, but her headache interfered with her ability to concentrate. She waited, trying to hum around the gag, but her chest refused to expand against the restraint of her arms. Just when she thought that she might vomit into the gag and choke, the vehicle veered and abruptly halted. The driver opened his door and got out; whatever they'd ridden in rocked in reflex. He swung open the door near her feet and cool, humid air caressed her soles.

Her captor leaned in and caressed her upper thigh, murmuring unintelligibly. Tamarind desperately soaked up as much of the moisture in the air around her feet as she could. Still, she felt parched.

Father, help me. The thought formed before she recognized it.

When the unknown abductor tugged her toward him, her feet touched the earth and again she felt the strange power flow through her soles. She urged it to fill her and something responded to her silent plea, swirling through her chest and into the far reaches of her mind. Almost she felt as if she could understand it. Seconds later, he launched her up and over his shoulder and her stomach heaved dangerously.

249

John. Why didn't you come for me?

The wind wrestled with her abductor as he walked and he cursed again. It snatched his words away and Tamarind sensed a thread of anger in its swift fingers—anger separate from the passion brewing the hurricane. The new power in her blood sang in response. Tamarind slumped against the shoulder he carried her over and waited.

He stopped and fiddled with something in front of him. She tentatively stretched a toe behind her. Her bare feet didn't recognize the smooth, hard surface. Abruptly he opened a door and the wind howled past them as he stepped forward. Tamarind sensed the room around them before he turned and pushed the door shut, leaning against it for a long moment. In the sudden quiet, his breathing sounded harsh and uneven. After a moment, he pulled her from his shoulder and she tumbled onto the floor, hitting her head and bruising her back. When he spoke this time, she recognized the voice. Its caress chilled her.

"Ah, *mi cariño*. That was *muy difícil*. But now we're alone, I can assure you that it was worth it."

Jesus knelt over her and rolled her onto her side. Then she felt the cold blade he wielded as he cut the bindings on her ankles. Pain prickled through her feet along with the rush of blood. He cut the blindfold away from her eyes, dragging the flat of the blade across her cheek as she looked at him for the first time in more than a month.

He clicked his tongue and shook his head slightly. "So wide, your eyes, *mi dulcinea*. Perhaps you are surprised to see me after all this time spent ignoring me. Perhaps you guess I have heard the stories you have been telling about me and you are afraid."

The gag wedged Tamarind's tongue back into her throat, which was so dry that she could only shake her head.

"Ah, *mi reina*, you pretended innocence all those weeks of turtle watching. Innocence when that *gringo* looked at you lustfully every night on the beach, innocence when I took you dancing and tried to touch you. But you weren't innocent when you returned and led me to Playa Melones to fuck, and you aren't innocent now. You know exactly what I'm talking about."

As he spoke, he used the tip of the knife to toy with several strands of hair near her left ear.

"Even when you came back that night, you wouldn't let me touch your hair." His voice sounded husky, strange. "Your hair. It's almost alive. You must be so proud of it. Too proud, perhaps."

The blade caught and tugged at the strands for a moment.

"There are some that say you are *del mar*, but I, I say you are nothing but a foolish woman."

He held up the severed strands for her to see, watching her eyes as he lifted them to his nose and inhaled. He dropped the strands onto her face and laughed as she blinked to clear hair from her vision. She was still blinking against the scratchy filaments rubbing against her eyeballs when he leaned over. Even so, she caught the bright flash of steel through the tangle of hair against her cheek.

Nineteen

ೞ

MARILYN BATTERED ST. CROIX, only 65 miles away, throughout the afternoon on its way north to the other U. S. Virgin Islands, St. John and St. Thomas, and Culebra. John, driving Valerie's Jeep north on Route 251, refused to turn the radio on and listen to the reports from Miami. He met almost no one on the way to Ana's small house; only a single black car turned east at the intersection of 251 and 250, away from Dewey. Many Culebrenses had fled their homes for the safety of the shelter built with relief money after Hugo had ripped through the island in 1989. Some huddled in the largest public buildings: the school and its library, the clinic and ferry terminal, and the two churches. Most of the owners of the guesthouses, including Valerie, had opened their doors to anyone looking for a place to hide.

John, his elbow propped on the window frame, looked out at the landscape as he drove. The treetops danced against the buttermilk sky and tired shrubs rustled, imitating the constant shushing of the ocean enclosing Culebra. Under a stand of palm trees on the east side of 251, a herd of wild horses huddled. The whites of their eyes showed even from a distance. Nothing else moved, on land or in sky. Valerie told John that morning that the seabirds had risen in dark sheets from their nesting grounds over the past few days and streamed away to the northeast and safety. The air, heavy and hot, smelled like kindling and dust—overriding the faint metallic scent of the ocean.

In the silence, he heard Tamarind's voice, clear and musical. Anguish rippled its edges.

John slowed down and looked around, half expecting to see Tamarind sitting next to him, her bare feet hanging out the window and her corkscrew hair filling the cabin. But no mischievous eyes peeked back at him, no fingers tapped in time with the radio on the seat beside him. Instead, an image of Tamarind hunched under the low-hanging night sky when he'd read *The Lion, The Witch, and The Wardrobe* to her filled his mind. Her rounded shoulders burned themselves on his soul's retina.

He'd just reached the access road to Tamarindo Estates when a dented blue Pontiac crested the hill and roared toward him. He almost ignored it, but then he caught sight of Ana's wild white hair as the driver turned south onto 251. Quickly he turned the Jeep around and followed after the speeding car, alternately banging on the horn and flashing the high beams. The driver didn't notice him until he'd turned onto 250 and even then he refused to stop, only slowing down enough for John to come along his left side. John leaned over while driving and jerked down the passenger window.

"Hey, you, Ana! Where's Tamarind!"

She looked at him. The contrast between her brilliant blue eye and the cloudy left one silenced the howl of the wind and the rumble of the two engines. In her look, she subsumed life and death. When she smiled, a chill split his cranium and discharged along his spine. Something gleamed on her breast.

John swerved the Jeep toward the Pontiac.

The driver swore in Spanish as the Jeep rammed his car and pulled hard on the wheel to veer away from John.

"Pull over, *amigo!*"

The driver darted glances at John and pulled ahead of him, but John punched the accelerator and swerved in front of the Pontiac. The old car went right and skidded to a halt. The driver jumped out, leaving his door open, and ran around the back of the Jeep where John met him.

"*Qué te pasa?*" The man's hoarse voice cut across the wind. He punched John's shoulder with the heel of his hand.

"*No hablo español.*"

John brushed past the man, knocking him into the Jeep's trunk as he did so. He'd almost reached the Pontiac's right taillight when the man grabbed his left arm and spun him around. The first punch landed on his chin, but the second one John blocked. He grabbed a handful of hibiscus flowers and pulled the man closer to him.

"Look, I bet you *comprende ingles muy bien*. So listen up: I need to talk to Ana and I'm either gonna do it with you standing or with you flat on your back. If you're in such a hurry to get somewhere that you won't stop unless someone runs you off the road, I'd think you'd want me to leave you able to drive when I'm done with her. Got it?"

The other man's eyes darted from side to side as John spoke, but when John finished, he nodded once sharply. John pushed him away and the man staggered into the Pontiac. He didn't move, but watched John make his way around to the passenger side where Ana waited, smoking a clove cigarette.

She looked at John, the cigarette held between her lips with the first two fingers of her right hand. She dragged on the cigarette and exhaled into the wind, which snatched the fragrant blue smoke and whisked it into oblivion.

"Where is she?"

She shrugged.

In the eerie bright overcast, John glimpsed a Goddess figure on a black cord around her neck. The stone in its belly winked as she moved. He reached into the window and snatched the cigarette out of her fingers and flung it away.

"I know you know where she is."

"*La mujer del mar?*" The wind tore at the driver's words, flinging them at John's head like darts.

John looked across the front seat of the Pontiac. The man bent now and looked back at him from the other side.

"*Sí.*"

"*Jesus la sacó.*"

"What'd he say about Jesus?" John held his face near Ana's wrinkled one.

"He said that Jesus took her." Her fingers dropped to the Goddess around her neck and lifted it. Almost immediately, she dropped it back onto her shirt as if it burned her. "She wanted to be with him during the hurricane."

"No." The other man frowned. "*No es la verdad. Jesus la agarró.*" He mimed putting his arms around someone and pulling her with him.

Ana scowled and pinched her lips together.

"Where did you get that?" John pointed to the Goddess.

Ana looked down at her chest. "I found it."

"Give it to me."

She snapped her face up and looked at him. "No."

John ignored her eyes and stared instead at the glistening wire-wrapped stone in the figure's belly. Suddenly he reached into the window, grasped the Goddess, and yanked. Ana yelped. The black cord broke at the juncture with the figure, which remained in John's fist. Ana screeched and lunged, but John pulled his arm to his side and stepped away from the Pontiac. She released the door latch and began to swing the door open.

"*Amigo*, don't you have someplace to go?" John backed away from the Pontiac.

"Ay!" The man opened his car door and slid into the driver's seat. "*Carme! Tenemos que ir ahora! No tenemos tiempo para esta tontería!*"

Ana paused, her right leg outside the open car door and her hand grasping the open window. She looked at Jaime and then back at John, who now stood near the rear bumper of the Pontiac. In this dark frame, she seemed shrunken, contained. The wind howled around her, tousling her hair, and nipping at her skirt hem. At its sudden ferocity, John realized that it had stilled during their conversation. Without saying another word, she tucked her leg back inside the car's cavity and slammed the door. Its rattle underscored her silence.

John ran back to the Jeep and jumped into the driver's seat. In its close interior, he brought the Goddess up where he could study it. He'd seen several dozen of these figures lying about Valerie's kitchen and at The Mermaid's Purse. This one appeared to be identical to all those others. Absently, he rubbed the stone with his thumb. After a moment, he set the figure on the dash behind the wheel and started the Jeep. He pulled out onto 250 without looking and drove, only vaguely aware of the road in front of him. Around him, the empty sky appeared a hazy bright citrine; where he could see the harbor on his right through the dark fringe of mangrove and thorny scrub, the sickly tint contrasted with the dull aquamarine of the seawater. The road hugged the ragged coastline, wending south and north along its many coves and channels as if nature would not be hurried. As he drove, the storm held its breath.

He'd nearly passed the Wildlife Refuge Office when he saw the black car that he'd seen a few minutes earlier parked on its far side. Teresa, the wildlife manager, drove a green Chevy. John braked and turned, cutting a wide swath across the dusty verge as the Jeep skidded toward the driveway leading to the office. He pulled in front of the low concrete building and shifted into park. As he did, he realized that his breath came in gasps. For a moment, his vision dimmed as his chest constricted and the heat enveloped him in its wet wool. Then he managed to wrench open the driver's side door. Overhead, the sky had darkened and the wind picked up again.

John started to get out of the Jeep when a glint caught the corner of his eye. He stretched forward and snagged the Goddess figure from the dash and pocketed it. He slid his hand into his pocket and his fingers found the smooth gemstone. Its warmth calmed him and his breathing eased. He walked to the office door, his eyes squinting to catch any sign of movement. Plywood covered the windows and he heard nothing.

He rapped on the door with his left hand. When he got no response, he tried the doorknob. It was locked. He backed up and rammed the door with his left shoulder. The Goddess lying against his palm thrummed as if alive. A moment later, the door burst open.

Overhead, a fluorescent light hummed, its bright light dazzling him after the near-twilight outside. In front of him stood an old metal desk, large and sharp-cornered and dun-colored like the decade in which it was manufactured. Forms and documents fluttered around the small room as the wind swirled in behind him, searching for something or someone in the stuffy space. On the wall behind the desk hung an institutional wall clock like the kind he'd seen throughout childhood at school. Underneath it stood two old metal filing cabinets, gray and impervious. The sharp scent of burned coffee mingled with the smell of dusty carpets, stale perfume, and body odor.

John took a few steps around the end of the desk and stopped. On the floor before him lay Tamarind, a gag in her mouth and her arms awkwardly wrenched underneath her. Her t-shirt had been sliced open down the middle and her breasts lay exposed. Other than the ravaged t-shirt, she wore only a pair of pink underwear. She stared at him, unseeing. The pupils of her eyes had widened so much that the ultramarine of her irises had nearly disappeared. She looked odd. For a few wrenching heartbeats, John couldn't comprehend why. And then he understood: her head had been shorn of its signature tresses. The manic copper curls lay forlornly in severed clumps about her on the floor and scattered across her chest. Long strands sprinkled her face and blurred her features.

"Tamarind!"

He crossed the distance between them without being aware that he moved and sank down on his knees at her side. She blinked several times and made no sound. Gently, he rotated her head until he could pick at the knot in the gag, but he couldn't untie it. The bindings on her wrist had also been tied too tightly for him to manage with his fingertips. While he struggled with the knots, Tamarind lay still and silent. John sat back and grunted, running his fingers beneath his hair and raking his nails into the scalp. As he did so, the

Goddess in his pocket burned his thigh through his pants and he yelped.

He dislodged the wire figure from the confines of his pocket and held it by the head away from him. Tamarind slowly turned her face towards it. Awareness precipitated in her eyes after the trajectory of her gaze intersected the gem's soft beam and her pupils shrank back to normal. Her eyes slid up to John's face and held his.

An electric shock surged through the figure and up John's hand to his spine. Something dark and steady swirled inside his chest and his eyesight sharpened. He leaned forward, rolled her onto her side and his fingers deftly untied what had seemed impossible only a moment before. Ignoring the tufts of hair clinging to the rough material, he quickly untied the gag. He picked it out of her mouth as carefully as he would have picked shards of glass from the sole of a child. When the cloth came away in his hands, he saw that it had rubbed the corners of her mouth raw. Tamarind worked her lips, but no sounds emerged. John laid a finger across her lips and she calmed. He flung the rough gag away and then set the Goddess into her palm, wrapping her fingers around it. He rested her hands across her heart.

The floor creaked behind him. Tamarind's eyes slid sideways and widened.

John swiveled his head toward the sound in time to see a blurred figure and metal winking. In the space between breaths, he flinched.

Twenty
❧

JOHN FELL AWAY FROM THE RUSH OF FLESH and shadow that descended upon him. Rasping breaths filled his ears and the office walls contracted around him, burying him underneath an avalanche of clothing, carpet, and a tangle of limbs and hair. Bodies squirmed around him and John flailed his arms and legs in response. As he jerked and heaved, memories surfaced and blotted out the reality of the office. Memories of seawater drumming in his ears, of salt burning his eyes, and of choking. White spots blossomed onto his darkened vision and his chest clogged shut.

Breathe. Just breathe.

Humming echoed inside his skull and his body responded of its own accord. His lungs opened a little and his vision cleared. His world had gone topsy-turvy. Papers flew around the office like dazed birds mistakenly trapped inside a glass building. Tamarind squatted near him on the floor, her shorn head forlorn in the fluorescent light and shadows obscuring her features. She held the Goddess between her knees. Her feet were bare.

John rolled a little to the left and saw Jesus propped on one hand and two knees; he held the other hand to the right side of his face. When he heard John move, Jesus lifted his head so that John saw the blood that streamed from his damaged right eye. He lurched toward John and tumbled onto him, scrabbling at John's neck until he'd found a purchase with his blood-glazed fingers. John clawed at Jesus' fingers, kicking his heels into the floor. Again, Tamarind's voice floated through his thoughts like a memory, or an epiphany.

Remember the pearl divers?

John closed his eyes. An image of a long dive filled his mind and he relaxed. He clearly saw the oyster shell waiting for him. Then Tamarind appeared next to him, her copper hair fluttering about her in the current and she smiled. She slipped her hand into his and together they swam to the bottom. Together, they reached down and lifted the oyster shell up. When John pried it open, a luminous pearl sat cushioned on the oyster's flesh. As he blinked, dazzled, Jesus' fingers released his neck.

John, surface now.

He opened his eyes and saw Jesus kneeling in front of Tamarind, who once again lay on her back. The Goddess gleamed in the dark recesses under the desk and the wind had taken on a life of its own. Now it was a banshee, howling through the office and sending papers whirling madly; now a poltergeist who ripped at the corkboard on the wall. The blinds on the windows danced and rattled. Jesus, impervious to the character of the wind, fumbled with his belt.

"*Ahora, mi cariño, ahora.* You will have a fucking like you have never had, *mi querida. Esto te prometo.*"

He lowered himself onto her.

John levered himself off the floor and launched himself onto Jesus' back. Clawing at Jesus' shirt, he managed to grasp enough cloth with both hands to wrench the other man off Tamarind. His breath grunted from deep in his chest, but his chest remained open, expanded—light. Again, the electricity that he'd felt only a few moments before while holding the wire Goddess charged through him; this time it rushed through every nerve in his system until he felt illuminated from within. He threw Jesus away from him.

Jesus fell into the desk and yelled. Clutching his side, he stood up and turned to face John, who had pulled Tamarind behind him. John darted a glance at her. She sat, listing to one side, one hand propping her upright and the other hand limp across her torn underwear. When he swung his head back, Jesus flashed his knife, which had fallen under the chair during their earlier struggle. The jagged gash along the inside corner of Jesus' right eye distorted his features and gave him a sinister, alien appearance. Dried blood and mucous—accidental war paint applied with fate's indifferent hand—bisected his cheek.

"Ssst." Air hissed through Jesus' clenched teeth. He swiped the knife at John, who barely arched his back in time to pull his stomach out of its path. "You think you're so *listo*, *gringo*. How smart are you now, eh?"

He tossed the knife to the opposite hand and swung at John again. Again, John avoided the blade. The third time, Jesus feinted to the right and John moved left; the blade traced a path across his abdomen. John understood that Jesus had sliced him, but he felt nothing. Instead, he watched as the wind caught Jesus on the far point of his pendulous arc, overbalancing him. For a moment, Jesus hung suspended in an invisible swing and then John stepped into him, shoving him into the desk. Jesus grunted as his battered side crashed into the sharp edge of the steel desk. John kicked at Jesus' bent legs and the other man collapsed, cracking his face on the desk as he fell. He lay in a crumpled heap and made no sound.

John ignored him and spun back to Tamarind, who had slid over onto her side on the rough institutional gray carpet. The t-shirt had fallen open and he saw her belly rise and fall in shallow breaths. Her skin had pallor to it that he'd never seen before. It clung to her frame, revealing fine details in bone structure and hollows under her ribcage and cheekbones. Tamarind had always been slight, but now she appeared almost emaciated, as fragile as onionskin stretched over a frame of hollow reeds.

He took a step towards her and the wound across his stomach burned and stung so sharply that he winced. She opened her eyes and looked at him. They were huge, too huge, and a dull blue like arctic seawater.

"You're hurt." Her voice no longer lilted. She sounded far away and traveling still.

"Not much. The other geeks will be in awe when I show them the scar."

He knelt at her side, consigning the pain in his gut to the recesses of his mind where it belonged.

"Tamarind, I know you're *del mar*. Did you–did you leave the sea for me?"

She took several breaths before she answered. Her eyes watched his face. "Yes." She raised a hand to his cheek; it was hot and dry. "I fell in love with you the day you came to Culebra and climbed that mangrove tree … near the canal."

John pulled her hand into his and then touched her lips with his other hand. They were cracked and bled a little.

"You need water, don't you?"

She nodded, almost imperceptibly.

"There's water in the Jeep." He glanced over at Jesus, who hadn't moved since he'd slithered to the floor. "I'll go get some and bring it back to you."

He stood up, feeling as if his gut had come unhinged and might swing open, spilling everything inside. He braced himself for the onslaught of compressed air from the doorway, but in that moment the wind abated. He hobbled toward the open door, anticipating a fresh blast, but it didn't come. He paused in the doorway. Outside, the sky had darkened to a premature nighttime and the air smelled wet. The oppressive heat from earlier in the afternoon had disappeared as the air pressure dropped. John looked south toward the harbor and saw the palms bent horizontal and the thorny thickets shaking as if in the grip of a fever; rain blurred the edges of trees and buildings alike. He ducked his head and ran.

In the trunk of the Jeep he found a case of water that he'd meant to unload for Valerie. He hefted it, resting it on his hip as a mother rests her toddler, and shuffled awkwardly back to the refuge office. Once inside, he stopped to catch his breath and swing his gaze from Jesus' body to Tamarind, lying with her eyes closed. The slight rise and fall of her chest reassured him that she hadn't been completely desiccated yet.

He set the water on the desktop and broke the plastic seal. Grabbing a bottle, he twisted the cap off and then knelt by her side, gently lifting her until he could prop her against his bent knee. Her head lolled forward and he slipped his left hand behind to steady it. His fingers snagged on her truncated tendrils, but he ignored his first touch of her head after so many weeks of imagining it and instead focused on tipping the bottle between her parted lips. Most of what he poured dribbled out of her and down her chin and neck, but he persisted. When he saw the water on her skin disappear as if absorbed directly, he poured more recklessly. Tamarind choked and coughed, her eyelids fluttering open and then she raised a thin hand to his holding the bottle. Their gaze met and held.

Tamarind drank five one-liter bottles of water without stopping. By the last one, John had surrendered the bottle to her and had opened three more with which to douse her body. Her skin and soft tissues rehydrated enough that she no longer looked as if she was on the verge of collapsing in on herself, but John suspected that her condition remained precarious.

"You need to get back into the ocean, don't you?"

Tamarind set the empty water bottle down and shifted so that she could lean more comfortably against his bent leg.

"Yes."

"You look so human, it's hard to believe. ..." Here he touched her legs delicately, just a brush of fingertips and nothing more.

"I *am* human—almost anyway. I've been living between two worlds, *mer* and human, all summer. Even though I have legs, I can't stray too far from Mother Sea."

"Where should I take you?"

She closed her eyes as if thinking about where they should go exhausted her.

"You've got to return to town, John, before the hurricane hits. It isn't safe to be out any longer."

"I won't return until I know you'll be all right."

She opened her eyes. The pupils had returned to their normal size, but they still looked as cold and hopeless as the arctic sea.

"Take me to the nearest water and leave me."

Before they left the wildlife refuge office, John shoved Jesus' limp form under the steel office desk. As he did so, he spied the Goddess figure lying on the carpet under the desk's dark bulk and he pulled it out and put it into his pocket. He'd found an old woven Mexican blanket in the Jeep's back seat and he brought it to wrap around the nearly naked Tamarind. Then he lifted her in his arms as if he were lifting a hatchling that had fallen from its nest. The knife wound in his stomach protested, but he ignored it. While he carried her to the backseat of the Jeep, the wind and rain avoided their path as if an invisible shield hung over them. John eased Tamarind down into a lying position and then returned to get the last of the bottled water and to shut the door.

When he got into the Jeep, he turned to look at Tamarind, who lay with her eyes closed. Her face had filled out again, but she was still pale; dark shadows smudged the skin under her eyes. The bright red and green of the blanket accentuated her pallor, nearly swallowing her in its cocoon. Too much space existed between them, a dark chasm of the unknown and the unknowable. He stretched out a hand and touched her on the hip. Her eyes fluttered open.

"We'll be there soon, I promise."

"I know."

He turned back around and his hand slipped away from her. The air remained eerily still around the Jeep and he found himself expecting the wind and rain to return and break upon them as waves break upon a rocky shore. It did not. So he started the Jeep and backed away from the office, heading west toward Dewey and shelter. As he drove, the stillness around the Jeep moved with them so that the rain and wind always remained thirty feet beyond them.

Earlier, he'd refused to listen to the radio. Now he turned it on: he needed to know how much time he had before hurricane winds reached Culebra and anyone left outside became chaff before Marilyn's obdurate scythe. Marilyn's eye currently passed over the east end of St. Croix and the airport on the southwest of that island reported winds ranging up to 97 miles an hour. The Miami Hurricane Center had upgraded her to category two and strengthening toward a category three. As she moved through the Caribbean, she dropped torrents of rain along her outer edges.

Even at her current speed, Marilyn wouldn't pass over Culebra for four or five more hours. John squinted out the window as the Jeep reached the intersection with 251. He would make it to Posada La Diosa provided that whatever kept the wind and rain at bay continued to do so for the next half an hour. He turned off the radio and turned north.

"Is there any music?" Tamarind's voice startled him in the quiet.

John looked at her in the review mirror. Her face held a little more color and the dark smudges had lightened. In the dim light of the Jeep's interior and with the blanket obscuring her head, she looked almost normal.

"I don't know. I'll see if I can find any."

He switched the radio back on and twisted the dial, looking for something other than weather, news, or pop music from the States. At last he found a Cuban station playing Lito Peña's *Yo Vivo Enamorado*. As its smooth saxophone and cheerful rhythms incongruously filled the Jeep, John found himself humming along and remembering the warm summer evening when he'd first heard the song with Tamarind. The memory of her singing and swinging a dripping Popsicle, her wild hair dancing around her face, brought tears to his eyes.

"I wish it was turtle-watching season right now." Tamarind hummed a little with the song, but her hum didn't reach her chest and none of her joyful clicking joined in as a counterpoint.

"Me too."

On the east side of the road, wild horses stood huddled under a tree. Several eyed the Jeep as it passed and John wondered what would happen to them when Marilyn's full force bore down on Culebra. He realized that no one had mentioned any of the wildlife, outside of the departure of the nesting seabirds, during the frantic preparations of the last twenty-four hours. What would happen to Valerie's beloved hummingbirds and bananaquits? Where would they go? Or what about the rooster and hens that walked so freely around town as if parading through their demesne? Would Marilyn devastate the wild things that galloped and strolled, hovered and glided, slithered and hopped around Culebra's preserves? He came to the fork in the road where the left branch headed toward Playa Flamenco and the right toward Punta Flamenco and Playa Resaca. Between the two branches lay Laguna Flamenco, protected from the Atlantic by the pristine sands of Playa Flamenco. He knew at once where to bring Tamarind.

He took the left toward Playa Flamenco and parked in the empty sandlot. When he slid Tamarind into his arms, she sighed and leaned into his chest. He lifted her from the seat and brought her closer, trying to block the wind and rain with his back even though neither wind nor rain touched them. A thickness sealed off his throat as he clutched her to him, but his breathing remained even and steady. In his pocket, he felt the Goddess burn and a dark, steady power buoyed him. When his wound began to bleed again, he scarcely felt it.

He trudged over the sandy path to the beach and then through the thorn thickets and between palm and mangrove trees to reach the lagoon. As he walked by the trees, an odd vibrating filled his chest and the rustling of their leaves almost made sense to him, as if their whisperings called to mind something long-forgotten that was on the tip of his tongue.

He reached the lagoon, winded and exhausted. Tamarind had lain still and quiet in his arms and he'd lost himself to the effort of getting to his destination, forgetting for the few minutes that it took him to get there why he'd come. He stood in front of the water in the gloom of the storm-darkened evening, his arms aching and his mind blank.

"John."

He looked down at Tamarind, who looked up at him with eyes as dark as a mountain river in winter.

"John, please put me in the water. I'll be fine."

He nodded once sharply and stepped forward. The surface of the lagoon frothed under the continuous caress of the passionate wind. He expected to struggle to the water's edge, but instead he felt again the dark energy that had aided him. Now it flowed from the ground and up through his legs, passing through the Goddess with an electric burst and up to his head where it settled into a thousand bees buzzing in his thoughts.

He dropped first to one knee and then the other, holding Tamarind against the rise and fall of his chest. She looked at him again, eyes wide and unblinking, and he slowly lowered her into the lagoon. The blanket opened a little and she struggled against its clinging folds. John freed one hand from under her knees and pulled the blanket away. Her lower half slipped under water and she sighed. John felt a faint

269

vibration in her torso and he knew that she hummed, even if the sound couldn't make it out of her chest.

"You must let me go so you can go."

"I know." Still he didn't lower her completely into the water.

"You're bleeding again." She touched his shirt with a fingertip. "You need someone to take care of you."

"I told you it's nothing."

She flinched at his tone and he felt his heart twist in his chest.

"Don't worry about me. I'll find someone at the clinic to take a look at me. I've got a few hours to kill before Marilyn gets here anyway." His words didn't come out flippantly as he intended. They sounded grim instead. "How will I find you after the hurricane?

"You won't." A voice growled at him from a few feet across the lagoon.

When he looked up, John saw a man in the water up to his chest. His long hair flowed in tangled rivers down his massive shoulders, one of which had an angry braided scar bisecting it diagonally. The blue of his eyes left no doubt who, or what, he was.

"Father!" Tamarind lifted her head and upper body away from John.

The hollow where she had lain only moments before ached with its cold emptiness.

Twenty-one

☙

TAMARIND PULLED HERSELF AWAY FROM JOHN at her father's voice, a sound of sand washing over broken rocks. She was a bare promontory, exposed and cold after the shelter of John's arms. Above them, the anxious wind, which had abated during their trip from the refuge office, keened through the treetops and whirled around her bare head. Fine icy raindrops prickled on her face and upper chest; she shivered even though the water in the lagoon was warm as blood.

"Release her, human." Her father spoke in a low, flat voice. His mind resembled the ocean at midday under a blazing sun; its impenetrable surface reflected Tamarind's silent entreaties, dazzling her inner eye.

John did as her father bid and she slid completely under the water, her face submerging. Her diving membranes, unused for months, slid noticeably into place. For a moment she lay there, soaking the water into her pores and extracting oxygen. Here, in the dense atmosphere so like her mother's womb, the raw world outside no longer threatened. Only distorted sounds reached her ears and for an instant even these soothed her. But the fluorescent light of the refuge office flashed across the murk in front of her, and again a dark figure bent over her.

She sat up. An awful sound met her ears and she flinched. Then she realized the sound emanated from her throat.

Before she could say anything, her father erupted across the lagoon, launching himself at John. He swept past her in the water, his powerful tail churning it until it foamed. His wake washed over her; when the water had streamed out of her eyes and nose, she blinked and saw her father gripping John's neck. She stared at his rigid, alien tail.

"What have you done to her, you vile squid? What happened to her hair?"

John clawed at her father's hands and arms, gurgling and choking over the implacable fingers.

Let him go, Father!

Her father ignored her. Instead, he shook John as easily as a shark brandishes a mouthful of whale flesh. John's head snapped back and fresh blood soaked his torn shirt.

No, Father, don't! Standing, she pushed her feet down into the mud of the lagoon and its ooze calmed her. The lovely dark energy she'd felt earlier at Playa Tamarindo surged through her and she stood. Water dripped off of her bare skin; she'd lost her ravaged t-shirt in the lagoon.

Father. The dark energy smoothed and deepened her voice, carrying it easily through the shrillness of the wind.

Her father looked at her, his eyes steely-blue and turbulent. John hung limp from his hands, rasping a few breaths around his grip. He'd lost his ponytail holder somewhere during the afternoon and his tangled hair hung

272

around his face. In the storm's twilight his skin had the bleached look of old driftwood or dead coral.

What is it, daughter?

Tamarind switched to speaking aloud. "Let him go. He's not responsible for my hair."

Her father kept his hands on John's throat, but he didn't shake him again.

Does it really matter? He's responsible for you putting off your tail, isn't he?

"No. I am."

I'll deal with you later. You're coming home. Back to the sea where we belong. Where you belong, with your sisters and your community.

"Not if you don't let him go."

You think you love this human, don't you? Don't you realize how vile, how abominable, they are?

"I know about Mother."

Her father's eyes dilated until she couldn't see any trace of the blue and his hands tightened around John's throat. John tugged weakly at them and then slumped into her father's grip.

How could you lie to me? How could you put off your tail and walk among these foul creatures knowing what they did to her? To me? He turned so that his scar gleamed in the dim light.

"They aren't like grains of sand, one as alike as another, Father. I have spent enough time with them to see them as they are. Many of them are worth knowing. Some worth loving." She kept her gaze on his face, but her heart beat against the cave of her ribs.

Bah! This jellyfish? He's only good for feeding bottom dwellers.

"If you kill him now, when he's done nothing wrong to you, then you're no better than the men who killed Mother." Her voice remained steady, but she heard her breath, ragged and shallow.

The wind calmed after she spoke, and so did the world around them. Trees and shrubs slumped at the respite and the lagoon, which had slapped at calves and the merman's muscular tail, subsided to a flat expanse of murky water. Her father stood immobile, silent and terrible.

"Put him down, Father, and I'll come with you."

When her father said nothing, she stepped forward and touched the back of his hands with her fingers. Her fingertips felt frozen on his cool skin and she dropped them hastily, waiting. He grunted and released John, who fell into the lagoon and crumpled to his knees so that the brackish water reached his chest.

Tamarind knelt beside him and touched his face. He raised his eyes, green as the leaves of mangrove, of tamarind, of palm—of all the trees and shrubs and flowers that she'd grown to love on Culebra. "Good-bye, John. May the Creator bless you."

His mouth opened, but nothing came out. His lips moved futilely, like a fish lying on its side on the beach suffocating in the open air. Keeping his eyes on her face, he fumbled for an instant with something below the surface of the lagoon and then lifted the small wire-wrapped moonstone Goddess, dripping and gleaming, up between them. He held it out to her and when she brought her hand up to accept it, his fingers clasped hers, hard.

Come, daughter, we go now before the fury of the storm whips the sea beyond my strength.

Tamarind extricated her hand from John's grip and looked steadfastly toward the sea as her father hoisted her onto his back, although she couldn't see it through the trees and scrub north of the lagoon. She knew from her walks on Culebra that the beach at the far northeastern corner narrowed until almost nothing remained between ocean and lagoon; her father would head there for the shortest path back to Mother Sea and safety. The full force of the storm loomed on the southern horizon and when it reached the island, it would devastate it. She felt nothing, no fear nor sorrow at the thought of mangled homes, trees ripped by the roots from the soil and denuded, birds and horses and giant anoles drowned or flung against concrete and rock.

Her father swam with one arm bent back to hold her around her waist—her own indifferent hands slack around his neck, the Goddess dangling against his chest—and they'd nearly reached the corner of the lagoon when the winds died again and she heard splashing behind them. Her father quit swimming and turned awkwardly in the shallow water to peer back toward the spot where they'd left John. The sky had darkened so much that she knew John would have trouble seeing.

"Tamarind! Tamarind!" The wind enlarged and directed his voice so that it reached them easily. "Don't go. Stay with me."

A faint surge of electricity prickled around them and her father shifted. The muscles in his back bunched and tightened. When she reached her thoughts out for his, his mind had darkened and again closed to her. He looked out toward John, whose head appeared as a darker splotch against the dusky lagoon. He said nothing, but waited. After moments long enough for them to reach the open ocean and race away, John neared, slapping the water with heavy arms that hardly cleared the surface of the lagoon. He stopped to look for them every few strokes. Against her father's chest, the Goddess glowed faintly even though the clouds hid sun, moon, and stars.

Her father took the Goddess from her hand and rubbed his thumb over the moonstone gem. *It calls to him.*

She didn't respond, only shivered against his back.

This stone is warm, almost alive. You imprinted a part of yourself on it when you wrapped it within this figure.

She clutched his neck. *It's only a piece of jewelry, nothing more. Throw it into the lagoon and take me away.* Even the rain now falling over them felt warmer than her chilled skin. *Please, let's go, Father.*

I cannot. His imprint is on it, too. His blood and his care for you have altered its essence indelibly. You are both bound by whatever magic lies wrapped inside it.

Tamarind closed her eyes, trying again to see into her father's thoughts, but they had taken on the polished sheen of obsidian.

"Tamarind." John's voice, a few tail lengths away, sounded frail. He'd stopped swimming and only his head bobbed above the water. As the sound of her name faded, his head disappeared. It appeared again, but only long enough for him to lift his face to draw a breath and then it slid a final time below the surface.

Before Tamarind could respond, her father lashed his tail against the lagoon, propelling them to the spot where John had slipped under. Without pausing, her father dived under the surface and black water pressed on Tamarind's eardrums and eyes. She started choking before the valve in her throat closed and her skin extracted oxygen from the water around her. Her diving membranes descended and she saw John's pale face; his open eyes stared at them.

Tamarind let go of her father's neck and swam towards John. She grabbed at his hand; his fingers curled around her wrist. She kicked her awkward legs against the enveloping water and reached upward with her free arm. Suddenly her father grabbed her hand and she soared to the surface. Next to her, John's head broke free, but she knew that he'd taken in water and couldn't breathe on his own. Before she could plead with her father, he'd pulled both of them up onto the bank and turned John onto his side. Sheets of rain washed over them until her father wove a spell in the air, surrounding them with an invisible bubble into which no wind or rain penetrated.

For several moments, they said nothing. Her father bent John's prone form over one thick forearm and began massaging his back with the other hand. In a moment John vomited copious amounts of brackish water and he coughed and choked violently afterwards. Her father waved his hand over John, murmuring until he grew limp and quiet. Then he lay John down again on the ground.

In the dark, her father's eyes glistened. He studied her face for some time before speaking. "Live well, daughter, and know that I'll love you until the stars fall from the sky and the oceans dry up."

Tamarind stepped closer to her father and into his embrace. Warm saltwater dampened her cheeks and blinded her eyes. Until now, she hadn't known what she would give up when she left the ocean behind. After the briefest interval, her father pulled back, kissed her gently on the forehead, and then eased her down onto the ground next to John.

Farewell, Father. Until the stars fall. Until the oceans dry up.

And then he'd slipped out of the bubble and heaved himself onto the sandy bridge to the ocean and disappeared into the roiling night.

They remained there on the lagoon's muddy bank, trapped between the ocean and Marilyn, in the protective bubble that Tamarind's father had woven in the air. Tamarind sat with her knees to her chest, shivering, while John lay inert at her side. Even though no wind penetrated the cocoon, its howling tore at her with vicious fingers. It sent rain at them with such a fury that Tamarind imagined waves crashing against rocky shores.

She had no way of knowing how long she sat there in the violent dark, but she'd grown so cold that her teeth began to chatter and her knees banged into each other even though she wrapped her arms around them tightly. She remembered the warm ooze at the bottom of the lagoon when she'd stood in front of her father and she wanted to lie down in that ooze, to wrap its velvety embrace around her. Occasionally the winds died down for a moment and she heard the lagoon slapping fitfully at the ground where they sat, unable to proceed higher up the bank. If John hadn't lain there next to her, she could have escaped into the lagoon and anchored herself among the mangrove roots. She shook her head and rocked on her buttocks a little. If John hadn't lain there next to her, she would have returned with her father to the sea.

She lowered her face to her knees and breathed into her cupped palms. As she did so, she saw the Goddess lying on the ground next to her. When she picked it up, it radiated a steady heat that set her to shivering even more violently. She curled herself around her hands, holding the figure against her abdomen where it warmed her enough that she finally stopped shaking.

"Hey." John pushed himself up to a sitting position, wincing. He looked towards her, but she knew that he couldn't see her. "Where are we?"

"Inside my father's glamour, on the edge of the lagoon. We won't be able to stay here when the heart of the storm moves over us. The waves from the waters to the north will surge over the beach and flood this lagoon. My father's protection won't be able to hold against them."

"You should have gone with your father. No need to save me a second time only to have a hurricane sweep me away."

"You won't be swept away." She reached out and touched his knee. She left her hand there. "We'll take the road up Mt. Resaca together and shelter in the tower until Marilyn is far out to sea."

"That sounds like a walk in the park." His tone belied his words. "Okay, let's do it then. I can't see so well in this crap so you'll have to take point."

"'Take point'?"

"Lead."

"Okay. You hold her then." She handed the Goddess to him. The moonstone glowed enough that his fingers found hers without fumbling.

"She's so warm. Makes the night seem colder still." He lifted the figure up next to his eyes and looked at Tamarind through the sphere of light she gave off. "Holy crap! You're blue!"

He scooted behind her and wrapped his arms and legs around her. The Goddess dangled in front of them, her beam swaying as John's arms pulled Tamarind closer.

She leaned back against his damp t-shirt. "My senses tell me we need to go while the winds are still gusting. In a few hours, they will shriek without let up."

He said nothing, only held her against him for a moment. When he released her, she pushed herself up and away to stand. Her toes splayed against the muddy ground and she wobbled a little until her balance asserted itself. Behind her, John stood up as well.

"Which way, sir?" She knew he meant it as a joke, but his voice trembled.

She took his hand. "This way."

Putting her hand through her father's protective glamour, she dismissed it and stepped away from the lagoon. Mt. Resaca loomed over them, a darker shadow within the night's enveloping penumbra. Together, they plunged into the cascade, their hands a lifeline between them.

❧❧❧

Tamarind clutched John's hand as hail tattooed her chest and stung her face and scalp. Not far off to her left the ocean, already frenzied beyond understanding, no longer offered her any strength or comfort. The alien drops in the air around them hissed static in her thoughts and refused to yield to her numb fingertips. She could weave no protective shield around them as her father had done and whatever benign force had aided them earlier as they drove from the refuge office had disappeared in the merciless onslaught. The gusts abated for a moment and she pulled John forward a few steps before bracing for another rush; as they walked across the grain of the storm's path, every fresh gust threatened to hurl them to the sea.

During one of these brief interludes, John swung the Goddess into the hand that held hers; now they cradled the figure between their interlocked fingers. Warmth radiated up Tamarind's arm and down her trunk, flowing into her feet and then into the ground. The dark, rich energy hummed inside her and flowed back through the Goddess to John, linking them more securely than their joined hands. When the wind next whirled around them, it barely rocked them where they stood. Tamarind lowered her head and trudged forward, moving through the rain as easily as if she swam in a calm sea. They passed through the first line of trees and thorn acacia lining the eastern edge of the lagoon and the strength of the winds diminished noticeably. John came up beside her and they picked their way side-by-side through the low-lying groundcover to the road that led up the western flank of Mount Resaca. He kept one arm across his abdomen as they climbed.

Half an hour later, they'd reached the top of Mount Resaca and the observation tower there, panting and bleeding from a myriad thorn scratches. When Tamarind twisted the doorknob on its only door, it remained stubbornly closed.

"It's locked."

"Of course it is."

John stepped around her and battered the door with his shoulder. It didn't budge. After a moment, he held the glowing moonstone figure up and studied the door, whose red paint had long been weathered to a pale echo of itself. In the faint light, he was a *moulos*, a dark water sprite with tangled hair and hidden eyes. She blinked and willed the image away. He reached above her and she felt him tugging at something along the doorframe.

"Good thing this is an old door and no one thought to put locking pins on the hinges. Here." He held a short stick-like item toward her. "Hold this."

She took it; it was rough and heavy and made of metal. John's body rocked beside her as he worked the second and third pins out of the hinges. After each pin slid free, he handed it to her and then he gave her the Goddess. She pressed the small figure between her breasts.

"You might want to stand over there for a moment." He gestured away from the doorway.

She stepped back a few steps and he lifted the door away from the doorframe and propped it against the doorway so that there was a space big enough for them to enter.

"C'mon." John turned and caught her hand before leading her into the black interior of the tower.

They shuffled along the curving outside wall toward the far side away from the partially open doorway. John, who walked ahead of Tamarind, stopped abruptly and swore.

"What?" Tamarind found herself whispering.

"I just ran into the stairs. Can you hold up that Goddess so we can at least make out shapes in this pitch black?"

Tamarind grasped the Goddess by the head and dangled her at the end of her extended arm. The stairs leading up to the top of the tower came into vague outline. She swung the Goddess to the right and saw another door beneath the stairs.

"Ah, storage. Let's see if we can open this one, too." John tried the door handle and the door swung open easily. "Let me hold Her."

He took the Goddess and waved her around the space. "As far as I can tell, there's enough room for us to squat in here. It'll be warmer, I think." He took her arm and pulled her into the closet and shut the door.

They sank down onto the concrete floor. Tamarind brought her knees to her chest and wrapped her arms around them. Her shoulder touched John's arm and her flank rested against his soaking t-shirt and shorts. In the muffling darkness, their breathing rasped in unison like some monster from the fairy tales that she'd read that summer. She hummed a little and her breathing smoothed and slowed.

John's own breathing calmed somewhat. "I've missed hearing that. God, I've missed *you*."

Tamarind dropped her head to her knees. She tried to hold herself still, but her body shook beyond her control. Fluorescent light haloed her mind's eye, defining the dark figure that kept bending over her.

"I should have come for you yesterday. I'm sorry, Tamarind." His voice fractured on the last words; they lay between them as sharp as slivered glass. "But that doesn't help you, does it?"

They sat there without speaking and Tamarind bit her upper lip so hard she tasted blood. Its salty, mineral taste evoked the sea so strongly that she gasped and then the saltwater washed over her face. Mucous mingled with tears and blood and for a moment she knew nothing of her surroundings. When at last the waves stopped rolling through her, she brought her hands to her cheeks and wiped beneath her nose.

"Here." John wiggled next to her and then handed her his wet shirt. "Wipe your face with this."

As she wiped her face off, they heard the howling of the wind. It sent fingers of damp air under the door to the closet as if searching for them.

"Men killed your mother?" She could barely hear him over the wind.

"Drug runners killed her years ago."

"How did they find her? Couldn't she hide from them?"

She felt the breath sigh from her. "Yes. We *mer* have cloaking spells and glamour to protect us from people. But she didn't want to hide. Humans fascinated her. I think maybe she wanted to be human too."

"No wonder your father wanted to kill me." He shifted next to her and she felt his upper arm brush her nipple. She tingled where his skin had touched hers. "You said you were almost human. Will you always have to stay close to the ocean?"

"I only have legs until the end of the rainy season."

"That's November, isn't it?" She felt him hold his breath for her answer.

"Yes."

"And then you get your mermaid's tail back."

"Yes."

"And there's nothing I can do to stop it, is there?"

She hesitated.

"What?" His voice sounded sharp. "*Is* there something I can do?"

"I can keep my legs if I mate with a human." She almost didn't get the words out of her throat.

"Well, then, you're all set." The saltwater of his voice stung the scraped hollow of her chest so that it burned.

"What do you mean?"

"Jesus was just coming back for a little more, wasn't he? I mean, maybe he's a prick of the highest order who deserves to burn in hell, but he didn't exactly imagine that you'd be willing to have sex with him, did he? After all, you've already had sex with him on Punta Melones."

"What?" The word scarcely escaped her numb lips.

"You know I saw you. You looked right at me that night."

"What night?"

"What night? You gotta be kidding me. The night you and he went dancing at Isla Encantada."

"I didn't have sex with him. He clearly wanted me to, but I went back to Ana's." She wanted to leave this tower, plunge down Mount Resaca, and throw herself into the sea.

"It was you. I know what I saw. I went back later to Isla Encantada looking for you and while I was out, I found your Goddess. When I picked it up, I had the strongest urge to go to Punta Melones, and there you were under Jesus. You smiled at me and I dropped her—" here he held up the Goddess, "on the beach."

"I didn't make her until after you left Culebra, John. Valerie gave this moonstone to me, to give me hope that you'd come back." Saltwater slid down her cheeks again. "It wasn't me. It might have looked like me, but it wasn't me. What if I *had* given myself to Jesus? Are you telling me that you've never been with a woman? Are you telling me that you and Raimunda only ever went dancing? I heard the stories, John. I know you were with her, many times since you and I met."

John squirmed next to her. "I—"

"I think you saw what you wanted to see so you could leave Culebra and me. And now you believe what you want to believe so you won't have to act. I've waited all summer for you. I've never lain with a human even though I could have, and in a few weeks, I'll return to the sea. I won't come back, John. I won't come back." Convulsions shook her breathing and she felt lightheaded in the stifling dark.

They sat there for a long moment. The sound of John's breathing vanished and Tamarind pulled herself away from him and balled herself around her knees. She closed her eyes and hummed, rocking and weaving an ellipse in the air above her head. If she rocked long enough, her humming would clear her thoughts and the spell she wove would take hold. She would disappear inside a cloak of darkness. And then, in a silence so complete that she'd nearly closed off all awareness of John, she heard him inhale audibly.

"Tamarind." He breathed her name out steadily. "Tamarind."

She could feel him release and expand next to her. She stopped rocking and waited. He reached for her and touched her shoulder with a fingertip as light as the brush of an angelfish. She didn't pull away but held herself still. He brought his full hand down upon her shoulder tentatively; his palm was warm and his fingers firm. A surge of electricity, warm and dark, flowed down her arm and through her body, reaching the base of her spine and radiating through all of her limbs. Her breath grew shallow and the air in the closet grew close around them. Outside, the hurricane had arrived and the winds careened through the tower after flinging the loose entry door aside.

"I don't want to lose you. But I don't deserve the gift you want to give me."

She leaned toward him and he moved his hand up to her shorn head. When she cried out, he bent and kissed her head, and then he kissed the top of her ears, first the left and then the right. He kissed the back of her neck, and then he traced her face with the tips of his fingers. He held her cheeks gently and waited. She lifted her arms around his neck and he kissed her mouth at last.

He slid slow fingers over her shoulders and down her flanks and when she'd stopped trembling, he moved away from her and tugged off his shorts and sandals. And then he sat next to her. She extended her hand carefully, searching with her fingers until she felt his nearest hipbone. Moving her fingers across his abdomen, she touched the tender skin above the cut. He flinched. Murmuring, she laid her palm over it. Gradually, he relaxed and she knew the pain had faded from his awareness and the risk of renewed bleeding had gone. She raised her hand to his face; he turned, pressing his lips against her palm. By degrees he pulled her on top of him, as carefully as if she were sculpted from tissue paper, and wrapped his arms around her. He rocked her as the madness and fury descended upon the breathless world outside their tower, ripping tree and wall, shrub and roof in an ecstasy of obliteration. Together they wove a spell so exquisite that the foundations of heaven might have crumbled and still they would have known only the utter stillness of their breath.

Twenty-two

ೞ

MARILYN SLOWLY LOST STRENGTH, becoming first a tropical storm, and then a storm front, and finally dissipating out at sea, miles north and west of Culebra days later. The morning after she passed, John awoke to find Tamarind's head resting on his shoulder, her body curled in his lap. The storage closet in the observation tower where they huddled had lightened imperceptibly. The screaming winds and gunshot spray of rain mixed with hail had vanished, leaving a profound silence. He absorbed the feel of Tamarind against his chest, her silky scalp lying against his neck, and the slight weight of her buttocks on his thighs. He wanted to sit in this place so far from people and research and proposals, until they'd put down roots and transformed into a tree like some Greek nymph.

The reality of a full bladder, an empty stomach, an aching slash across his abdomen, and the soreness of scratches and bruises kept him from pursuing this option.

"Hey." He touched Tamarind's cheek.

She stirred and sighed. "It's quiet."

"Yeah, I guess we slept through the rest of the hurricane. I think it's still raining though."

She moved a little and he grunted. "Sorry." She brushed his wound with a fingertip.

"Oh, that's not the problem. You just pushed against a full bladder."

"Ah." She sat very still. "We can't stay here much longer. There's no food and I need something to wear."

"You sound disappointed."

"It's just that it seems so safe here. And private."

John ran his free hand along her flank, around the slight curve of her hip, and down her thigh. "Yes, private is good. Perhaps we can wait a bit longer to venture out into the world."

࣪ࣧ࣪ࣧ࣪ࣧ

Tamarind and John remained in the observation tower on Mount Resaca until the sun chased away the last of the rain later that morning and then they trudged down the road toward Playa Flamenco. John wore only his shorts and shoes; Tamarind had pulled on the remnants of his bloody t-shirt. She'd regained enough water since leaving the refuge office that she no longer looked emaciated and frail, but bruises purpled her arms and legs and angry scratches slashed her skin. A single long scratch marred her right cheek.

All around them lay scattered thorn acacia, ripped by the roots from the ground, and broken limbs from palm and mangrove trees. The rain and wind had gouged chunks from the land, leaving it pitted and vulnerable. Overhead, sooty terns and laughing gulls dotted the clear sky and they heard birds calling as they always did, as if the world below hadn't been devastated.

They found Valerie's Jeep sitting alone in the lot near the beach, thorny scrub caught under its chassis and in its rearview mirrors. A dead Puerto Rican ground dove lay on the Jeep's hood, its neck broken and its head lying sideways. They cleared the Jeep of the brush and carcass and drove to Ana's cinderblock house to get Tamarind's belongings. Fragments of the chicken coop and seagull house had embedded in the branches of nearby tamarind trees and littered the ground; patches of the blue tarps that had covered them had been caught on limbs and wrapped in eddies around rocks and tree trunks.

The plywood covering Ana's small windows had been hurled from sight and the glass shattered, but in the corner of her house the temporary chicken roost and its occupants remained unharmed. The birds chuckled and squawked when John and Tamarind entered. Tamarind tiptoed through the debris of Ana's home and peered into the plywood box. The chickens fluttered and complained; they had large raw-looking bald patches on their rumps and piles of feather and dung cluttered the floor. She hummed and clicked a little until the birds quieted and settled into sleep, their beaks tucked under a wing.

Together, she and John maneuvered down the hidden path to Playa Tamarindo where her cache of clothes, jewelry, and books remained untouched by the rapacious waves. She stripped John's t-shirt off after exposing her things, flinging the scrap away from her and into the waves where the current caught it and sent it south before it grew waterlogged and disappeared. He watched as she waded into the saltwater of the Luís Peña Canal until it covered her head. He waited without taking his eyes from the spot where she'd gone under. When she emerged, the sun glistening on water droplets in the stubble on her scalp, he let out his breath.

Tamarind stood for a moment on the empty beach among the litter of shells and seaweed, plucking something invisible from the air around her as she murmured. Within moments, the water on her had disappeared. She seemed scarcely to notice the pile of silky underwear lying like treasure near her clothes and grabbed the first one that her hand touched. After she'd stepped into these, she remained bent over while she pulled on a clean t-shirt and shorts. She knelt down and picked through the jewelry pile until she found a pendant on a gold chain. She stripped the pendant from the chain and dumped it onto the rocks without a second glance. The chain lay curled on her palm like a tiny glittering serpent.

"Can I have my Goddess?" She held out her hand to John, who searched in his pocket for the small figure.

"I've just been keeping Her safe for you."

Tamarind accepted the gleaming figure. Grasping it around its belly, she threaded the chain through a small loop on the Goddess's head. She raised it up to her neck, but before she could fumble with the clasp, John had stepped behind her. Brushing his fingertips across the back of her neck, he took the chain from her fingers and latched the clasp for her.

She smoothed the figure between her breasts. "Thanks."

Tamarind tossed the clothes and books into a small travel bag that Valerie had given her for their trips to San Juan. The last item she packed was a small hand mirror. This she lifted to her eyes, before twisting and turning as she struggled to see more of herself in the mirror than was possible. While they lingered on Playa Tamarindo, the sun climbed to its apex and the day grew warm. As they walked back up the hidden path toward Ana's house, sweat glistened on John's shoulders and trickled down his spine. Tamarind watched it run toward the waistband of his shorts until she realized sweat also wet her shoulder blades and the hollow between her breasts. In wonder, she touched the moisture on her chest and tasted it. It tasted like the ocean.

They returned to the Jeep and drove down 251 to Dewey. For the first time since he'd driven Zoë around Culebra, John paid attention to the landscape beyond the road. As with Mount Resaca, trees and shrubs had been yanked up and raw wounds in the earth gaped. At the airport, all of the light planes were overturned and scattered, like so many pieces upended from a giant chessboard after a bitter loss. In place of the scrappy small houses clinging to the slope leading to town, there was nothing more than scattered debris, resembling an abandoned fairground for an army of careless giants. Here and there he could make out sheets of metal roofing, wooden planks, doors, piles of clothes, odds and ends of home life: pictures, a mattress, a broken chair. But mostly what he saw was unrecognizable, twisted and thrown in meaningless clumps and individual pieces as far as the eye could see.

Dewey had also been transformed. Marilyn had ripped off sheets of plywood and smashed store windows, broken light poles trailed wires like spilled entrails, and paper and glass carpeted the ground. Waves from the harbor had surged over the shore, canal, and docks, before reaching hungrily along Dewey's streets. Where they had passed, a salt residue rimed the pavement and glittered in the sun.

John drove slowly, the Jeep's tires crunching over the fragments of humanity and nature mingled on the pavement, pulverizing the smallest.

"There's Valerie." Tamarind pointed as they neared La Virgen del Mar.

Valerie stood with Sister Maria Margarita on the steps of the church, her hands covering her mouth. The nun's hands rested on her hips and her lips were pursed as she surveyed the houses and shops around them. When her gaze crossed over the Jeep, they widened and she stared at them.

She put her hand on Valerie's arm. "My friend, look, there is John and Tamarind whom you worried so much about."

Valerie looked where Sister Maria Margarita pointed and screamed a little. "John! Tamarind!"

She came to the Jeep, picking her way through the debris so quickly she was like a bananaquit fluttering. When she got to the driver's side, they saw the puffy grooves under her gray eyes and her uncombed hair. John recognized her shirt from yesterday.

"John! Tamarind! You're safe! Thank God!" She leaned as far into the Jeep as she could, wrapping her arm around John's neck. Then she pulled away and looked at Tamarind. "Oh, my God. What happened to your hair?"

Tamarind blinked and touched her head. "I–"

"We survived a bit more than a hurricane. We'll tell you about it later." John looked at Valerie, who gazed back at him for a long moment and then nodded. "Is everyone okay?"

"So far as we know. Only old Captain Joe hasn't radioed in yet, but he's a salty dog so we hope for the best. The power's out, but the Dockside has a generator so we can get some hot food once in a while until the power's restored on the island. If you two are hungry now, Sister's got a kerosene stove and has soup in the sanctuary."

"We are." John looked around for a place to park. "Just let me park your Jeep over there where the mess is only a couple feet high first. I don't suppose you could find me a t-shirt someplace, or a blanket?"

Valerie's gaze dropped to his bare chest and she saw the slash there, dark and wicked. She inhaled sharply. "Sister's got some blankets and a first aid kit, too."

"Thanks."

"I'll see you two inside then." Valerie looked at each of them in turn and then returned to the church.

After John parked and they'd scrabbled through the uneven litter to the church's steps, they heard voices and laughter. A moment later, a mewling threaded its way among the chatter. Just inside the church's doorway a group gathered, oblivious to the destruction only a few feet away. Tamarind recognized Jaime, the father-to-be from yesterday. Tucked between his left arm and his chest, he held a blanketed bundle that appeared to have a coconut wedged into one end of it. When she and John drew near, she saw that instead of a coconut, the furry brown sphere had a small mouth and cloudy blue eyes that studied the sky above its father intently. Jaime held his baby.

He turned at their footsteps. "*Madre de Dios. Qué pasó?*"

All of the people around them stopped chatting and looked at John and Tamarind, who stood just outside the church's entrance. Their eyes, so lively only moments before, lost their dark luster and their faces closed in on them as anemone tentacles close around prey. A few of them stepped back, and ducking their heads, turned away. The ones that remained shifted closer together and watched John and Tamarind, their lips pursed and their arms around each other's waist. Tamarind's hand flew to her scalp before she realized what she was doing. She let it brush the prickly soft hairs at the top of its arc and then it fell back to her side.

John wrapped an arm across her shoulders. "When *una mujer del mar* casts off her tail, she cuts her hair to show that she has left the sea forever."

"*Es la verdad*?" Jaime looked at her.

Tamarind nodded.

"So it's done then, young one?" The scent of cloves parted the watchers and Ana leaned against a pew, her legs crossed at the ankles and a hand-rolled cigarette gripped in her left hand. Blood spattered the front of her blouse and the bird's nest of white hair around her face lay matted against her forehead.

"Yes." Tamarind turned to look at Ana and her chin lifted a little. She touched the Goddess at her breast without knowing that she did so.

Ana nodded and dropped the cigarette onto the tiled floor where she ground it with her toe. She walked over to them and stopped. Without looking at John, she brought her hand to the Goddess, holding it up and away from Tamarind's chest so that the sunlight shone on the moonstone.

"She's a powerful one, this one is." She spoke so softly that only Tamarind heard her words.

Without warning, a laughing gull dropped from overhead and swooped alongside Tamarind, nipping at her chest. The delicate chain snapped and the bird continued flying through the open doorway into the sanctuary with the Goddess dangling from its beak. Tamarind cried out, lifting her hand at the same time. John lurched toward the bird as soon as his mind processed what had happened, but the bird escaped his reach. It flew on, flapping strongly as it navigated around the inside of the church; first, it sped toward the altar and then veered to the right as Sister Maria Margarita appeared in its path. It zoomed in a low curve toward the side of the sanctuary and continued on around the far side to come full circle at the altar. People crouching in the pews ducked their heads.

Tamarind kept her gaze on the gull and the Goddess in its mouth. John stood nearby, his attention also focused on the mad flight of the bird. Dark, steady energy crackled in the air between them. While they watched, the laughing gull's wings flapped a little less strongly and its height wavered. Again, it circled the sanctuary in its desperate flight. As it came around toward them, Tamarind held out her hand once more. The bird shied from her hand and wobbled toward the middle of the church where Valerie stood. It tried to veer away from her, but as it tipped, the Goddess slipped from its beak. She caught the figure before it fell to the floor.

The laughing gull swung back toward the open doorway, its wings flapping unevenly. As it passed over Tamarind and Ana, it let out a cry like an apology and then it had gone through the dark frame of the door into the brilliant sunshine where the air currents lifted it up as easily as if it were ash from a bonfire.

"I think this is yours." Valerie walked from the sanctuary to where Tamarind stood. She lifted the gold chain up and studied the break. "It looks like the clasp gave way. I can fix it easily."

Tamarind nodded her head once and Valerie closed her hand around the Goddess.

"She'll be ready in time for your wedding, and I'd like to give you two gold bands to exchange that I picked up in San Juan." Valerie looked at John, who blinked. After a moment, he grinned. He looked at Tamarind, clasping her hand in his.

"Perfect."

"Great! Sister!" Valerie turned around and called back up the center aisle to the nun, who stood in front of a table at the front of the church with a huge aluminum soup pot on it. "Go find Father! We're going to have a wedding while we wait for the clean-up crews from the mainland!"

They got married on Playa Flamenco as the sun melted orange into the waves. Tree branches and bits of thorny acacia and cactus scrub had been cleared away and the white sand had been raked until it was smooth. Citronella stakes burned in a semi-circle around the wedding party and their flames danced in the growing dusk. John wore a pair of jeans and a t-shirt; Tamarind wore a blue batik dress purchased from the Mermaid's Purse that afternoon and the repaired chain from which the Goddess hung, mysterious and radiant. Julie, the owner of the Mermaid's Purse, presented her with a fringed black shawl decorated with huge *flamboyan* flowers that Tamarind draped over her head like a *mantilla*. They stood before the priest barefoot, their hands clasped.

During the brief ceremony in which they promised to honor each other before God and to love without end, Valerie and Sister Maria Margarita stood on either side of John and Tamarind with the gold bands that Valerie had given them. Chris, Pablo, and Teresa, John's closest friends on the island, sat on woven blankets behind them. Twenty feet away to the west, Ana squatted alone on the beach and smoked a clove cigarette. Her green peasant skirt puffed around her spindly legs and her white hair tangled in the breeze. If anyone had glanced at her, they might have seen her lips moving as the priest spoke.

Afterwards, the sun dissolved into the water, leaving behind a rich red afterglow in the deepening blue of the horizon. Stars spread north and west in the wake of the advancing night, their tiny white lights revealed against the darker background. Ana unfurled herself and came over to Tamarind, who stood apart from John and the priest while they talked. She carried a small wooden box in her hands.

"I haven't given you my gift yet, young one."

Tamarind dug her toes into the sand; the warm grains yielded to her nervous prodding and covered her feet almost to the ankles.

"Ana, you don't have to give me anything. Without you, I wouldn't have any legs."

"True, young one. But I still want you to have this. It's a box fashioned from mangrove wood and this symbol on the top is a sacred *mer* symbol for the ocean. It's inside this circle, which represents the earth. The mangrove has its roots in the ocean but isn't of the ocean. You are like the mangrove in reverse. You may try to put your roots in the earth, young one, but you will always belong to the sea. Like the mangrove, you will always live in the border between the sea and earth."

Ana's clove-rough voice abraded Tamarind's heart and she shivered even though the night was warm around her.

"I have imbued it with powerful spells for your marriage. Take it and remember me whenever you look at it."

"Thank you." Tamarind whispered as John stepped behind her and wrapped his arms around her waist.

Ana handed her the box without taking her eye from Tamarind's face; the hasty dark shadowed the normally bright eye and blurred the edges of her features. Ana glanced at John and nodded slightly before turning away from them and heading toward the dunes edging the beach. In a few minutes, she'd disappeared over the slight rise to the path that led to the sand lot and then to Route 251 South.

"It's time to go. The others want us to go with them to the Dockside for dinner. Chris stopped by there and asked them to keep some tables open. Since they're the only ones with a generator, I'm sure they've got more business than they can handle right now. If we don't go, they may just give our tables away."

Tamarind still stared at the spot where Ana had disappeared. She cradled the box in her palms.

"Can I have a moment alone on the beach?" She didn't turn to look at him.

She felt him stiffen and draw in a breath. She hummed, a faint throbbing that didn't reach his hands on her waist. After a moment, he expelled the breath softly.

"Sure. I'll be in the Jeep waiting."

Tamarind waited for him to get to the other side of the beach before moving. Although the sensory pores on her sides had shrunk to almost non-existence with her final transformation, she still knew when he'd crossed over the dunes and gone out of sight. Setting the box down and dropping the scarf next to it, she tiptoed to the ragged edge where the waves lapped the soft white sand. Hitching her dress up to her waist and clutching it in her left hand, she knelt down.

Humming again, she traced her fingertips across the damp sand and sang low a *mer* parting song, the song sung when a loved one died or faced mortal dangers, such as from sharks or encounters with rogue *mer*. Or humans. The water rolled over itself in increasing intensity, foaming and washing toward her knees, adding its voice to hers in a rising crescendo until she'd finished and then it seemed to fade away, taking the sweet sadness of her words with it.

"My God, that was haunting." It was Valerie. "Saying good-bye to your home, to the world that gave birth to you?"

"Yes." Tamarind realized that her cheeks had grown wet with more than spray. "Mother Sea has blessed me and blessed my union with John. I can leave in peace now."

Valerie came and laid her hand on Tamarind's shoulder. "Always remember, Tamarind, that you carry the Goddess's strength inside you. And that is no small gift."

Tamarind said nothing, simply stared at the phosphorescent white cresting along the edge of the waves in front of her.

After a time, Valerie spoke again and her cheerful voice rang across the susurrus of the ocean. "Come! It's time to eat your wedding feast where your friends will toast your happiness and fertility. And I must go transform John's pathetic room into a bridal suite."

৶৶৶

As they flew northwest over Culebra toward San Juan two days later, Tamarind looked down at the island, which reminded her of a spiny lobster. Below them, on Playa Tamarindo, Ana's knotty form squatted on the shore's stony mosaic, but she didn't lift her face towards their small plane. Instead, she stooped and reached, moving articles too small for Tamarind to distinguish, her arms spidery in their movements. Seaweed wove a loose web around her, forming an intricate bed for the unseen objects that she dropped. Tamarind sensed, rather than saw, a pattern to these tiny offerings, the way that memories sometimes hover at the edge of conscious thought, but the brilliant sky filled her mind instead. If she ignored the frame of the plane's window at the edges of her vision and looked straight ahead, she forgot everything and flew with the sooty terns and brown boobies above the immense blue ocean.

Beneath them, Ana patiently worked. As the plane approached the far horizon, she sat back on her haunches and aimed her single eye on it.

"You'll be back, young one. Mark my words—you'll be back."